Maggie Weston is a Victori
Though she grew up voraci
classical literature, she stum
first romance novel at the age of eleven and
never looked back. When she's not writing, or
researching all the weird things our predecessors
did, she can be found reading, taking on home
improvement projects that she thinks she can
handle (but can't), and watching period dramas.
Maggie lives with her husband, two dogs and
innumerable houseplants in California.

One Night with the Duchess
is **Maggie Weston**'s debut title
for Mills & Boon Historical.

Look out for more books from **Maggie Weston**
coming soon.

Discover more at millsandboon.co.uk.

ONE NIGHT WITH THE DUCHESS

Maggie Weston

MILLS & BOON

First published in Great Britain 2024
by Mills & Boon, an imprint of HarperCollins*Publishers* Ltd,
1 London Bridge Street, London, SE1 9GF

www.harpercollins.co.uk

HarperCollins*Publishers*, Macken House, 39/40 Mayor Street Upper, Dublin 1, D01 C9W8, Ireland

One Night with the Duchess © 2024 Maggie Weston

ISBN: 978-0-263-32096-1

10/24

For my parents,
who have always been irrationally confident
in my ability to succeed.

Chapter One

London, 1840

'Excuse me, my lord.'

'What is it, Taps?' Matthew Blake, Lord Ashworth, regarded his butler over the rim of his crystal whisky glass.

Taps, who had served the Blake family for nearly twenty-five years, was a contradiction in motion, a man as firm and stout in appearance as he was fidgety by nature. Even as Matthew watched him, Taps shifted from one foot to the other.

'There is a young lady here to see you, my lord.'

Matthew raised one dark eyebrow and spared a glance at the rosewood clock on the mantel. The delicate brass hands indicated that it was nearly one o'clock in the morning. 'Who?'

'She refused to give a name, my lord. However, she said it was a matter of great urgency.' Taps paused almost imperceptibly before adding, 'She seems quite distressed.'

'Is she alone?'

'She is accompanied by another woman, perhaps her lady's maid.'

Intrigued despite his fatigue, Matthew asked, 'What does she look like?' He didn't know any young woman who'd risk visiting his private residence unchaperoned at such a time.

'She is in mourning, my lord.'

He waved one large-palmed hand lazily. 'Show her in.'

Taps paused and cast a subtle look at Matthew's attire—or lack thereof. 'Would you like some time to make yourself presentable, my lord?'

'Taps,' Matthew chided without looking down at his partially unbuttoned shirt, 'it is one o'clock in the morning. Any woman coming to see *me* now doesn't give a fig about propriety.' He slouched further into his chair. 'At this time of night, she's lucky I'm clothed at all.'

While his butler would never dare to question him, Taps had long ago perfected a tone that displayed disapproval while somehow sounding nothing but polite. He used it now, issuing a crisp 'My lord' before bowing and leaving the room.

Matthew ignored his butler's subtle reprimand and pondered his unexpected visitor instead. He wasn't aware of anyone he knew having died recently, which could only mean that either he didn't know the lady in question or she was wearing mourning garb as a disguise. Considering whose house she had entered, he considered that wise. Bold, undoubtedly. But wise.

There was a gentle announcing knock on the door before Taps re-entered the room, this time with a small woman in tow. Her slight frame was hidden under a mass of black fabric, her face completely obscured by the weeping veil that fell in one smooth sheet from the brim of her hat to the exact point at her throat where her high-collared dress started, leaving not even a single inch of skin exposed.

Seeming at a loss for how to introduce the woman, Taps floundered for a second, then gave up entirely, bowed, and left the room.

Curious as to what she'd do, Matthew said nothing. He made no move to greet the stranger, essentially breaking every rule of decorum that had been drilled into him from birth. He took a sip of his peated whisky, crossed one booted ankle over the other, and waited in silence for her to say something.

The woman bowed her head in greeting. 'Lord Ashworth.'

Her voice was cultured and young—young enough that he instinctively knew nothing good could come of their meeting. 'If you're going to barge into my house in the middle of the night, I at the very least deserve the courtesy of knowing to whom I am speaking.'

Her head tipped forward, almost as if she were trying to regain her composure—or pray. 'My name is Isabelle Con—' She took a small breath and slowly straightened her spine. 'I am Isabelle St Claire,' she corrected, 'the Duchess of Everett.'

Matthew's heart constricted in his chest. Slowly, he

put his drink down. 'Your Grace,' he greeted her politely, but his mind warred with this new information. He knew the name, of course. There were, after all, less than thirty dukes in all of England.

There'd been news lately… At the club, maybe… No, he remembered, *at Giovanni's School of Arms.*

'Your husband died a few days ago?'

'Yes.'

Her affirmation was all he needed to have the memory surfacing. His best friend—Leo Vickery, Lord Pemberton—had told him about the Duke of Everett, who'd had a sudden heart attack at the age of fifty-five. A sad event, to be sure—made all the more unfortunate by the fact that he'd left behind a bride of eighteen, a woman barely out in society. *This* woman, as fate would have it.

'My condolences.'

'Thank you.'

'Your Grace,' he chastised gently, 'it is hardly proper for you to be here at this hour. If anyone were to see you in my home…'

There was no need to explain further. Matthew's reputation aside, some things simply were not done, and visiting a strange man in the middle of the night was certainly one of them.

'I am well aware,' she countered immediately, her tone leaving no room for further argument on his part.

Hopelessly fascinated, Matthew leaned back in his chair. 'Your Grace…?'

'Isabelle.'

Uncomfortable with the familiarity, he simply nodded.

'I am going to be frank, Lord Ashworth.'

She sounded like an ancient matriarch, chastising an errant toddler, but Matthew found the contrast of the stern tone and the young, birdlike woman intriguing.

'Please do,' he said, and although he did not move from his position, he fought the insane urge to go to her and tear the weeping veil off. For some unholy reason, he wanted to see her face.

The Duchess did not mince her words. 'I was married a mere two weeks before my husband died.' She anxiously clasped and unclasped her small gloved hands. 'The marriage was decided upon when I was just thirteen.' She cleared her throat daintily. 'The Duke was a trusted friend of my father's.'

The Duchess took three quick steps towards the door, spun around, and then hurried in the opposite direction like a mouse trapped in the corner of a barn.

'You see, my husband was not a...' She paused to consider her word choice before settling on, 'He was not an *unkind* man. He was older, to be sure, but rather... soft...'

She tugged at her bodice with both hands, as if she could somehow rip the heavy dress off her body.

Matthew pushed himself to a stand, getting warier by the second. 'Your Grace,' he said, interrupting her nervous chatter, 'please speak plainly.'

The Duchess spun around to face him. She inhaled a huge breath and as the black veil was suctioned inwards, plastering the dyed lace to her lips, she spluttered. Reaching up with both hands, she frantically ripped the entire hat off, scattering pins and scraps of fabric on the floor.

In any other circumstance Matthew might have been amused. His mouth even momentarily fought a smile as he watched the hairpins bounce across the carpeted floor before settling. But the moment he looked up his smile faded and any humour died.

The Duchess of Everett blinked at him from worried eyes the colour of onyx…eyes framed by impossibly long, inky lashes. Her skin was golden, stark against the cascade of black hair that had come undone and fell in thick ringlets down her narrow waist to her flared hips. Her sharp features were softened by a small, straight nose and a delicate mouth. She was a vision.

'My marriage was not consummated,' she blurted, and then immediately slapped a hand over her mouth, clearly mortified by her admission.

Matthew watched, fascinated, as a pink blush spread from the high collar of her dress up her neck and through her cheeks. At a complete loss for the appropriate thing to say, he merely repeated, 'My condolences.'

The Duchess opened her mouth, closed it. She placed both hands on her hips and began to walk around his parlour.

'With all due respect, Your Grace. How may *I* be of service exactly?' he asked.

'Is it not obvious?'

'I'm not sure that it is.'

'My late husband's cousin is insisting upon a doctor's…*proof* that I am really the Duchess of Everett.'

Matthew scowled at that. 'Why did you not refuse? I'm sure most doctors would find such an examination archaic.'

'I should have,' she agreed. 'However, that only occurred to me after the fact, and now the risk is that my marriage will be annulled.'

Matthew began to see her dilemma. 'And you would lose your new title… *Duchess*.'

The Duchess straightened her spine and shot him a look that would have sent a lesser man running. For Matthew, her narrowed eyes and tight mouth had the complete opposite effect, and for some absurd reason he suddenly wondered what it would be like to tease those seriously set lips into sighing open for him.

'I am a virgin,' she stated, and although he'd inferred that much, hearing the actual words turned his momentary fantasy to dust. Though she tried to hide her embarrassment, she fidgeted with her gloves again. 'A new match, however humiliating for my family, could be arranged…'

Her voice was clear, but Matthew could hear the heavy dread in it still. He did not move; he barely breathed.

'My concern is for the new Duke of Everett—my husband's son by his previous wife.' She spun around again, making her stiff skirts sway back and forth like an ancient church bell. 'Luke is only seven.'

Matthew saw her logic then. 'And you fear what would happen to him should you be sent away?'

'My husband's cousin—Gareth St Claire—is an unbearable man. And he is next in line for the Dukedom after Luke.'

'Common law would prevent him from assuming guardianship of Luke if he is next in line for the title,' Matthew pointed out, even though he knew that such things rarely mattered. Without protection, a titled child alone in the world was easy prey.

'Yes, I am aware,' she replied dryly. 'But my late husband named his wife—if there should be one—as Luke's guardian in the event of his death. That is me.' Her voice rose with her panic. 'If my marriage is annulled, Luke will be placed as a ward of the Chancery. He's a *child*, my lord. It will be years before he's of age and able to assume the responsibilities of his title, and in all that time there will only be one stranger appointed to come between Luke and his uncle.'

'You think he would harm the boy?'

Although he kept his tone cool, Matthew saw her distress was genuine. He knew even if it weren't for her obvious anxiety, the facts remained. No man was as close to power and wealth than when he was separated from an inherited title by a single child—nor would he ever be that close again.

'There are many ways to damage a child irreparably, my lord. More ways to manipulate and control one. I don't know if Gareth would physically harm Luke, but I would not put anything past him. And I am the only person with the means to do something.' She took two bold steps closer. 'Many of my childhood summers were spent at the Everett country home, Moorhen House. I was always a bit…solitary. An only child. When the previous Duchess died in childbirth, Luke was completely alone. He is a little brother to me in many ways.'

'Some might even say a son?'

'Yes. Although he is only eleven years younger, some would say he's like a son to me.' Again, those thin shoulders squared, those black eyes slowly rose to meet his. 'It's my responsibility to ensure his well-being.'

'And secure yourself the title in the process?'

'I'm not denying that I would benefit, Lord Ashworth. Merely that benefit to myself is not my primary motivation. Being the Duchess of Everett is a duty I take seriously. However, Luke's safety is my only concern.'

Matthew was no idiot. He had an inkling of why she was in his house, hiding in her widow's weeds, at one o'clock in the morning. And even though he'd never touch an unspoiled daughter of the peerage, he couldn't help but push her to her point. He needed to hear her say the words.

'And you're here because…'

She exhaled a deep breath. 'I've come because…'

'Yes?' It was a single word, a simple word, but it left Matthew's lips weighted with anticipation.

'May I ask a favour?'

'You may ask,' he countered, 'but I will most probably refuse.'

'I would like you to bed me.'

Having become somewhat used to people expecting such behaviour from him, Matthew smiled grimly. But, in spite of that, when he said, 'No,' the word left his lips tasting bitter.

Isabelle was startled at the abrupt answer, issued from Lord Ashworth with no hint of doubt. 'You're not even going to *think* about it?'

The giant man standing in front of her grinned, his white teeth flashing wolfishly. He ran one large hand through his unstylishly shaggy hair.

'There's no need. I don't *bed* virgins. I don't ruin reputations—'

'That is not what I heard.'

Matthew ignored her comment. 'And I certainly will not be led by the nose into a situation where you could hold any sort of power over me. I'm not the man you're looking for, *Duchess*.'

Isabelle couldn't help the slightly hysterical giggle that worked its way up her throat. 'You... You think that I would trick you into *marriage*?' she asked, somewhat stunned by the notion. 'Have you not been listening to anything I've said?' She waved both hands down towards her heavy black dress. 'I'm in *mourning*. I will be for *years*!' she practically shouted. 'And even if I wasn't, marriage to you is the *last* thing I'd want!'

Because she felt hot and flustered by his looming presence and the entirely inappropriate conversation they were having, she started to pace.

She lowered her voice. 'I'm a *duchess*. I don't need your title. And marrying again before my mourning period is over would cause a scandal that would be completely antagonistic to my main goal—helping Luke.' When he only raised his eyebrows, she continued, 'Moreover, I have no *desire* to get married again.'

'But you're not a duchess—technically. And am I just supposed to trust whatever you say?'

Isabelle turned abruptly to find that he'd closed the space between them, and that instead of looking at his face she was staring at a patch of tanned skin where his collar lay open. She slowly craned her neck back, shifting her eyes away from his chest to his steel gaze.

'Do you honestly believe that I'd be here with any other motive? That I'd want to lose my—' she lowered her voice '—my *maidenhead* to a stranger whose name I picked off a list?'

Lord Ashworth did not try to fight his grin. 'You have a list?'

Isabelle ignored the unsteady fluttering in her stomach, and even though it had not really been a question she felt compelled to clarify. 'A list of ne'er-do-wells that I got from my very well-informed companion.'

'Ne'er-do-wells?'

She waved her hand flippantly in his general direction. 'You know…' And when he just shook his head, she leaned closer and whispered, 'Rakes.'

Lord Ashworth threw his head back and laughed. It was a lovely sound, deep and rusty, as if he wasn't in the habit of using it often. But instead of appreciating the way it rolled over her skin, Isabelle felt the first true panic stick in her throat. It had been easier to get her feet moving once she'd had a plan and made up her mind, but now… Now her plan seemed as ridiculous as Lord Ashworth clearly found it.

Hot tears prickled her eyes.

Panic clawed through her chest.

Her breathing grew tight, each whoosh of air grating up her throat as if it were being forced.

If she couldn't convince one of the five men whose names she and her cousin Mary had carefully selected to help her, she'd lose Luke mere weeks after she'd been put in a position to help him.

Luke was the entire reason she'd agreed to marry the Duke in the first place. Every time she'd thought of running away, of leaving to go and stay with her aunt Angela in Italy, she'd thought of Luke, alone and neglected at Moorhen House. And so she had stayed.

She'd stayed because it wasn't Luke's fault that his birth had killed his mother and practically estranged him from his grieving father. She'd stayed because on her worst days, including the day she'd been told she was to marry the Duke of Everett, she'd had only one person whom she knew loved her regardless, who looked at her as if she could solve any problem in the world, protect him from anything…*slay his dragons*. She'd stayed because she remembered what it was to be alone in a nursery with only speechless dolls and an uninterested nursemaid for company, and she could never abandon Luke to the same fate.

Remembering now had her taking a deep, calming breath. She removed the list of names from the inside of her glove and opened it with fumbling hands and blurred vision.

Leo Vickery, Lord Pemberton, was next.

Isabelle had met Leo before at a birthday celebration held for her dear friend, Wilhelmina Russell, which made things a little less awkward... Or at least one might hope it made things less awkward. Unlike the brooding Lord Ashworth, whose illicit affair with the Marchioness of Dunn had marked him a reprehensible rogue, Lord Pemberton was the quintessential peer— for, while he kept an expensive mistress, he did so fairly discreetly, and did not ruin any marriages in his pursuit of his own pleasure.

Isabelle took a harried step towards the door. Paused. When she turned back, Lord Ashworth was no longer laughing. Those cold, grey eyes were studying her with a quiet dread that she felt in the depths of her soul.

'If it's all the same to you, I would appreciate your discretion in this matter,' she said.

She didn't wait for a reply.

She got all the way to turning the brass knob before that deep, gravelly voice called, 'Wait.'

She swallowed nervously and turned back to face Lord Ashworth.

He held her hat in his hand.

'Oh. Yes. My hat.'

Isabelle strode across the room and attempted to pluck the hat from him, but instead of releasing it, his strong fingers closed tighter around the brim. She yanked— *hard*—but he didn't move a single inch.

'Is there a problem, my lord?'

'Who else is on your list?'

Shame suffused her, heating her blood and crawling unpleasantly over her skin. 'I'd prefer not to—'

Before she could finish the sentence, he'd plucked the crumpled paper from her hand and held it up to read.

With an indignant gasp, Isabelle tried to snatch the list back; however, Lord Ashworth merely placed one heavy hand on her shoulder and held her in place, stopping any further attempt. Humiliated beyond reason, she stood still and stared at a loose gold thread in the plush rug beneath her feet.

His big palm on her shoulder was heavy, almost comforting despite the restraint. His clothes carried the familiar scent of cigar smoke, but it was faint—as if he'd been standing in proximity to someone who'd been smoking. And instead of making her ill, as it had when she'd been a girl, curled up with a book in her father's study while he'd smoked, the bitter tang soothed her now.

Her father, who was not an affectionate man by nature, had never minded Isabelle's company, so long as she had remained quiet and not interrupted his business. And, Isabelle, who had never had much opportunity to interact with him otherwise, had spent many an hour sitting in silence in her father's office, making herself ill on tobacco smoke in the hope of a casual word or a glance of affection that never came.

Lord Ashworth finished reading the list and released her, leaving Isabelle oddly unsteady. It was as if he had been grounding her, keeping her panic at bay, so that the moment he let go, it all came flooding back.

'You can't do this, Duchess.'

'I *have* to,' she insisted. 'I *lied*. I told everyone my marriage was consummated. The physician is coming in *two days* to put Gareth St Claire's mind at rest.'

'No. I'm telling you now, Leo—Lord Pemberton— won't touch you. He likes to have fun, but he'd never go through with something like this. Atkins and Williams might—but they wouldn't keep quiet about it, which would not only ruin your reputation, but risk your marriage's annulment anyway. And even if Cedric Finchley didn't say anything it'd be because he had far worse intentions. His family's fortune is in dire straits. He's more likely to spend his entire life hounding you, blackmailing you to pillage Luke's inheritance. Is that really what you want?'

A cold tendril of fear snaked through Isabelle's resolve. 'No. Of course that's not what I want!'

'There are other ways, you know… To make it seem as if you've…' Lord Ashworth sighed deeply as his eyes studied the ceiling. Her hat dangled forlornly in his hand.

The hope that rose in Isabelle's chest was so sharp, so real. 'How? Tell me.'

'It's really just a matter of…penetration. You… I mean.'

Isabelle frowned. 'I… I don't understand.'

'I apologise, Your Grace. But explaining the basics of

screwing to a young woman wasn't exactly something I'd prepared myself for when I got home an hour ago.'

Isabelle ceded his point with a small nod. 'I'm not a child, Lord Ashworth. I am a widow—one who wouldn't even be having this conversation if I'd been brave enough with the Duke that first time.'

Lord Ashworth pinned her with those unsettling eyes. 'He tried…?'

'He *tried*,' she admitted tartly. 'It was horrifically awkward. Once he started removing his clothes I just lay there and cried, and he couldn't…or wouldn't… He left. He said I needed some time to "grow accustomed" to the idea.'

'I doubt time would have made it more appealing,' Lord Ashworth drawled. 'What was he? Fifty-five? And fat as a Christmas goose, if memory serves.'

Isabelle didn't argue. 'It doesn't matter. I should have been braver. I should have done my duty—for Luke.'

'It does matter,' he snapped. 'You should never have been betrothed to him—and age is the least of it.'

Seeing that he was growing increasingly frustrated with her, Isabelle calmed her tone. It didn't matter that she agreed with him, or that she still sometimes woke in the night drenched in sweat and terror before she remembered that it was all over. She had married the Duke, as her father had demanded. And she had survived it as her mother had said she would.

'If I don't do this, *nothing* will change for me. I will be marked a virgin, my marriage will be annulled, and I will be married off a second time—this time to someone whom I don't know and who very possibly isn't as understanding as the late Duke was. I have lived through it once, and by God I could survive it again.' Just the thought made her stomach roil with dread, but Isabelle pushed through it. 'But Luke will be shipped off to boarding school. He'll never be given the love and attention he needs. And that's the best-case scenario.'

'That I do understand,' Lord Ashworth surprised her by saying.

'Well, then.' She held out her hand, palm up, fully expecting him to hand her the paper and send her on her way.

Instead, he turned and threw it straight into the blazing fire.

For a long moment, all Isabelle could do was stand and stare at the rapidly disintegrating paper. It flamed and curled, turning as black as the rage that snapped through her.

Instead of storming out, she simply lifted her chin defiantly. 'It was five names; I can remember all of them.'

'You don't have to.' Lord Ashworth walked back to the large tufted chair he'd previously vacated. He collapsed into it and picked up his whisky, the picture of a man up to his neck in trouble. 'I'll help you.'

'You *will*?'

'Yes.'

'Why?' she couldn't help but ask, given his sudden change of heart.

He shook his head. 'My options are either to let you try with someone who'll undoubtedly ruin your life. Or explain to you the mechanics and then pray to God you don't impale yourself on something. My way is quicker, and less dangerous to everyone involved.'

Isabelle couldn't quite believe what she was hearing. 'You'll help me? Do…*this*?' A shiver of nerves crawled over her body.

'Yes. And just in case you get any ideas, I leave for a tour of the continent in two days' time. I won't be back in England for two years.'

Desperate to sidestep his remaining doubts, Isabelle crossed her heart on the bodice of her heavy black gown. 'I swear on my life, my lord, I won't ever contact you again.'

He nodded once and then, setting his whisky down, stalked to the door. For one mortifying second she thought he might call someone to come and remove this insane woman from his house, but instead he turned the key, locking them in together.

Chapter Two

The Duchess looked so terrified when he turned around that Matthew didn't dare go to her straight away. Instead, he wove around her—frozen in the centre of the room like some morose statue—and proceeded to where his whisky decanter sat on the sideboard.

He still wasn't sure why he'd changed his mind. But there'd been a moment when she was talking about Luke, about needing to help him, when Matthew had understood her motivation perfectly. Moreover, he'd admired her for it. He didn't know a single woman who'd be more invested in her stepchild's wellbeing than her own under the same circumstances.

So, her determination to help Luke had admittedly struck a chord. Then, once he had seen the names on her list, his resolve had started to crumble. All it had taken was the steely determination in her eyes and her rigid march to the door and he hadn't had a choice. Matthew was not the perfect gentleman—nobody would argue that—but he would never deliberately hurt or expose Isabelle, as Michael, Andrew or Cedric might. And

Leo… Leo wouldn't harm her, or betray her confidence, but for some absurd reason that he didn't want to dwell on Matthew couldn't quite explain why the thought of the Duchess approaching his best friend unsettled him. It simply did.

Taking his time now, he poured himself another whisky, all the while achingly aware of Isabelle's eyes on him. 'If I'd had some warning, I might have been a bit more prepared.'

'I think decisions such as these are best made without time to dwell,' she countered fluidly.

'So, it was a strategy, then?'

'I think *desperation* would be a more accurate term.'

Matthew finally turned to face her. Isabelle was watching him warily, but her hesitation did nothing to detract from the long, slow slide of lust through his system.

She was a gorgeous woman, all sharp and delicate with those remarkably large witch's eyes. For one so young, she had a courageous spirit and a backbone of steel. Any man would want her, but in some uncanny twist of fate she was his—at least for tonight.

And wasn't that how he preferred it? Although his reputation as a rake had been somewhat exaggerated, due to an affair that had ended badly, the unfortunate event had served as a self-fulfilling prophecy of sorts. Because Matthew had only needed to be humiliated by a woman once to understand that it would never happen again. Now, if he accepted an invitation to a woman's bed, he did so knowing it would be a welcome distraction for one night—and only one night.

On impulse, he passed Isabelle the drink he'd poured for himself. He couldn't quite hide his grin when she snatched it out of his hand, as if she were afraid he might grab her and ravish her. 'You still have time to walk away.'

'I won't.' She swallowed the peated whisky in one go.

Matthew took a step forward, fully prepared to rescue a gagging, gasping female from the shocking burn of the expensive Scottish whisky, but Isabelle merely closed her eyes and curled the glass against her chest, exhaling deeply as if she were enjoying the hot slide of it down her throat.

He stared at her for a long moment, studying the way her dark lashes rested against her golden skin. 'You drink whisky?'

Her eyes fluttered open, revealing dark irises heavy with nerves. 'I would occasionally sneak some of my father's spirits to the head groom, Henry. On his birthday and for Christmas. He used to scold me horribly— and then tell me we had to "dispose of the evidence".'

She smiled her first sincere smile. Matthew felt its effect like a punch to the stomach.

'It became a tradition of sorts,' she said.

'Would you like another?'

'No.' She placed one slender hand across her stomach. 'I need my wits about me for this.'

'It's not a mathematics test, Isabelle.'

'But it's painful?'

He sobered immediately. 'I hadn't thought of that. I haven't…'

He rubbed at the back of his neck, unsure of how to proceed. He wasn't one to struggle with words, but for the first time ever he wasn't in a situation he could talk his way out of. He wouldn't lie to her. He wanted her to understand what she was asking of him.

Isabelle saved him from having to reply. 'I remember: you don't bed virgins.'

'I've heard that it's uncomfortable, but that it will ease after a little while.' Realising that she was growing paler with each word that came out of his mouth, Matthew changed tack suddenly. 'I'll make it pleasurable for you.'

'I don't care,' she insisted bravely. 'I just want to get it over with.'

And, so saying, she took a bold step forward, coming so close that he could smell the honey-toned whisky on her breath when she tipped her head back to look at him.

'Tell me what to do.'

Matthew reached out and gently took the glass from where she still pressed it against her heart. He tried not to think about how cold her fingers were through her netted gloves, and avoided looking at her as he turned to place the glass on the side table. He tried, rather unsuccessfully, to calm his galloping pulse. He was thirty years old and no green lad, but she was such a contrast— so brave and yet so innocent—and the contradiction of her had him trembling with a foreign anticipation.

He looked around the room. His townhouse, a stone's

throw from Piccadilly, was ideally located and luxuriously furnished. The parlour was neatly organised, with intricately carved wooden furniture and thick rugs imported from India. The fire in the grate cast a warm glow, softening a room that he'd never considered too masculine until now. His parlour was fit for a viscount—but by no means fit for a duchess.

'For what it's worth, I'm sorry for the situation you're in. If I could think of some other way to help you, I would.'

She tugged at her bodice again. 'You are helping me.'

Matthew gently grasped her, circling her thin wrists with his hands. 'May I help you with that?'

Isabelle froze. Her eyes widened. 'Do I need to take *everything* off?'

'In the interest of me not suffocating under all that fabric—'

'Crepe.'

'For what I have in mind, we're going to take the *crepe* off.'

But because he could see that she was scared, he gently turned her around so that her back was to his chest.

She stood completely still in front of him as he ran his hands up and down the stiff black fabric covering her arms. The scent of whatever soap she'd washed her mass of hair with reached him and, unable to resist, he leaned closer and nuzzled the soft skin of her neck as he breathed her in.

Isabelle tensed immediately, and Matthew drew back enough to whisper, 'Don't be afraid of me, Duchess.'

He buried one hand in the mass of her silky hair and tilted her head back so that she could see the truth in his eyes when he promised, 'Any time you want to stop, you tell me. I'll stop.'

She nodded shyly, and although she didn't speak she stepped back and removed her black gloves with a few deft tugs.

There were so many ways he could make this quick and efficient—clinical, even. But even knowing *how* to, Matthew wouldn't. If he was going to be with this woman only once, he was going to show her what it could be like, so that years from now, when she eventually took a lover, she'd know not to accept anything less than complete pleasure—*her* complete pleasure.

'I'm going to take this off now.' He started on the dozen tiny buttons down her back, but when she still didn't reply, he paused. 'Isabelle? Is that all right?'

'Yes.'

His fingers kept working, undoing the tiny pearls from their clasps. Matthew, who'd always seen the layers of women's clothing as an irksome impediment at this juncture, was perfectly comfortable with the thick erection pressing against his trousers. What he couldn't quite make sense of was the new tremble in his hands.

'Are you afraid?' he asked.

'No.'

The question had been issued gently, so as not to scare her, but Matthew couldn't quite stave off his chuckle at her no-nonsense reply. Who was this strange woman?

And, more importantly, where had she been hiding all these years? If he'd met *her* in a ballroom…

'I'm a little afraid,' he admitted as he unclasped the last button and spread the back of her heavy dress open, revealing the tight corset laced over a short-sleeved chemise.

'*You're* afraid?' She sounded horrified. 'Why are *you* afraid? You are supposed to be quite a Casanova.'

His stomach flipped uncomfortably as he walked around her and crouched down to help her out of her gown and petticoats, now puddled on the floor up to her knees. She steadied herself by putting her hands on his shoulders and stepped out of the heap of black fabric. There was something so new in the gesture, something so trusting and intimate, that Matthew couldn't quite help but compare this moment to every other time he'd bedded a woman. There was no rushing now—only the strange urge to keep the Duchess with him for as long as possible.

He looked up the length of her body, from the place where her drawers travelled beneath the long chemise at her shins, up the centreline of her corset to her nipped-in waist, the gentle swell of her breasts, and finally to her face.

'You're the most beautiful woman I've ever seen. You're also innocent.' He pushed to his feet. 'I'm afraid I'll hurt you. Or embarrass you.'

He was bloody terrified that he'd lose his self-control and embarrass himself too.

'You don't have to worry about me,' she told him primly.

But he didn't miss the way she crossed her arms over her chest to hide herself, and he certainly couldn't miss the wide-eyed fear unspooling in her inky irises.

'I'm only reminding you that it's normal to be afraid, given the circumstances,' he replied gently, and draped her dress and stiff petticoats over a nearby chair.

'But I'm not afraid.'

Rather than argue, Matthew stepped up to her again. He trailed his fingers up her bare arms, giving her time to become comfortable with his touch. Beneath his fingertips, despite her insistence that she wasn't afraid, he felt each tremble that passed through her. It was as if their nerves were connected by some phantom thread that compounded every touch until he was suffused with an unbearable level of awareness.

When he pressed up against her, letting her feel the weight of his hard length against her corseted stomach, she issued a small, strangled swallow, but he calmed her by cradling her face with both hands and forcing her gaze to his. He traced her high cheekbones with the pads of his thumbs even as his fingers sank into her thick, silky hair to frame her skull.

'I'm going to kiss you now.'

Her hands rose to grip his wrists tightly, but it wasn't fear in her eyes any more. It was confusion, layered with need.

'Yes,' she whispered, in reply to a question that hadn't been asked.

He lowered his mouth to hers. It didn't matter that she didn't return the kiss. The moment his lips touched hers, Matthew groaned against a fiery flood of desire. She was impossibly soft and sweet, and just this, the faintest, most innocent of kisses, was enough to have a torrent of wicked fantasies corrupting his imagination.

'Open your lips for me, Duchess.'

'I—'

He wasn't sure what she'd been about to say, only that he didn't give her the chance. The moment she opened her mouth to speak he slid into her wet warmth and tasted her, his tongue gently coaxing hers to return the kiss.

After a few long, torturous seconds, she tentatively stroked him, and her innocent offering was enough to have him throbbing against the fabric of his trousers. Matthew sank deeper into the kiss, basking in the way Isabelle grew bolder, meeting his increasing urgency with her own with each second that passed.

Although she couldn't be aware of it, she pressed her body up against his, almost as if she might angle herself to take him. Her hands released his wrists, but she didn't push him away. She roped her slender arms around his neck and held on as if her life depended on it…on *him*.

Feeling the edges of his self-control begin to fray, Matthew broke the kiss first. He exhaled deeply and, resting his forehead against hers, took a moment to pull himself back together.

'For an innocent, you pack a sinful punch, Duchess.'

When he opened his eyes she was staring up at him, her small, panting breaths escaping through her parted lips to whisper against his throat.

'It is wrong,' she said seriously—so seriously that he couldn't help but smile. 'But I… I enjoyed that. Very much so.'

Matthew had never needed words—had always counted sexual success in his partner's release, in moans and gasps—but the simple words from Isabelle tore at him. They disassembled what he knew about pleasure and rebuilt something entirely new and exhilarating in his mind.

'Did you, now?'

Instead of answering, she flushed scarlet and plonked her face against his chest, hiding her innocent embarrassment.

Overcome by an impossible urge to comfort her, to eradicate her self-consciousness, he raised one shaky hand and ran it over her hair. 'Can you hear my heart racing, Duchess?'

In a gesture that undid him, she turned her head and rested her ear against his chest. She nodded.

'That hasn't happened to me before.'

She pulled back to look at him, her dark brows dipping inwards. 'It's not always…like this?' She lowered both her hands to one of his and lifted it to the centre of her chest, pressing his palm over her heart.

Matthew, understanding what she wanted to tell him, ignored the urge to palm her breast and focused on the excited cantering of her heart instead.

'Not always,' he said.

Never, his confused mind corrected.

Unsure how exactly she could remedy the fact that she'd placed Lord Ashworth's hand directly on her bosom, Isabelle simply let his hand go in the hope that he'd drop it.

He didn't.

Instead, he stroked his thumb over the small swell of her breast above her corset. 'How about this?' he asked, and brushed over her skin again. 'Do you like this?'

His eyes, silvered with focus, flickered to her face.

Isabelle wasn't entirely sure how much of what was happening inside her was due to pleasure and how much was due to nerves—only knew that she definitely felt both. Her skin felt alive, and every time he touched her it seemed to respond to him. A quiver here. A shiver there. Her stomach fluttered uncomfortably, and there was an odd heaviness building between her thighs.

'I do,' she admitted unsteadily.

The sound he made in the back of his throat was the closest thing to a growl she'd ever heard a human make, and in her mind, she couldn't help but think it must prove why Mary had added Lord Ashworth to the list. Isabelle rather liked it. He reminded her of a mercurial cat, one who seemed *laissez-faire*, but had eyes that tracked her as if she were easy prey and he was waiting for an opportune time to pounce.

Lord Ashworth raised his other hand to her left breast

and repeated the same stroke, this time with a murmured 'So beautiful…'

Isabelle couldn't help the stuttering whoosh of air that left her lungs. Unsure of what to do with her hands while his were so skilfully employed, she raised them stiffly to his shoulders. With only his thin shirt separating her palms from his skin, she could feel the hard, muscular shape of him, so different from anyone she had touched before. There were no angles, no softness. Only sinew and brawn pulled tight beneath golden skin, and when he turned her around again, this time to unlace her corset, she felt the absence of him.

He gave a few sharp tugs to the laces at her back, but when the corset collapsed around her, and the cool air slipped over her sweat-slicked chemise, her forgotten nerves began to resurface.

As soon as he'd freed her from the confining garment, Isabelle wrapped her arms around herself. Gone was the momentary pleasure she'd felt when he'd kissed her and touched her. Now all that was left was embarrassment. And shame. Here she was, undressed and about to sleep with a stranger, mere days after her husband had died.

This is the only way to help Luke, she reminded herself. But even that didn't settle the pang of dread settling low in her stomach.

'Isabelle?'

God, if people find out, I'll be ruined. And then I definitely won't be able to help Luke—Gareth will make sure of it.

'Isabelle?'

She came to the second time he said her name. 'Yes?'
'What's wrong?'

Isabelle was mortified to feel the cool trail of tears down her cheeks, but not nearly as mortified as when she saw the look of dread in Lord Ashworth's grey eyes.

Needing to remedy the situation immediately, she cleared her throat. 'Do you remember when I told you I wasn't afraid?'

His kind smile softened the hard steel in his eyes. 'It wasn't exactly true?'

'Not exactly.'

'I can imagine.'

He didn't stop her from covering herself, or try to talk sense into her. He leaned down and lifted her, holding her close against his chest.

'What are you doing?' she whispered, painfully aware of the thin layers separating them. Even through his clothes, his body heat reached for her like an embrace.

Matthew didn't reply to her question right away. Instead, he carried her to the settee and sat down, settling her on his lap with her feet resting on the plumped red cushions next to him.

'I'm trying to help you to relax, Duchess.'

'I don't know if this is going to help.'

He tipped her chin back, forcing her eyes to his. 'Trust me.'

Isabelle squirmed, trying to get comfortable, but when Lord Ashworth groaned, and pinned her in place with his large hands, she stopped moving immediately.

He nudged her with his hips, pressing upwards into the back of her thigh. 'Do you feel me?'

'Of course,' Isabelle said pertly.

She had, after all, helped bathe Luke when he was a baby. And once she'd accidentally stumbled upon a stable boy urinating at the back of the stables. Although… neither of those experiences had given her the impression she felt so firmly beneath her now.

'I know basic anatomy, my lor—'

'Matthew,' he corrected. 'Given the circumstances, I'd say we're on a first-name basis, Duchess.' He leaned in close and blew a deliberate breath against the column of her throat. 'Wouldn't you?'

Isabelle shuddered helplessly against the sensation. 'Y-yes.'

'Isabelle… What exactly do you know about screw—?' He cleared his throat and corrected himself. 'The marital act?'

'That I should not fidget, *never* talk, and always listen to my husband's instructions.' She parroted her mother's tone. Frowned. 'Or, in this case, your instructions, I suppose.'

He sighed and, closing his eyes, pinched the bridge of his nose. 'Fantastic.'

'I guess that would depend on what you tell me to do,' she observed. 'It could be terrible.'

The deep chuckle that rumbled through his chest and into hers pulled a genuine smile to her face. When he laughed, it made what they were doing seem less consequential, somehow. More natural. If she'd been any less nervous, Isabelle would have tried to imagine that this was her wedding night—*their* wedding night.

'You mentioned your head groom earlier, so I'm assuming you have horses?'

Isabelle frowned at the odd question. Maybe he was trying to distract her. More than willing to oblige, she replied, 'Yes. There are many at Moorhen House. But I have two of my own. Both are thoroughbreds that I brought with me when I was married. Saskia and Truant.'

'Have you ever *bred* horses?'

'Yes,' she answered seriously. 'My father's horse stock has prime bloodlines, descended from Silver Prince.' She saw his mouth twitch. 'Oh, you mean...' She leaned in and whispered, 'Have I *watched*?'

'Yes.'

She nodded happily for a moment, but when she saw the pointed look on his face, felt the hardness pressing into her again, her blood froze. 'But... Good Lord, are you certain?'

Though his eyes sparked with amusement, he explained, 'I fit inside you.' Reaching down, he cupped one big hand over her chemise and drawers. 'Here.'

She shifted under his hand as an uncomfortable tension gathered between her thighs. Matthew didn't move away; he gently rolled the heel of his hand against her, turning that sliding weight into something tight and aching.

'I suppose that makes an odd sort of sense,' she said

breathlessly, trying her best to be brave. 'We are, at our most basic selves, mere animals.'

'Are you always this rational?'

Matthew's smile took any mockery out of the question.

'I try to be. My father always tells my mother that hysterics solve nothing and merely waste time for everyone.' Although she didn't say it, that exact phrase was what her father had used when she'd cried at the news that she was to marry the Duke of Everett. 'But sometimes, when I get very angry, I lock myself in my room and…' She looked over her shoulder in an instinctual habit to check that nobody was nearby.

'And?'

'I *throw* things,' she whispered.

'You… You throw things?' Matthew asked, and raised the hem of her chemise to slide his palm up the fabric of her drawers, following the line of her inner thigh.

As absurd as it was, Isabelle wished she hadn't hurried to change and left her stockings off. Impropriety aside, it would have made her infinitely more comfortable to have an additional layer between her skin and Matthew's now.

She held very still, trying her best not to panic as that heavy hand brushed her in sensation after sensation, moving closer to her most private part.

'Yes. I—I throw things,' she managed with a shaky breath. 'Shoes at the door, pillows at the window, bonnets at the floor. Once, I even threw a vase. It—'

She inhaled sharply as he ran one finger through the slit in her drawers, touching her for the first time.

Her breath stuttered out as he gently traced her seam. Caught between the pleasant coiling sensation low in her womb and complete humiliation, Isabelle buried her face against his warm neck, inhaling linen and the lingering scent of tobacco.

'I don't know…' *Anything.* Whatever he was doing felt sinful. Wicked. But she didn't want him to stop either.

'Don't hide from me, Duchess. Look at me when I touch you.'

Mortified, but wanting to be brave, Isabelle slowly prised her face away from his neck and looked into eyes the colour of a brewing storm.

Matthew lowered his head and crushed his mouth to hers, dragging her into a kiss that stole any objection. When he would have pulled away, she placed one palm against his cheek and drew him back to her; it was easy to forget what she was doing when he kissed her.

Matthew's chest rose and fell quickly beneath her, as if he'd just finished some strenuous activity. The arm supporting her back tightened around her, holding her close, while the hand between her legs continued to tease and coax. Just when she thought she'd got used to him touching her, he parted her folds and slid his finger up and down, over her damp inner flesh.

'Can you feel how wet you are, Duchess?' His deep voice was tight, hoarse.

Incapable of voicing a reply, Isabelle simply nodded.

'That's to make it easier for you to take me. Here…'
He caught her hand in his and began to lower it.

Horrified, Isabelle resisted. 'I don't want that. I *can't*.'

'Duchess, touching yourself is no sin.' Raising her
hand to his lips, he gently kissed her fingers, encouraging her to relax. 'Let me show you,' he whispered, and
carried her hand to her own centre when she acquiesced.

He placed his hand over hers and guided her fingers
through slick warmth, showing her where he'd slot in
and the bundle of nerves that he said would help bring
her release. When Isabelle could take no more, and
tugged her hand back, he caught her fingers and, instead
of kissing them as he had done before, he suckled them.

She watched with wide-eyed horror as his warm
tongue curled around her digits. She should have been
shocked by the crudeness of it. She should have pulled
away with scorn. But instead, the heavy tightening in
her centre grew by degrees, turning almost painful—so
painful that a small mewl slipped from between her lips.

'Duchess, you are the most exquisite thing I've ever
tasted,' he whispered, and when he brought his lips back
to hers she could taste it—*her*—on him.

Isabelle was too hot. She felt sick with excitement
and nerves. And when he lowered his hand back to her
centre and touched her she was helpless to stop herself from writhing against his touch. Every brush of his
fingers against her pulled her nerves inwards, coiling
them tighter and tighter, and when he began to gently ease a single finger inside her she roped her arms

around his neck, clinging to him even as she arched against his hand.

Matthew groaned. 'Duchess, you're so tight.'

Isabelle couldn't reply. She merely closed her eyes and fought the sensations racking her body.

'Does this hurt, sweetheart?' He moved inside her, pushing deeper.

Isabelle tried to make sense of her body beneath the building pressure between her thighs. 'No,' she replied. 'It burns a little,' she whispered, pressing closer as her instincts took over.

'Hold on to me, Duchess,' he whispered. And the moment she wrapped her arms around his neck he took her mouth in a fierce kiss and, adding a second finger, pushed into her completely.

Beneath the heady kiss Isabelle was aware of discomfort as her untried flesh stretched to accommodate him. But then Matthew was moving, sliding his fingers in and out of her rhythmically, and instead of discomfort she felt a pleasurable tightness that preceded a painful roll of pleasure.

She tore her mouth away, moaning his name. 'Matthew... I...' She didn't know what she wanted to tell him, only knew that as he curled his fingers inside her it seemed quite urgent that he either stop or hurry up.

'I know, Duchess,' he whispered, and circled his thumb against the nerves at her apex.

Isabelle's stomach tightened as the new sensation consumed her. She moaned helplessly as it crested, cried out his name when she could no longer contain it, and when it burst through her, draining her muscles of strength, she could do nothing but collapse against him as her body greedily clung to him, trying to pull him deeper, keep him closer, hold him longer.

Tremor after tremor coursed through her, trailing shivers over her skin. It was the most unusual sensation Isabelle had ever felt—as if she was somehow satisfied and exhausted and energised all at the same time.

Matthew kissed the side of her head and then gently moved his hand to grip her thigh above her knee. When he moved away they both saw the smudge of blood he'd left behind; it was stark against the white of her drawers, but also rather underwhelming compared to the virgin blood she'd expected.

'It… It is done?' she asked, confused by how simple it had been.

'Enough that they won't suspect anything, Duchess.'

'But… You didn't…'

He gently picked her up and settled her onto the settee. 'You shouldn't have to give yourself to a stranger just to help your family.' Taking her hand, he placed her fingers over the distinct ridge in his trousers. 'I can ache for you and still believe that to be true.' He gently lifted her hand away.

'Matthew…' For some inexplicable reason her eyes burned. Her body, so satiated moments before, felt empty. As if she had been deprived of something— something *integral* that was supposed to have happened but hadn't.

'Your secrets are safe with me, Your Grace.'

Isabelle hated the honorific—hated that he'd used her title moments after…*that*! She watched helplessly as he stood and walked to the fireplace, distancing himself from her.

'I trust you,' she whispered, staunching her inexplicable sadness.

Matthew leaned heavily against the arched mantel, as if he needed to support his own weight with it. He didn't look back at her, but she saw the bunched muscles in his back and shoulders and the tired lowering of his dark head.

'We need to get you dressed.'

Unsure of what was happening—unsure of herself—Isabelle merely replied, 'Yes.' But she didn't move from the settee.

She watched Matthew take a deep, steadying breath and straighten. He turned to face her again, his eyes now calm and placid. If it hadn't been for the protrusion in his trousers, she'd have thought him completely unaffected.

Isabelle's mind raced. 'Matthew…'

'Isabelle?'

'I just had a rather dreary thought.'

'Oh?'

He took a step forward. Stopped. He linked his hands behind his back, as if to physically stop himself from reaching for her, and it was that hint of subtle restraint that steeled her courage.

She folded her hands in her lap and tried to calm the nerves dancing in her stomach. 'If I don't remarry, I'll never be able to experience…' She instinctively placed her hand on her chest, over her thumping heart. '*This* again.'

'Isabelle, you're young.' He gave an exasperated shake of his head. 'Beautiful. Brave. Kind. You'll remarry.'

There was no doubt in his tone.

'But what if he's not…?' *Like you*. That was what she'd been about to say. Instead, she blurted, 'If this is going to be my only chance to feel *this*… I'd like to do it properly.' And then, because she'd rather die than verbalise any more, she finished with, 'If you know what I mean.'

'I'm afraid you're going to have to clarify, Duchess.'

'You know exactly what I'm talking about.'

Matthew took one large step in her direction and then stopped abruptly. 'I'm not sure that I do.'

'I would like you to finish what you started.'

And even though a hot blush rose to her cheeks, Isabelle didn't back down. Somehow she knew that any sign of doubt on her side would send Matthew running.

'Isabelle, there's no need. I—'

'*I* need,' she interjected.

The statement rang loudly through the room, embarrassing her. Still, somehow knowing that it felt *right*, she persisted.

'Years from now, when I'm old and childless and alone, I want to look back and remember that I chose this for myself. Not my parents. Not my husband. *Me*. And I want you to show me.'

His eyes widened with surprise, and Isabelle used it to her advantage.

'Please, Matthew. Aside from Mary and Wilhelmina, you may be the person I trust most in the world. A literal stranger. A notorious rake. How pathetically sad is that?'

Isabelle had no idea where her passionate speech had come from, but even through her naïveté she was distinctly aware of one fact: not all men were like Lord Ashworth.

'Mary and Wilhelmina?'

'Mary is my cousin and both are my dearest friends,' she explained.

Lord Ashworth nodded once before continuing, 'Isabelle, once we go there, neither of us can go back. I'd love you for one night and then leave England. I depart in two days' time.' He watched her face closely, as if searching for the truth there. 'Is that really what you want?'

'Yes.'

He visibly winced at her blunt admission, and she wondered if he was rejecting or relenting.

'You've made me no promises.'

His eyes darkened. Raising both his hands, he linked them behind his head and swore. 'And what if there's a child? I don't have any protection with me…'

'Protection?'

'Sheaths.' At her blank look, he swore. 'Condoms. Rubbers. French letters.'

'Is the risk so great?'

'It is not insignificant, Isabelle. I could try to…to prevent it, but there is no guarantee.'

After that admission, Isabelle couldn't think any more of the possibility of a child. If she did, she'd balk. So, for the first time in her life, she chose to be reckless and simply took what she wanted.

She rose off the settee and slowly crossed the room to where he stood. When he still didn't move, she placed her palm on his cheek and drew his mouth down to hers.

Matthew did not resist, and the moment their lips touched she knew she'd won. His control broke. His tongue prised her mouth open and swooped inside, daring her to keep up with his unrestrained need. His hands reached for the top of her chemise and, instead of undoing the three small buttons there, he merely ripped the garment open, sending the buttons to join her hairpins on the floor. He yanked the chemise down to her waist, exposing her bare breasts.

Matthew seemed to drink in the sight of her for a long moment, before leaning down and sucking her aching nipple into his mouth. Isabelle mewled in pleasure and surprise and he gentled immediately, replacing his greedy sucks with long, slow swirls on his tongue and gentle scrapes of his teeth.

That same building pressure started up between her legs again.

Her hands found his hair, brushing the thick locks back from his face. Then his muscular arms coiled around her and lifted, forcing her to kick off the torn chemise as it slid down past her knees. She wrapped her legs around him.

Matthew carried her back to the settee and gently laid her down. He removed her drawers and took a step back as he stripped his own clothes, his eyes on her the entire time.

Isabelle lowered her hands, trying and failing to hide herself.

'You are magnificent, Duchess,' Matthew murmured. 'Don't hide from me. I could spend my whole life just looking at you.'

Emboldened by his words, humbled by the honesty in his eyes, Isabelle let her hands fall away.

And only minutes later, when he whispered her name as he edged inside her, she felt no pain, only an impossible fullness, toe-curling pleasure, and the dizzying sense that she'd somehow traded her soul for a favour... for one perfect night with a stranger.

Chapter Three

London, 1842—two years later

'I don't quite understand why Mary and I must attend, Willa.'

Isabelle flipped through a fabric sample book at the modiste, gently separating out fabrics of different colours and textures that appealed to her.

After over two years in dreary blacks, greys and grey-purples, Isabelle was determined to choose only those colours that would momentarily startle anyone who saw her. She wanted to appear like a rare tropical bird or an exotic plant: bright, colourful, and potentially dangerous. She had already removed a velvet the deep red of port wine, and a green silk that reminded her of the fields of Moorhen House after a long rain.

For her new day dresses, among others she had chosen a lilac cotton dress with small white daisies printed whimsically over it, and a navy-blue linen gown that Madame Tremblay had trimmed in cream lace.

'It's your first ball since the Duke died—God rest his

soul. Wouldn't you rather it be in a home familiar to you, surrounded by people with whom you are already acquainted?' Willa nestled back on the tufted pink settee and sipped her tea. 'The season is underway, Izzy. Before you know it, sessions will be over and you will have missed your chance.'

Alone with her friends, Isabelle felt comfortable speaking her mind. 'I wasn't actually planning on re-entering society.' She enjoyed the life she'd built over the past two years. Her widowhood afforded her a quiet existence, with little interruption, while motherhood kept her active and entertained.

'Nonsense. You're only twenty, Izzy. You've no need to hide away from the world.' Willa's brown eyes glazed over. 'The things I'd do if I were in your position… Filthy rich and widowed. Young.' She sighed wistfully. 'Why, I'd walk around my estate in breeches—'

'I should never have told you I did that!' Isabelle laughed. 'And I don't wear them all day—only to ride.'

'I'd curse in public.'

'Scandalous!' Isabelle said in mock horror, enjoying the game. 'You could take a lover?' she suggested.

Mary spluttered on her tea.

Willa raised her eyebrows. 'Oh, no. Were my husband to die, I would never let another man touch me.'

Isabelle didn't point out that not all men were like Earl Windhurst, Wilhelmina's horrible husband, and that some men could make a woman feel *everything*.

'Please, Izzy. I need you there. As a duchess, you're one of the only people Windhurst still approves of.'

Mary and Isabelle exchanged a worried glance. It was no secret that Willa's marriage to the Earl was an unhappy one. While Willa often refused to partake in society for weeks at a time, her husband had set his mistress up in an extravagant terraced home in Regent's Park and was often seen gallivanting about with her in public. The resulting humiliation had been too much for Willa, and over the eighteen months of her marriage she had been transformed from a beautiful, joyful girl into a woman well accustomed to the realities of life.

To Isabelle's surprise, it was Mary who interceded. 'I agree with Willa, Izzy. You cannot simply ignore your position in society for the remainder of your life. And Lord and Lady Russell's ball would be an opportune time for you to make an appearance.'

Isabelle, who had gone from her father's house to her husband's house and then into mourning, without coming out into society first, hadn't had a chance to practise being a duchess. Instead, she still felt very much like the odd, lonely girl she had been growing up. She wasn't accustomed to swarms of adults vying for her attention either. And, as a duchess, she'd found attention came whether she wanted it or not. She couldn't go for a walk without people greeting her as if they were old friends and not very slight acquaintances—her mother's cousin's best friend, or her father's friend's brother's son.

'I never know what to say,' she admitted finally. 'And the worst thing about not knowing what to say is that I

am a duchess, and people always wait for me to speak
first.'

'For heaven's sake, Isabelle. You *are* a duchess,'
Willa reiterated. 'And a widow to boot. Say whatever
the hell you want to say. What are they going to do?
Flog you? Scorn you? Declare you scandalous?' Willa
rolled her eyes. 'And even if they did, what difference
would it make? You could go back to your reclusive
life having proved me wrong.'

Mary, who rarely disagreed with Isabelle on anything,
nodded. 'Willa is right. It's time, Izzy.' As if she could
sense Isabelle's anxiety, she added, 'It may be trying at
first. But it will become easier over time.'

'I dare say you might even learn to enjoy yourself,'
Willa drawled. 'Besides, I'll be right there to curse or
say something alarming should you flounder.'

Unlike Willa, who didn't give a damn, and Mary,
who never made any mistakes, Isabelle was glaringly
self-conscious over all her shortcomings. 'I can't—'

'*Please*, Izzy,' Willa urged quietly. 'You and Mary
are my only true friends, and it's so hard to pretend to
enjoy myself. I don't want to be a burden, but I would
be happier knowing you were nearby, in case…'

'Yes?' Isabelle prompted.

Willa flashed a smile that never reached her eyes. 'In
case it's a dreadful bore.'

Isabelle wasn't fooled, but she didn't press the matter either, understanding that it was Wilhelmina's private life, hers to share or keep close as she saw fit. Still,

a friend in need was possibly the only thing that could sway her.

'I suppose one night won't kill me.'

Mary clasped her hands together excitedly.

Even Willa managed a small smile. 'Thank you.'

Madame Tremblay chose that moment to re-enter, with her three assistants each carrying several day dresses which Isabelle and Mary had ordered during their last visit and were now ready to undergo final fitting.

'I'd best be going.' Willa levered her slight frame off the settee. 'My mother is supposed to be visiting. I shall inform her that you both plan to attend.'

Isabelle watched Willa as she left the private fitting room, her back ramrod-straight, her head held high— and her doe-brown eyes completely empty.

On his third day back in London after nearly two and a half years away, Matthew meandered out through the stately doors of his social club, Barber's, at the side of his closest friend, Leo Vickery, Lord Pemberton. The London air in spring was still crisp, despite the time of day; however, there seemed to be a renewed vigour about the city now that winter was slowly sliding behind them.

As the two men walked together, they talked of mutual acquaintances, most of whom Matthew had not seen or heard from since he'd been gone.

'Both Heathcote and Tramley got married,' Leo said. 'Heathcote to a merchant's daughter who came with a dowry that puts the royal family to shame, and Tramley to Lady Louise Eastfield—you remember her. Her mother was always throwing you two together.'

Matthew grimaced, thinking back on his interactions with the shy, awkward girl. Louise had been so scared of him that it had made every encounter unbearably uncomfortable. 'She wasn't much of a conversationalist, if I remember correctly. She tended to simply circumvent discussion by saying, "Yes, my lord" or "No, my lord".'

Leo sighed deeply. 'I should have made her an offer…'

Matthew, who knew his friend's taste in women rather well, raised one brow in surprise. 'You courted her?'

'No. But if I'd known she didn't talk I might have. A wife who says nothing except to agree with my opinion would suit me very well, don't you think?'

Matthew laughed. 'If you paused to listen once in a while, Pemberton, you might find that some women have interesting things to say.'

'I have yet to meet such a woman. Unless you consider embroidery, music and the latest fashions interesting.' Leo distractedly removed his hat and twirled it between his hands. 'Tell me about the women you met abroad. I've heard that Italian women are—'

'Bloody hell!'

A frustrated feminine voice cut off what was undoubtedly going to be a crude suggestion from Leo.

Matthew watched with amusement as a tall, slim woman rushed past them, her hands holding her skirts indecently high, as if they were an impediment she needed to overcome. A short lady's maid struggled to keep up with her long strides.

'Why am I always late?' the lady queried.

Clearly assuming that the question had been directed at her, her maid replied breathlessly, 'You get distracted easily, my lady.'

'My husband is undoubtedly going to have something dreadful to say about this, Peggy.'

'Yes, my lady.'

Matthew turned to Leo, but his friend was staring after the woman, his blue eyes glazed with recognition. Just as she was about to go out of earshot he cupped his hands to his mouth and called, 'Willa!'

Up ahead, the woman came to an abrupt stop. Matthew watched as she turned around slowly, her posture straight and stiff. She leaned forward slightly, eyes narrowed.

'Leo!'

Leo grinned and, without a word of explanation to Matthew, hurried forward. 'I *knew* that mouth could only belong on one woman,' he teased.

Matthew raised both brows. Leo might be a mischief-maker, but there were certain things even he didn't do, and mentioning a lady's mouth so suggestively was certainly one of them—or was supposed to be anyway.

As they approached, Matthew took stock of the stranger. She was tall, and looked as fragile as glass. Her upper arms couldn't be thicker than his wrists, yet despite her startling thinness she exuded a strange, frenetic energy, as if she couldn't quite stay still for more than a second at a time. Her mass of blond hair had been curled and swept back to reveal an enviably angular face and sad brown eyes that seemed oversized when compared to the rest of her features.

'Because I'm the only woman you know who swears in public?' Her tone was clipped with dry humour.

'Because you're the only woman I know who swears at all,' Leo countered.

Matthew didn't miss the way his friend's eyes flickered over the woman with surprise—and neither did she. She shifted uncomfortably under his gaze, passing her slight weight from foot to foot as if she were preparing to run.

Matthew bowed and, ignoring Leo's lapse, introduced himself. 'Matthew—Lord Ashworth.'

'Wilhelmina, Countess Windhurst.' She studied his face for a moment as if she were trying to piece something together. 'Have we met before, my lord? You look awfully familiar.'

'Willa was the youngest of the Russells,' Leo informed him, having regained himself. Turning back to Willa, he explained, 'Matthew went to school with me. I spent as much of my childhood with him as I did with Jameson and your other brothers. You two will have undoubtedly met somewhere over the years.'

'I believe I was a guest at a ball your parents hosted before I left for my tour of the continent,' Matthew supplied. 'Perhaps we were introduced?'

She seemed unconvinced. 'Perhaps. You'll have to

forgive my memory; my brothers have introduced me to so many acquaintances over the years.'

'Where are you running to?' Leo queried.

'Home. I'm supposed to be meeting my mother.' She waved a thin hand. 'Although heaven knows why I have to keep a social engagement with the woman. We see each other all the time.'

Leo laughed lightly. 'Allow us to escort you part of the way? We're heading in the same direction.'

The offer was in no way suggestive or improper, but Wilhelmina took a full step back. 'I would like that, Leo—it's been so long since we talked. But...' She cast a glance over her shoulder, as if searching for her maid to come and rescue her.

'We won't tell Windhurst if you don't,' Leo said, and when Wilhelmina didn't reply, only opened and closed her mouth uncertainly, he simply stepped forward and gently took her elbow. Wilhelmina hesitated for a small second, but it was long enough for Leo to use his superior weight against hers. He simply started walking, leaving her to fall into step with him or be dragged along.

Matthew remained politely quiet as they resumed their walk, but his curiosity had been piqued by this strange interaction—by Lady Windhurst's show of fear and by Leo's quiet possessiveness. Matthew had known Leo for almost twenty years, and he'd never seen his friend treat a lady with such unpractised deference. His typical approach was simply to avoid any eligible young woman as if she had the pox and flirt with every ineligible woman as if she were Aphrodite herself.

Matthew listened intently as Leo gently drew Lady Windhurst into conversation.

'We saw your brother at the club,' Leo said.

'Which one?'

'Jameson,' Leo clarified. 'He said that Grayson is engaged to be married?'

'Yes. And his fiancée, Rose Hudson, is exquisite. He's so besotted I'm almost convinced it's a love match.' She paused for a small moment. 'In fact, were she not *quite* so beautiful, I'd be sure of it.'

Matthew found himself smiling at the comment and the casual affection it was made with.

'And the rest of your brothers?'

'About the same. Gambling, whoring, and—perhaps worst of all—getting away with it.'

Leo's laugh rumbled.

'You laugh, Leo, because you will never know what it is to be born a woman in a family of men.'

'Thank God.'

Willa's mouth turned upwards in the first hint of a smile. 'I have to watch them live in freedom, with complete disregard for any social compunction. It's awfully annoying.' She turned her gaze to Matthew suddenly, as if remembering he was there. 'You will forgive my manners, Lord Ashworth. Leo and I are old friends. I sometimes forget myself when we're together.'

'There's nothing to forgive,' Matthew assured her.

He found that he liked her candid manner. There

was no pretence, no feigned incompetence or missish manners.

Wilhelmina regarded him as they walked with Leo between them. 'You do seem rather unoffended,' she affirmed. 'I dare say I like you.'

'Matthew has just returned from a two-year tour of the continent,' Leo supplied. 'He was about to describe all the scandalous women he encountered when you barged past.'

'I do not *barge*, Leo—I *glide*.' When Leo merely shook his head, Wilhelmina returned her focus to Matthew. 'I am intensely interested to hear about these scandalous women, Lord Ashworth.'

'Fortunately they are a figment of Leo's imagination.'

Leo scoffed.

Willa's eyes glistened with humour. 'As much as I doubt that, I do understand your moral dilemma.' She sighed wistfully. 'My dear friend Isabelle's aunt lives in Italy. And she's always writing us scandalous accounts of the Italians.'

Though the years had done nothing to dull his memory, Matthew barely flinched at the name. After all, it was a common enough name, one he had heard spoken numerous times over the years and learned to steel himself against—until Wilhelmina added, 'You know Isabelle, Leo. The Duchess of Everett.'

'I do.'

Their voices dimmed as Matthew's mind was flooded with images of the Duchess, her golden skin and bewitching eyes. He had never forgotten her…never been able to recapture the feeling of her in his arms.

Wilhelmina and Leo kept talking, oblivious to Matthew's sudden interest in their conversation as he listened intently for snippets of the Duchess, though none came. He wanted to stop Wilhelmina from rambling and direct her back to talking of her friend. He wanted to ask this strange woman how Isabelle was and if she'd maintained guardianship of her stepson. He wanted to know everything. *Anything.*

'My parents are having a ball next Friday,' she was saying. 'I expect you'll be there.'

'I have accepted your mother's invitation already,' came Leo's firm reply.

'Lord Ashworth, may I presume to extend to you an invitation on my mother's behalf?'

Matthew had no need to think it through. 'It would be my pleasure.'

'I'll send a formal invitation to you via one of my brothers.'

Matthew bowed politely as their party stopped at the edge of the park.

Leo reached out and took Willa's hand, holding it for a moment longer than was proper. 'We'll see you next Friday, Willa.'

She bobbed her head in a quick gesture. 'Thank you for walking with me.' Her brown eyes turned to Matthew. 'Both of you.'

They murmured appropriate replies and then watched

as she glided away, her lady's maid hurrying behind her once again.

'Good God,' Leo said as soon as she was out of earshot. 'I almost didn't recognise her.'

'She's changed?'

'She's so slight…' Leo's brows dipped inwards.

'Perhaps marriage doesn't agree with her,' Matthew suggested. 'Windhurst has always been a lout. I'm surprised Lord Russell agreed to the marriage.'

'Yes,' Leo replied quietly. 'Jameson objected to the match. But Grayson and her father thought Willa needed to be reined in. She's always been…'

'Unconventional?'

'Wild,' he corrected, but there was no judgement in his tone and a smile on his lips. He absently twirled his hat again, an anxious habit that he'd had even as a young boy, but his eyes never left the corner Wilhelmina had disappeared around.

Intrigued by his friend's obvious attachment to the lady, Matthew tried to offer some consolation. 'She's smart. Canny. She'll be fine.'

Remembering himself, Leo grinned suddenly. 'Well, at least you can now prove me wrong on one point.'

'Oh?'

He shot Matthew a wry glance. 'I stand corrected on my earlier observation about women. Wilhelmina Russell has always had something interesting to say—even when she shouldn't.'

Chapter Four

Matthew saw the Duchess the moment she stepped into Lord and Lady Russell's ballroom—and so did everyone else. A rippling murmur passed over the gathered guests as Lady Russell welcomed the widow who, despite her young age, had surpassed the older woman in rank when she'd married the late Duke of Everett.

Time had not altered her. Isabelle was still striking. Her black hair was piled atop her head and adorned with a single rose that complemented her burgundy dress and contrasted with the golden skin of her exposed shoulders. Though her posture was perfect, her rigid spine and neutrally set mouth somehow gave her the appearance of being extremely uncomfortable in her surroundings. In fact, she looked like a startled deer that had stopped to assess the danger and was contemplating bolting at any moment.

His stomach danced with nerves as he watched her murmur something to her companion, and when the women turned in the opposite direction to him he exhaled deeply and loosened his vice-like grip on the crystal punch glass he held.

He hadn't been sure of what his own reaction would be after all this time. But he would never have guessed that he'd be stunned senseless by her—again. He'd blamed his reaction all those years ago on her sudden appearance in his home and her outlandish request, but now… Now he realised that he hadn't been quite honest with himself all this time. The Duchess of Everett was everything that he remembered—and more.

'Would you like an introduction?' Leo asked. 'The Duchess is a friend of Wilhelmina.'

Realising that he had been staring after Isabelle, Matthew turned his back in the direction she'd gone. 'Perhaps later.'

It wouldn't do to make a fool of himself—and, considering his history with the Duchess, he thought it best to let her discover him by herself rather than have his company thrust upon her. She would be mortified if he suddenly appeared before her for an introduction, and although she was one of the more pragmatic women he'd ever met, Matthew didn't know if she'd be able to school her reaction to seeing him again adequately. Better to be seen by her first—better to give her time to come to terms with the fact that he was in attendance at the ball.

Easier said than done.

As the night progressed, and he and Leo made the social rounds and danced countless dances with the numerous girls that Lady Russell insisted on introducing them to, it became clear to Matthew that the Duchess would not be one of them. It wasn't surprising, really. Unlike the other young women at the ball, and even though she was barely older than many of them, Isabelle was a widow. And a duchess to boot. The result was that she and her companions seemed to be spared Lady Russell's attention.

Instead of dancing or talking with the other guests, they sat in a corner with Wilhelmina. They talked and laughed amongst themselves as if they were at a private tea party, not a formal ball, and the close-set layout of their chairs discouraged interruptions of any kind.

'If you keep staring at them like that, people are going to talk,' Leo commented during one of their brief respites from dancing.

'As three young, attractive women, they are decidedly uninterested in being social.'

'And why should they be? Willa is married—and a countess.' Matthew noted Leo's odd tone when he spoke of Wilhelmina. 'And the Duchess of Everett and her companion are both widowed. If you ask me, they're damned lucky. They've done this already, and now—unlike the rest of us poor sods—they're spared the inconvenience of having to dance with every unattached person of the opposite sex.'

'I wouldn't call being married and widowed before the age of twenty *lucky*, Leo,' Matthew chastised.

'I'll wager the Duchess wouldn't agree with you,' Leo quipped, pulling a quick laugh from Matthew.

'Irrespective, it appears as if your opportunity for an introduction has come and gone.'

Matthew spun on his heel just in time to see Isabelle and her companion walking around the edges of the room towards the door. At first he thought she hadn't seen him, but then Isabelle turned and looked back directly at him. When their eyes met, her face paled.

For one long second they stared at each other.

And then she whipped around again, continuing her escape at an increased pace.

Matthew cursed. 'Leo—can I trust you?' he asked urgently.

Leo frowned at him. 'Of course.'

'Stop her.'

'What?' Leo arched back to stare at him. 'Are you quite all right—?'

'There's no time. I'll explain later.' He nudged his friend in Isabelle's direction. 'Hurry.'

Leo took off without a backward glance, cutting through the crowd easily. He didn't circumvent the dancing, as Isabelle had, merely sliced right through the quadrille, interrupting the structured dance and earning several reproachful glances.

Matthew didn't care. Leo got to the ballroom door seconds before Isabelle and her companion and, bowing at the waist, greeted them both.

Not wanting to be too obvious, Matthew turned back to where Wilhelmina now sat alone. The Countess was watching him, her head tilted ever so slightly, her brown eyes narrowed on him. He approached her warily, aware that she must have seen Leo's mad dash through her mother's ball.

'Lady Windhurst,' he greeted her with a small bow.

'Lord Ashworth. I thought it was you.'

'Apologies for not greeting you sooner. You and your friends seemed occupied.'

'Oh…' Willa waved her hand dismissively. 'Izzy, Mary and I see each other all the time. It would have been no interruption.'

Her gaze flitted behind him, and he didn't have to look to know that Leo was leading the Duchess back through the room towards them. Matthew could feel her at his back. The fine hair at his nape pulled tight, and even though he desperately wanted to turn and watch her approach, he braced himself against the urge. He needed a few more seconds to acclimatise himself to the panic spreading through his galloping heart.

'It would seem that you are acquainted with my friends,' said Wilhelmina.

It was not a question, but Matthew replied anyway. 'To my regret, I am not acquainted with either of them.'

Willa made a non-committal sound. 'I will have to introduce you, then.'

She stood and boldly linked her arm through his just as Leo approached, Isabelle and her companion on either side of him.

'Leo, what on earth were you thinking—accosting my friends like that?' the Countess chastised. 'It's a wonder you didn't cause injury to one of my mother's guests.'

'My apologies, Willa.' Leo relinquished formalities,

using Wilhelmina's nickname instead of her title. 'I realised that Her Grace was leaving and remembered that I had not had the privilege of introducing her and her companion to my friend.' Leo took a small step back and sent Matthew a pointed glance. 'Your Grace, may I present Lord Ashworth? Lord Ashworth—the Duchess of Everett, Lady Isabelle St Claire. And her cousin, Mrs Mary Lambert.'

Matthew bowed even as his heart lurched in his chest. 'It is a pleasure to make your acquaintance, Your Grace... Mrs Lambert.'

The women returned the pleasantries, but Matthew was looking at Isabelle, and he noticed the red blush of embarrassment riding high on her cheekbones. Even her small mouth seemed to be struggling, her lips wobbling slightly before settling in a nervous half-grimace.

'Lord Ashworth has just returned from a tour of the continent,' Willa offered, breaking the awkward silence. 'The last time we met he was on the precipice of telling me about his scandalous Italian women.'

'Oh...' Mary said awkwardly.

Isabelle remained silent, but he saw her risk a peek at him from under her heavy lashes.

Willa and Leo grinned like a pair of feral children who'd been tossed a bone.

Unsure of anything except that he needed a moment alone with the Duchess, Matthew asked, 'Would you do me the honour of dancing with me, Your Grace?'

He braced himself for the refusal he saw in her eyes.

'I'm—'

'Oh, she would love to!' Willa exclaimed. 'Isabelle was just telling me how much she misses dancing.'

Isabelle turned to stare at her friend. If he hadn't had a vested interest in getting her alone, Matthew might have laughed at the way her eyes narrowed in Willa's direction. But instead of arguing, the Duchess deferred and gave the polite response. 'Yes. It would be an honour, Lord Ashworth.'

Matthew, seeing her discomfort, didn't offer her his arm. Instead, he bowed again, and indicated for her to lead the way to where couples were preparing to waltz.

Isabelle stopped in the centre of the ballroom, in the hope that the other dancers would shelter them as much as possible, and turned to face Lord Ashworth. He was immaculately turned out in traditional formal attire, his skin dark against the stark white of his linen shirt and silk waistcoat. His black hair, although trimmed and styled, was still too long, yet Isabelle could not deny that he made a striking image.

She opened her mouth to speak, to say something trivial about the weather or the ball, but no words came. Instead, her tongue felt thick and clumsy. A hot flush worked its way up her neck, and even though she hadn't eaten anything she had the most awful feeling that she might be ill.

The waltz started. The music gently drifted to them through the crowded room. Matthew tipped at the waist, his gaze never leaving hers, but all Isabelle could do was stare at him. His grey eyes, so familiar to her, did not calm her, though they were gentle and filled with understanding.

When she did not move, Matthew gently arranged her in the waltz position, placing his right hand lightly on her upper back. The barely perceptible touch somehow burned through all the layers of her garments more than any ham-handedness could have done. Their bodies remained politely separated, but he was still too close. The heat from his skin seeped into her hand, and when she dared to meet his eyes again he was close enough that she could see the black rings around his grey irises.

'Were you running away from me, Duchess?' he inquired, his deep voice lowered and only for her.

No etiquette existed for a situation like this—Isabelle knew that. So, unsure of how to behave, she merely nodded honestly, and in a small voice that was so pathetic, and so unlike her, replied, 'I once promised that I would never seek you out…' She straightened her spine and with more force added, 'I have kept my word.'

Together, they turned in a gliding circle, easily following the dance, though neither of them was paying any attention. Matthew was watching her face so intently that Isabelle feared he would see that she was hiding something far more scandalous than their past encounter.

But instead of ceding her point, as she'd expected, he surprised her by leaning forward, shockingly close, and whispering, 'Did you ever, even once, think about breaking your word?'

Isabelle was too shocked to reply, though the word *yes* echoed loudly in her head.

Matthew's strong arms held her close. 'After what we shared, one truth could hardly make a difference, Duchess.'

Isabelle shook her head, overwhelmed by the strange turn this night was taking. 'I made you a promise,' she repeated.

'And you've certainly kept it.'

Isabelle arched backwards, the better to see his face, and when she met his eyes she was shocked to see her own memories, her own awareness, reflected in their depths.

'What do you want?' she whispered, panicked by the conversation they were having. 'My situation—'

'Your situation is secure, Duchess. I am a man of my word.'

Isabelle didn't know what to do. Every instinct was telling her to politely excuse herself, leave the ball, and remove her family to Moorhen House without delay. She could not be in town with this man; even London was too small. Somehow she knew that they were fated always to intercept one another and that she could not hide from him for ever.

'Matthew…'

His fingers jolted against hers at her use of his first name. His dark head lowered. 'Duchess?'

'There is something I need to tell you…'

She looked up at him again. For a long moment all she could do was stare, trapped by his expectant gaze.

Chapter Five

'May I escort you back to your seat?'

The Duchess didn't even seem aware that they had stopped dancing and were now standing in the middle of the ballroom while other couples skilfully tried to avoid bumping into them. A group of women nearby were watching them closely, their fans covering their mouths—and their undoubtedly speculative words.

She leaned heavily on him, as if she might faint at any moment. Over the music, Matthew became aware of her short, panting breaths. Her eyes were dark with panic, her face contrastingly pale.

Alarm coursed through him. 'Isabelle?'

She eased away from him and slowly raised a hand to her chest. 'I can't…breathe…'

'Duchess?' he urged, keeping his voice low to avoid attracting more attention. 'Look at me.'

She raised her eyes to his, and although she held his gaze her chest heaved with panic and her sharp breaths became more and more pronounced.

'I'm going to take you back to your friends and then escort you to your carriage.'

Without waiting for her reply, he linked her arm through his and led her quickly from the dance floor.

Matthew was aware of all the eyes in the room watching them, watching *her*, with thinly veiled curiosity. 'I am sorry, Duchess,' he murmured, 'to have caused you so much distress. It was not my intention.'

'It's not what you think,' she replied breathlessly. 'There's something I need to tell you… I—'

'Your friend abandoned us at the first opportunity, Lord Ashworth,' Willa said, unknowingly talking over Isabelle in her attempt to move attention away from the fact that he and Isabelle had only managed half a dance together.

Unsure of how to behave, torn between wanting to console the Duchess and grab the lifeline Wilhelmina had thrown him, he replied, 'Leo has never had the ability to stay in one place long.'

'Nor in the company of one woman long,' Willa retorted, eliciting various reactions from the nearby eavesdroppers.

The Dowager Countess Radcliffe gasped dramatically. Lady Pembroke fluttered her fan in a dramatic display of distress. Lord Wickmore, who knew Leo rather well, nodded in agreement.

But as Lady Windhurst's unladylike observation drew nearby attention to her, Matthew looked down at Isabelle. She was staring at him as if she was afraid—as if she wanted to get as far away from him as possible. And, of all the ways he'd imagined she'd react at their reintroduction, he'd never thought that she might be *afraid* of him. Were their memories of that night so different?

'Her Grace is not well,' he said gently, hoping to give her some small relief. 'Mrs Lambert? Perhaps I could escort you both to your carriage?'

Mary immediately took charge of the situation. 'I think that would be best, my lord,' she said.

Willa's eyes narrowed on Isabelle, then widened with concern. 'Izzy, I dare say you *do* look rather pale.'

'It is nothing,' Isabelle replied shakily. 'Only too long since I have been in society. I'm afraid it is all rather overwhelming.'

Willa pushed herself to stand and, instead of politely bidding the Duchess farewell, yanked her into a tight hug. 'Thank you so much for coming, Izzy.'

Although he was certain he was not supposed to hear the next part, Matthew was aware that Lady Windhurst murmured, 'The Earl has departed already, thank God. I shall leave as soon as I have said goodbye to my mother.'

'You will come and visit us soon?' Isabelle managed, still sounding breathless.

'Tomorrow.'

As soon as she had released Isabelle, Matthew exchanged farewells with Lady Windhurst. He led the Duchess and Mary Lambert out of the Russells' ballroom, using his significant height and brawn to part the crowd for the two women who followed close behind.

He waited with them in silence for fifteen minutes

as their carriage was called, too conscious of Mrs Lambert's elbow-to-elbow stance next to Isabelle to speak to her as he would have liked. He had so many questions—so many things he wanted to say to her. But most of all he wanted her to stop looking at him out of the corner of her eye, as if he was a predatory cat out to hunt her.

Did she not remember the way they'd fitted so perfectly together? Or the way she'd slotted into his side for the short thirty minutes they'd taken afterwards to come to terms with what they'd done? Had she really not thought of him all this time as he had thought of her—daily? Some nights he'd fallen asleep thinking of her lean, lithe body and her quick-witted mind, only to have her plague him in his dreams too, so that he'd woken up exhausted and angry and yearning for a person he barely knew.

The rumble of an approaching carriage and the Duchess of Everett's palpable relief indicated that their time was up, and Matthew swallowed down his flaring disappointment.

He waited until the carriage was abreast of them, and then, when the Duchess stepped forward, he reached out and grasped her hand, halting her escape. He passed her and held out his other hand for Mary Lambert—something that would have been considered an affront to the Duchess had anyone noticed.

Instead of taking his hand, Mrs Lambert looked at Isabelle, who gave her consent with one curt nod.

He handed Mary into the carriage and then turned his

back on her to face the Duchess. 'I am sorry to have distressed you.'

'I know.' She bowed her head, almost as if she were shy or confused. 'Matth—' She caught her breath. 'Lord Ashworth—'

'You may always call me Matthew, Duchess. Surely, after everything, we can remain friends?'

Those words were the furthest thing from the truth—perhaps the greatest lie he'd ever spoken. He could never be friends with this woman. For a martyr he was not. He knew what it was to make love to her, and he found that he would rather end their acquaintance now than see her about and pretend that she had not shaken him to his very core.

'We cannot.'

She raised those dark eyes to his and he saw the way she pulled herself upright, straightening her spine with resolve.

'As you wish,' he replied and, bending over her gloved hand, turned it so that he could kiss the inside of her wrist one last time.

But when he raised his eyes to her face he saw that she was blinking rapidly, her eyes glossy with tears.

'Duchess…' He shook his head, trying to make sense of her odd behaviour.

Before he could say more, Isabelle hurriedly wiped her face and forced her lips into a tight smile. 'Thank you for escorting us to our carriage, Lord Ashworth.'

He held out his hand, ready to help her in, but Isabelle raised her hands to her chest instead and took a single step back, before quickly climbing into the carriage without his assistance.

Matthew's hand curled in on itself as if he were scorched. He stood back as a nearby footman came and closed the door, watching as the carriage started moving, taking the Duchess away from him. With each yard the carriage travelled, his disappointment sank deeper.

Matthew turned on his heel and marched back towards the Russells' ball. All this time he had thought of her, *dreamed* of her, hoping that she thought of him, too…

Growing increasingly frustrated with himself, Matthew pushed all thoughts of the Duchess out of his mind and went in search of a bottle.

He of all people should know that nothing good could ever come of him pursuing the Duchess. Hadn't he told himself that over and over again in the past two years? Hadn't he brought the memory of past scandal, of Christine's frenzied begging, to his mind countless times, in an attempt to remind himself why he avoided attachments altogether?

But it was done now.

It took him only three minutes to get to Lord Russell's study. He had, after all, spent many years visiting Jameson Russell in this very house.

Matthew opened the door—and pulled up short when he saw Leo and Lady Windhurst were in the room. There was nothing scandalous about their situation except the fact that they were alone. They were both kneeling on the floor, on opposite sides of a small table, a chessboard open between them. From what he could see, Willa was giving Leo a thorough fleecing.

'Ah, Lord Ashworth,' Lady Windhurst drawled. 'You have walked in on a most embarrassing situation: your best friend, your closest ally, is being beaten at his best game—by a woman.' She sighed dramatically.

Leo snorted, completely at ease. 'Chess is not my best game. Not by far.'

Wilhelmina tilted her head in agreement. 'Yes. But I don't think we can politely compete in all the other things you are so renowned for.'

Leo choked on the sip of brandy he'd just taken. Matthew did not try to hide his laugh. He stepped into the room, making sure to close and lock the door behind him.

'There's no point in locking us in,' Willa said calmly. 'I seem to get away with quite a lot now that my husband has taken to flaunting his whore.' She refocused on the board and, after a moment's deliberation, moved her last pawn two spaces forward. 'It is rather nice to have such leeway. Don't you think?'

Leo didn't comment, although Matthew would have been a fool not to notice his friend's downcast gaze.

Matthew considered his reply for a brief moment, before settling on the blunt truth. 'I have never for a single moment considered Earl Windhurst an intelligent man, my lady. But his behaviour now proves him the greatest fool that ever lived.'

Lady Windhurst looked up at him in surprise, her serious brown eyes lightening perceptibly.

Matthew held a hand dramatically over his heart. 'Were you mine, I would sail the world to bring you only the best of everything. Spices from India! Dresses from Paris! Caviar from Russia!'

As he'd intended, Lady Windhurst laughed. And, although she hadn't been looking at Leo, Matthew saw his friend's eyes snap to Willa as the sound left her mouth.

'You forget, Lord Ashworth, that I have seen the way you look at Isabelle.'

Matthew's grin faltered, but instead of denying it he shrugged nonchalantly. 'The Duchess is a beautiful woman.'

Willa made that same non-committal sound and went back to the chess game, but she kept on talking as she considered her next move.

'Your taste cannot be faulted. Isabelle is the very best.' She moved a knight expertly, placing Leo's king in check. 'She is cultured and beautiful and rich as sin— her late husband left her a sizeable jointure. She is also *revoltingly* kind and loyal—often towards people such as me, who are entirely underserving of it.'

Having made her move, Willa sat back from the board and frowned.

She turned to him. 'Although she does come with the additional burden of two children.'

Two children.

Time simply stopped.

The sound of his own heart pumping filled his ears as Willa's words registered.

Two children.

'Oh…?' He managed the single word through the block lodged in his throat even as his brain fought to deny it.

Impossible.

It couldn't be…

She would have told me…

And yet even as he thought it, he remembered Isabelle's promise never to contact him again—the very promise she'd reminded him of only tonight. And the look on her face, pale and afraid, as they'd danced. And again as she'd got into her carriage.

Her words, 'It's not what you think', suddenly took on new meaning.

Willa didn't raise her head as she watched Leo try to extricate his king from checkmate. 'Yes. The late Duke of Everett had a son—Luke. He's about nine now. And Isabelle conceived in the few short weeks she was married to the Duke. Seraphina, her daughter, is one and a half.'

Matthew felt the blood drain from his upper extremities. His mind flailed at the calculation even though his heart was constricted by the truth. Because he knew beyond a doubt that Isabelle wouldn't have approached anyone else after she'd accomplished her goal of securing Luke's guardianship.

'Isabelle has a daughter?' he rasped.

'Yes.'

Willa looked up at him. Her smile had died. And maybe it was because Seraphina had just been in Willa's thoughts, but Matthew saw the exact moment that recognition flared in her brown eyes.

He looked away, trying desperately to appear uninterested.

But Wilhelmina wasn't so easily fooled. After a long, drawn-out silence, she said, 'It's so peculiar, though… Sera looks nothing like the late Duke. If I knew less about Izzy, I'd say she'd been thoroughly debauched by someone else before the wedding.'

'Doubtful.' Leo chose that moment to comment. 'The Duchess doesn't have it in her. Too cool. Aloof. Practical.'

Matthew wanted to argue. He wanted to say that she was not cool, but fire in his hands. That she was never aloof, only shy and inexperienced. But practical… He would give Leo 'practical'. The Duchess was perhaps the most practical woman he'd ever met.

He didn't say any of that, though, too overwrought by the sudden certainty that his life had just taken a drastic turn.

'I think I'll retire for the evening,' he said to nobody in particular.

He had to go.

He had to *know*.

Leo waved him off casually. Wilhelmina pushed herself to her feet.

'I'll lock the door after you.' She followed him to the door, lowering her voice significantly as she added, 'I was wondering why she panicked this evening, you know. Before she saw you she was managing her first foray into society since being widowed quite well.'

'Where is she?'

'At home, I imagine.'

'Lady Windhurst,' he said quietly, his tone beseeching. 'Please...'

'She is at Everett Place. In St James's. The house is impossible to miss.' She unlocked and opened the door. 'Had I known I was divulging something I shouldn't have, I would never have said anything.'

'I do not doubt it.'

Wilhelmina stared at him for a long moment. 'If you hurt my friend, there will be hell to pay.'

Matthew didn't reply—what was there to say?

And although she tipped her head in farewell, he felt Wilhelmina's gaze burning into his back as he marched down the corridor.

He didn't let her warning stop him. He exited the house, and the moment he was on the street he started running.

Chapter Six

Everett Place, although technically a townhouse, was probably better described as a town mansion. The six-storey residence had an exterior façade comprised of yellow malm brick. The entrance, offset to the left, was framed by two white Doric pilasters beneath the large Venetian windows that lined the entire front of the house.

It was nearing midnight and, suddenly unsure of himself, unsure of the situation, Matthew leaned against a lamppost on the opposite side of the street and considered his options.

He knew what he *wanted* to do. He *wanted* to storm into Everett Place and demand the truth from Isabelle. But then what? What happened once she'd told him?

Matthew, who was typically so sure of himself, felt new panic at his lack of direction.

I should go home, he thought. *Think this through.*

He even moved off to do just that. But then, just before his eyes left the windows of the house, one of the dark rooms was lit with the warm glow of a candle, and before he could think to move his feet the Duchess herself drew back the lace curtain. She leaned one shoulder against the windowpane and stared out into the night, as if she were searching for someone in the dark…as if she were searching for *him*.

Matthew held his breath as he watched her from the shadows opposite. The Duchess was a beautiful woman, her sable hair still piled atop her head, her skin warmed by the candlelight behind her. She was still dressed in her burgundy gown, and as he watched she wrapped her arms around her waist and looked down on the empty street.

He thought she looked rather sad. And he couldn't help but wonder if she was sad because of him—because of their encounter. The manner in which she'd tried to run from him was indication enough that he had terrified her. Or, maybe, he thought now, he had simply threatened the secret she protected.

The thought that he had scared her shamed him. Had he been less eager to see her again he might have thought his reintroduction through more.

Like now, his mind screamed at him.

He was standing outside her home, spying on her like some deranged madman, and for what? What would he do if the child was his?

Seraphina, Willa had called her. *Seraphina.*

As if his thoughts had somehow conjured her, a second woman approached—a maid. She was carrying a small child who had the same round, cherubic cheeks and dark, riotous curls that Matthew remembered on Eleanor, his youngest sister, at the same age.

The child was crying, her eyes scrunched closed, her tiny hands fisted in frustration.

His heart simply stopped beating for one perfect moment, before resuming at an accelerated pace.

His stomach roiled with nausea.

Sweat broke across his brow.

His mouth watered, and for one long moment all he could do was close his eyes and swallow down the anxiety clogging his throat.

He should turn and walk away. He should leave. Only Matthew couldn't get his feet to move. Instead, he opened his eyes again and stared, in a daze, as Isabelle turned away from the window.

Her sadness simply lifted. Her lips curled into a genuine smile as she extended her arms for the crying child. Seraphina went to her and immediately nestled her head in her mother's neck, seeking comfort.

The maid left, casting the room into dimmer light as she took her candle with her, silhouetting the Duchess and her child in the window. Together, they looked like one of Raphael's *Madonna and Child* paintings. Isabelle was beautiful—if not virginal. The dress she wore would have evoked purely carnal thoughts in the most decent of men. And Seraphina… She was a cherubic replication of…*him*.

Isabelle brushed Seraphina's curls back from her forehead and placed a single kiss on her cheek. Although he couldn't hear what she said, he saw her lips move as she cooed words of comfort.

Matthew would have given anything at that moment to be standing there with her—with *them*—listening to her maternal chatter. What words did she speak to calm her child? What stories did she weave for her? Or were they not stories at all, but simple nothings measured out in that universal tone reserved for young children?

Hating to leave, but knowing that he was intruding on a private moment, Matthew finally moved to go. He'd go home—for now. At least until he could plan his next steps.

He took a step forward, inadvertently bringing himself out of the shadows—and realised his mistake too late.

In the still, dark night, his movements were amplified. He hesitated as the Duchess saw his brief advance and turned to look out of the window.

Their eyes met.

There was one horrific second in which she recognised him, followed quickly by her terrified retreat—a retreat that left him more certain of the child's identity than her physical appearance ever could have.

He looked up at the dark window for a long moment, daring her to step back into the light and face him.

The Duchess did not.

Of course she did not.

And so, helpless to do anything else just then, Matthew simply turned and walked away.

If he'd imagined that his life would change once he'd

returned from his tour, he never could have imagined that it would change so soon—nor so drastically. For there was no doubt in his mind that he had been looking at *his* child, *his* daughter.

Seraphina.

Isabelle had almost managed to convince herself that she had imagined Matthew, Lord Ashworth, standing outside her house and looking up at her bedroom window the night before by the time she went down to breakfast the next morning.

She'd tossed and turned all night—one moment convincing herself that it had certainly been him, and that she would have recognised him anywhere, and the next telling herself that she'd imagined the entire episode and that Matthew had far better things to do with his time than follow her home and wait beneath her bedroom window like some sinister Romeo.

'Good morning, Mary,' she said as she entered the dining room.

Mary, who was sitting at the family dining room table reading a letter, looked up at her and smiled. 'You slept rather late this morning.'

'On the contrary,' Isabelle replied, 'I barely slept at all. And then couldn't find the energy to actually get out of bed once the sun had risen.'

She walked to the sideboard to peruse the breakfast that had been laid out and, sensing that her uneasy stomach wasn't ready for the full English fare, settled on pouring herself a cup of tea instead.

'Is anything the matter?' asked Mary.

Isabelle considered her cousin over the rim of her teacup. 'I don't know,' she admitted finally.

Hearing the uncertainty in Isabelle's tone, Mary put the letter she had been perusing down on the table and turned, giving Isabelle her full attention.

'Last night, once we'd returned from the ball…'

'Yes?'

'Well, I was in my bedroom…' She trailed off, unable to finish.

'And?'

'Well, I could have sworn I saw Lord Ashworth standing on the street below, looking up at me.'

Mary paled. 'Are you certain it was him?'

Yes. Isabelle exhaled a huge breath, but didn't answer the question out loud, settling on 'I had Sera with me' instead.

'Oh.' Mary sat back in her chair, but instead of calming Isabelle, maybe telling her she was delusional, or reminding her that Lord Ashworth probably had no interest in his illegitimate daughter, she asked, 'Do you think he knows?'

Isabelle moved to sit opposite Mary at the table, her worry suddenly amplified by her cousin's. 'If it was him, he most certainly knows—or at least suspects,' she whispered. 'How could he not?'

'What will he demand?'

'Demand?' The idea that Lord Ashworth would demand anything of her hadn't even entered her mind.

He wouldn't…would he?

'Izzy, you are a *duchess*,' Mary replied quickly, leaning across the table. 'One with a considerable fortune and no husband's protection. And Lord Ashworth is a notorious womaniser with a highly questionable character. He could demand anything.' She shook her head rapidly, as if wanting to deny the statement, even as the words 'And you'd have no choice but to give it to him' came out of her mouth. 'Seraphina looks too much like him,' she said.

Isabelle took a deep breath and tried to calm herself. 'As far as I know, the Heather earldom is intact,' she countered, trying desperately to ignore the frantic ticking of her pulse. 'His family fortune is considerable. Why would he need to demand anything from me?'

'Well…' Mary's brows drew together as she considered the question. 'What *else* could he want?'

'I… I have no idea.'

They were saved from having to speculate by a light knock on the door.

Both she and Mary resumed their respective breakfasts, and Isabelle called, 'Enter!'

'Good morning, Your Grace.' The butler came in and bowed, holding out a silver tray with the morning mail.

'Thank you, Gordon.' She took the three letters off the tray. 'Have you seen Luke this morning?'

'Still abed, Your Grace. Though I passed Tess in the hall, on her way to wake him for your walk.'

'Thank you.'

The butler bowed and left the room.

Isabelle flicked through the letters. The first, from

her mother, she decided to leave until later in the afternoon, knowing that it wouldn't contain anything urgent—she'd seen her at the ball just last night, and her mother had had nothing to say to her beyond a cursory greeting. The second was from her solicitor, Mr Briggs, who was undoubtedly writing to confirm the monthly estate meeting that she had insisted Luke partake in since her husband had died. The last…

Isabelle stared at her name, written in a neat, masculine hand, for a long moment. There were two parts of her, each vying for control. One wanted to tear open the letter and read what he'd written. The other wanted to throw it into the blazing fire and pretend she'd never received the missive at all.

'Is it from him?' asked Mary.

'I don't know.'

After a long moment, she opened the letter with trembling hands.

Duchess,
Meet me at Hyde Park Corner. Two o'clock. We have much to discuss.
M

'He wants to meet me,' Isabelle said finally. 'Today.'

She read the note to Mary, making sure to keep her tone neutral despite the heavy dread collecting in her stomach.

'Oh, Izzy, what are you going to do?' Mary's face was still pale, her eyes wide with fear.

'I'm going to meet him,' Isabelle replied matter-of-factly. 'There's no way around this, Mary. Whatever he has to say to me—whatever he wants from me—cannot be ignored.'

She tucked the letter into the long sleeve of her dress so that she could destroy it later.

'You're awfully calm, Isabelle.'

Isabelle didn't feel calm at all. She felt quite ill, actually. However, there was one thing keeping the worst of her panic at bay: the memory of that night. Matthew had been kind and gentle with her. He'd never laughed at her situation nor made her feel scandalised or cheap.

'I don't remember him being cruel,' she said quietly. 'Quite the opposite, in fact. Perhaps he just wants to know the truth? Perhaps he has heard that I have a child and put the pieces together?'

'I suppose there is only one way to find out.'

Isabelle nodded her agreement, and they both lapsed into silence.

Mary finished reading her own letter and soon rose from the table. 'I will be ready to accompany you.'

'Could you tell Luke that we'll delay our walk until then?'

Mary hesitated. 'You think it a good idea to take him?'

'I don't see the harm in it.'

But internally Isabelle thought that the more people between her and Lord Ashworth the better. Last night, when he'd held her in his arms, she'd wanted to rest her head against his chest and breathe in the scent of him—

the scent that still haunted her sensory memory two years later. She'd wanted to lean into his touch where it had burned through her clothes…

'And Sera?'

'No,' Isabelle said immediately. 'I… I can't.' She raised one trembling hand to her tired eyes. 'People would talk, Mary. Only weeks out of mourning and spotted gallivanting around the parks with Lord Ashworth—and a child who looks eerily like him? No,' Isabelle repeated, straightening her spine. 'I want to keep Sera away from this. She must stay here with Tess.'

'I think we should have Willa accompany us too.' Mary turned back from where she stood at the door. 'That way it will seem as if we are out together and have just happen upon the Viscount.'

Isabelle considered Mary's suggestion. Not only did Willa know Lord Ashworth, she'd also provide a necessary distraction. After all, he could hardly threaten or expose her in front of two other people and a child— could he?

'Yes. We shall ask her when she arrives.'

'What do we say?'

'That we would love her to join us for a walk in Hyde Park.' Isabelle shrugged, but the gesture did nothing to dispel the heavy weight of guilt sliding through her. 'To be entirely honest, Mary, I… To have done what I did…'

'You didn't have a choice.'

'There is always a choice. And I knew the consequences of mine when I made it. Now there is nothing to do but face Lord Ashworth and reap what I have sown…' The knowledge calmed her. 'There is no way around it. And to be entirely honest… Even if I could take it back, I wouldn't. He gave me Seraphina.'

Suddenly, the door to the dining room burst open and Willa herself strode in, her quick steps filled with anxious energy.

Gordon hurried to keep up with her, bowing quickly before Willa could speak. 'Lady Windhurst, Your Grace,' he wheezed, his breath coming in uneven gasps.

'Heaven knows I don't need an introduction, Gordy,' Willa teased, using the pet name that only she used for Isabelle's elderly butler.

Gordon merely frowned, bowed again, and repeated, 'Your Grace,' before departing.

As soon as the door had clicked shut behind him, Willa spun around to face Isabelle. 'You little hussy!' she declared, her brown eyes wide.

Mary gasped.

Isabelle froze for one perfect second, before a small, hysterical giggle escaped from between her lips. 'I suppose our promise to keep silent won't be necessary after all, Mary.'

'How?' Willa threw her hands in the air. *'When?'*

She began an agitated march around the dining room. 'I mean, I always wondered at Sera's looks, but… *You.* I would have lost that wager a hundred, nay, a *thousand* times over! You…' she glanced around the room as if to check for eavesdroppers, lowered her voice, and stage whispered '…and *Lord Ashworth?*'

'Wilhelmina, dear,' Isabelle chastised. 'Could you perhaps *actually* whisper instead of *pretending* to whisper?'

Willa hurried over to the seat Mary had just vacated and dragged it out with little grace or ceremony. She plonked into it and rested both elbows on the table. 'Tell me *everything*, Izzy!'

'How did you…?'

'I didn't. Not until you came up in my conversation with the gentleman last night.'

Isabelle listened as Willa explained how she'd put the pieces together.

'I'm sorry to have brought it up,' Willa finished. 'By the time I realised, it was too late.'

'It's not your fault.' Isabelle sighed. She related her own story to Willa, ending with, 'I always had a feeling that there would be a bigger price to pay one day…'

'What do you mean?' Willa asked, looking back and forth between Isabelle and Mary.

'He has asked me to meet him at Hyde Park Corner today at two o'clock.'

'Drat.' Willa raised one hand to her face and tapped her index finger against her lips as she considered. 'Do you know what I would do?'

'What?'

'I wouldn't go.' Willa slammed her palm on the table. 'I would show him that I cannot be cowed. You are a *duchess*, Isabelle!'

'Mmm…' Isabelle mumbled, considering.

'You don't think that would push him to do something rash?' Mary, ever calm and rational.

'Like what?' Willa countered. 'He's hardly going to run around the park shouting his sins for all the world to hear.'

'True.' Mary nodded slowly. 'He wouldn't dare. Not after his last scandal.'

Willa looked back and forth between them. 'What scandal?'

'He was…*involved* with the Marchioness of Dunn—Christine Dalmore—when he was quite a bit younger,' Isabelle offered, feeling vaguely guilty for sharing the gossip. 'It was how he came to be on our list.'

'It didn't end well,' Mary finished.

'Oh, I remember something about that…' Willa tapped her fingers on the table. 'She caused a scene when he broke it off.'

'*Caused a scene* would be putting it lightly.' Mary glanced at Isabelle, as if to make sure she had her approval to talk of such things. When Isabelle nodded, she added, 'The Marchioness went to his club and threatened to kill herself if he did not take her back. Apparently, she had to be sedated before her husband could transport her to the country. Soon afterwards she travelled abroad, and to my knowledge has not returned.'

'How odd. He doesn't *seem* the callous type.' Willa turned back to Isabelle. 'What do you think? You know him best.'

'On the contrary. I do not know him at all.'

Although she did not say it, Isabelle reminded herself that, even if Matthew had been nothing but kind and gentle with her, he had a past that proved him a reprehensible rogue, a man who should not be trusted. She briefly fought an internal battle, pitching the memory of her night with him against her knowledge of his previous scandal, but when she factored Sera into the equation it was an easy decision.

Pointing to the small writing desk in the corner of the room, Isabelle said, 'Mary, pass me that pen and paper.'

Mary hurried to oblige.

Willa grinned wickedly. 'You think he deserves the courtesy of a note?'

'No.'

Fuelled by thoughts of the Marchioness's ruination, by memories of Matthew, and by a new fear for herself and her family, Isabelle hurriedly scrawled a reply. And if, through her determination, the memory of his gentle manner and quiet care flared, Isabelle did her best to ignore it. Her own potential scandal aside, Matthew had the power to ruin Seraphina—and that she would not abide.

'I think *I* deserve the pleasure of refusing him.'

The note was short and borderline rude.

M,

In answer to your request: no. I regret to inform you that I am otherwise engaged at home for the remainder of the day. Nonetheless, I hope you have

*a pleasant walk. The weather looks promising for
a promenade...*
D

She didn't know why she signed it 'D' for Duchess,
instead of 'I' for Isabelle. Knew only that she rather
liked the way he turned her title into an improper endearment.

'What I wouldn't give to see his face when he reads
it!' Willa laughed.

Even Mary offered a small smile. 'Hopefully, he
doesn't retaliate.'

Chapter Seven

Matthew couldn't help but scowl when he read the Duchess's curt reply—her *refusal*, as it were.

'Taps!' he called, his voice booming through his study and out into the hall.

His butler appeared in the open doorway almost immediately. 'My lord?'

'Have one of the footmen fetch me some flowers.'

Taps's white bushy eyebrows rose high on his forehead at the strange demand—or perhaps at the angry tone it was delivered in. 'Flowers, my lord?'

'Flowers, Taps.'

'Any specific *type* of flower?' he asked, bewildered by the request.

'No. My only requirement is that the arrangement be *very* large.'

'My lord.' Taps bowed, and then left the room in a hurry to complete the task.

Matthew read the note again. He could imagine her, reading his own demanding letter, her dark eyes narrowed in frustration, her pretty lips pursed as she thought of how best to refuse him… But instead of making him angrier, the image cooled his temper.

He raked both hands through his hair and expelled a tired exhale. He didn't quite know what the right thing to do was—not when it came to Seraphina.

And when it came to Isabelle… Oh, to say he didn't know what he *wanted* to do would have been a flagrant lie. He wanted to see her naked breasts again, her rosy nipples peaking with desire. He wanted to run his hands over the petal-soft skin beneath her navel and work his way down to her thighs. He wanted to dip his fingers into her and hear those shocked little sounds she made each time he did.

But what he wanted to do barely seemed like the right or even the *civilised* thing to do, given the circumstances.

Matthew shifted in his seat, trying to dispel the heavy weight of his need. He picked up the ivory letter opener on his desk and restlessly spun the short blade between his fingers.

I should court her—openly and for all of London to see.

Isabelle might be a widow and a duchess, but she was only twenty years old. The *ton* could hardly fault him. And even if they did, Matthew would try not to care. He had been considered a rake since the age of twenty-five, when his ill-advised affair with the Marchioness had imploded. But even with that scandal looming over his head, mothers still tried to foist their daughters upon him at every available opportunity. He was, after all, a viscount, and would one day be an earl—a fact that seemed to override any maternal hesitation regarding the number of scandalous things he was supposed to have done in his past.

But still, the possibility that his past might taint Isabelle—or, God forbid, Seraphina—gave him pause. Despite his restlessness, despite his urge to act, he would have to be careful. Now, more than ever before, he would have to proceed with caution.

Matthew was so lost in thought that he didn't notice the hour slipping by. His correspondence—which included some business that he had intended to conduct on his father's behalf—lay forgotten in front of him as he pondered Isabelle and Seraphina, and when Taps re-entered, saying that the flowers had been procured, Matthew practically jumped to his feet.

'Have them ready for me. I will be out momentarily.'

'May I have the carriage brought round, my lord?'

'No, I'll walk.'

Taps opened his mouth as if to comment, or perhaps to protest, but then seemed to think better of it at the last moment. 'Very well, my lord. Shall I have a footman assist you?'

'No. Thank you, Taps. I believe I can manage flowers.'

'My lord.'

Taps bowed and left the room, leaving Matthew to put on his own coat and gloves.

It was only five minutes later, when he stepped into the hall and saw the monstrous flower arrangement, that he realised he might have been too hasty in refusing the carriage. The blasted thing had to be four feet tall and nearly half as wide, leaving him to wonder how he was going to see his own footfall through the foliage.

He frowned down at the flowers for a long moment, identifying white and red roses, blue forget-me-nots and white daffodils before his floral knowledge ran out. He wondered if Isabelle was as enamoured of floriography as his sisters were—and then hoped to God that none of the flowers included in the arrangement would give offence.

'Is something the matter, my lord?'

'It's rather larger than I expected, Taps,' he drawled in reply.

'Carriage, my lord?'

'Please.'

Willa, Mary and Isabelle all sat in the receiving room, talking and laughing as the day passed languidly by. While Mary sat on the settee, drinking her tenth cup of tea, Willa played a game of chess at a nearby table with Luke, and Isabelle sat on the floor with Seraphina, rolling a ball back and forth on the carpet between them.

They all paused in their conversation when the sound of a mighty crash echoed through the cavernous foyer of Everett Place.

'Goodness!' Willa exclaimed, her eyes wide with curiosity. She pushed herself to her feet. 'What on earth was that?'

'I have no idea.'

Isabelle followed suit, instinctively picking up Seraphina and hurrying towards the receiving room door without hesitation. She opened the door with one hand, pulling up short when she saw the chaos that had been unleashed into her home.

Gordon and Lord Ashworth were both lying on the floor beneath a rather dishevelled mass of flowers. The small Sutherland table in the foyer had been overturned and the vase upon it—a blue French enamel one she'd received as a wedding gift from her cousin—was broken into numerous pieces that were scattered around the pair like jagged confetti.

Matthew was the first to move, heaving the ridiculous arrangement off both himself and the elderly butler before pushing himself to a stand and extending a hand to help Gordon up. As soon as both men were upright, he ran a hand through his hair, scattering tiny leaves and petals about the foyer.

He surveyed the carnage around him. 'Blast.'

Seraphina giggled, and the joyous sound echoed loudly in the otherwise silent foyer.

Matthew's attention snapped to her.

His grey eyes widened perceptibly.

His chest heaved with a shuddering in-out breath, and although his thoughts must have been running rampant he didn't say anything at all—just stared at his daughter in mute shock.

Isabelle, too, was not quite sure what to do or say.

'Apologies, Your Grace.' It was Gordon who broke

the silence. The butler was red with embarrassment. 'I was trying to direct Lord Ashworth where to set down the flowers, but there was an…impediment.'

'I see,' Isabelle replied. She cleared her throat, curious as to what 'impediment' Gordon had been referring to, but no further explanation came. 'Please fetch a maid to come and clean this up, Gordon.'

'Yes, Your Grace.' The butler disappeared, his mortification clear in his hurried footsteps as they echoed down the hall.

'Here, let me take her.' Mary took charge and came forward, her arms extended for Seraphina.

Isabelle let her go, knowing that it was best that she spoke to Lord Ashworth alone. 'Thank you, Mary. I'll only be a moment.'

Isabelle took a deep breath and turned to face Matthew again. Except he wasn't looking at her. He was watching Seraphina, his eyes tracking her intently, as if he were absorbing every detail of her in the finite time he had. Seraphina peered at him from around Mary's shoulder, oblivious to the tense situation, her baby smile wide, her little hand clenching and unclenching in a little wave in his direction.

'I take it you did not receive my reply to your letter?' Isabelle asked, trying desperately to ignore the confusing pull of awareness spreading through her body.

When Willa gently shut the receiving room door behind her, leaving her alone with Lord Ashworth, he finally turned to look at her.

'I did,' he replied. 'But, seeing as you thought to mention you'd be at home, I thought I'd call.' Leaning down, he picked up the flowers off the floor and bowed. 'Though I must admit this is not quite how I imagined it would go.'

'No. I don't suppose so.'

Were it any other man, she might have laughed. The flower arrangement was absurdly oversized, the foyer a mess of overturned furniture, petals and broken pieces of vase. But it wasn't *any* man. It was Matthew—and they both knew why he'd come.

Isabelle had lost the ability to say more. She just stood there in front of him, speechless in her fear and shame.

'You didn't tell me.'

As if sensing that polite small talk would be wasted, Matthew cut straight to the point. He shook his head, his familiar grey eyes filling with confusion and, surprisingly, pain.

'*Why*, Duchess? I...'

He ran one large palm through his shaggy hair—hair that Isabelle remembered the sliding, silky weight of with absolute clarity.

The scurry of an approaching maid prevented her reply. Isabelle swallowed down the panic clogging her throat and indicated for him to follow her as she walked across the hall to her late husband's study.

Once they were inside, she leaned her weight against the door, supporting herself against the sudden exhaustion that swept through her. Of all the fears and worries that had plagued her since Sera had been born, this had not been included among them. Not necessarily the fear that Matthew would find out—he'd only have had to see Sera once to know that she was his—but that he would *care*.

They were both quiet, each wondering what to say and hoping that the other would fill the heavy silence.

'I made you a promise,' she said eventually. He opened his mouth to speak, but she talked over him, needing to purge herself of the truth after all this time. 'And every time I sat down to write you, to tell you, I remembered how kind you had been. I remembered that you had briefly thought I was trying to trap you, and I couldn't... I thought you'd see it as just that— a...a trap.'

Matthew placed the flowers down on the large desk. He didn't come towards her, just watched her face as if he were gauging her every expression. 'I might have at first. But I would have come home, Duchess.' His sincere eyes bored into hers. 'I would have done the right thing by you. I would have—'

'You didn't *have* to,' she countered. 'I was safe. Nobody knew—nobody *knows*,' she corrected hurriedly. 'Matthew... Seraphina will be raised as a lady, the daughter of a duke. You can have your life free from the burden of us.'

'The *burden* of you?' He took one large step closer, his features darkening with anger. 'Did you ever stop to think that I wouldn't want her raised as someone else's? That I'm not the type of man who'd let my child—irrespective of the circumstances of her birth—walk through life unprotected?'

'No,' she admitted honestly. And even though her heart softened at his possessiveness, she couldn't allow it. 'We could never say anything.' He opened his mouth to argue, but she hurried on. 'Even if you wanted to claim her, you couldn't. She would be *ruined* before her second birthday,' she added desperately. 'Is that really what you want?'

'No.' He frowned down at her. 'Of course not.'

'So, why are you here?' she asked, raising her hands to her heart in a forlorn gesture. 'If people saw you two together, they would know. And even if they couldn't prove it, the rumours would be enough.'

His eyes clouded with regret. 'She looks too much like me.'

It wasn't a question. Still, Isabelle could only nod.

'Oh, God.' He collapsed onto the nearby settee as if he'd lost his legs. 'I think it's only dawning on me now,' he whispered. 'I assumed when I saw her last night… But hearing it confirmed…' Leaning forward on the chair, he hung his head and raised his right hand to his face, his index finger and thumb pressing down on his eyes. 'Oh, God,' he repeated, and expelled a shuddering sigh. 'I have a child. A…a *daughter*.'

His words came out laced with blatant shock and fear and wonder.

Isabelle wanted to offer some comfort—some words that might make him feel better. Yet she didn't know where to begin. What words were there? So she stood in silence like a scared schoolgirl—not a grown woman who'd traded her body for a favour from the very man in front of her.

After a long moment, he slowly turned to face her. 'May I assume that you won't marry me?'

Isabelle was so stunned that for a full three seconds she merely stared. But when she replied she did so with the confidence of a woman who knew she would never marry again. 'You may assume so.'

'Still so worried about your title, *Duchess*?' His eyes flashed. His tone oozed bitterness. 'You realise that you outrank me? And that you would keep the title Duchess of Everett even if you married me?'

Isabelle tried to stave off the hurt that lanced through her at his callous words, but the only way she knew how to defend herself against it was to let the rage come.

'I do not think only of myself! Seraphina *and* Luke are mine to protect. If people were to find out I could lose my guardianship of Luke. And you… Matthew, you have a scandalous past—or have you forgotten your marchioness so soon?'

He flinched against the accusation. And his voice was filled with bitterness when he spoke. 'It is rather difficult to forget when it drags behind me like a chain!'

'If you became involved in Sera's life, your past would follow her too. I am saving you, Matthew—from a loveless marriage to someone you would never have considered were the circumstances different.'

Her words were sure, her resolve true. And if Isabelle allowed herself one small moment to imagine what it would be like, to be married to Matthew, she did not linger on it long.

Matthew's eyes snapped with emotion. 'Don't presume to know what I think, Duchess.'

She didn't know what he wanted from her and so, at a loss for the right words, Isabelle fell into a restless silence.

'We won't say anything, then,' he suggested after a long while. 'As far as anyone would know, Seraphina would still be the daughter of a duke. But Duchess, if you married me, I would protect Sera—and Luke. I would treat him as my own. I would love and protect him and ensure that his estate and interests were being sufficiently managed until he was of age.'

'At what cost?' Isabelle cried out, overcome with an emotion that wasn't all fear. It was desperation too. A longing for him to stop painting a picture of a future that could never be practically realised.

Isabelle's life had taught her many hard truths—the first of which was that a woman tied to a man would always be trapped, whether she be wife or daughter or sister. As a daughter, she had been passed on with thought only of the title she would marry into and the benefits that the union would reap. As a wife, irrespective of how short the marriage had been, she had very quickly realised that there would be no escape at all.

But when Matthew talked, when he spoke of hypotheticals that involved them *together*, she couldn't help but become caught up in the possibility.

'Nobody could prove anything.'

Matthew rose off the settee in one fluid movement and rounded the furniture to face her again. He stood so close that she had to crane her neck to meet his eyes.

'It would be a rumour—maybe a minor scandal. And it would eventually die down.'

'Until she comes out and society scorns her! Until what happened between us ruins her chances,' she argued, knowing that she was right in this one instance.

'Chances for *what*?' he demanded, exasperated. 'Duchess, together we have titles, land and more money than we could ever spend! We could give her the dowry of the century. Seraphina could choose anyone she wanted. *Anyone!*'

'That's not true!' Isabelle raised her voice to match his. 'Only a man would think that being raised a bastard wouldn't have consequences!'

'She's not a boy.' He lowered his voice again, his tone growing colder with each point he made. 'She can't inherit. She loses nothing by people merely *suspecting* she is illegitimate.'

'How could you even say that?'

'Because it's true.'

'Rumours will do far more damage than you are able to repair by throwing money at them.'

'How can you—?'

'I won't allow it, Matthew.'

He recoiled as if she'd struck him.

'I'm sorry,' she said.

'So, that's it?' he asked. 'I'm never to meet her, speak

to her or know her—my own child—because you are
a coward?'

'A coward?' Isabelle whispered as the blood drained
from her face. Pain and fury mingled in her chest, stealing her breath. But when she replied, she let it come in
a torrent. 'Do you know how afraid and alone I was
throughout my confinement? Do you know the pure
agony of birthing a child with only a friend and a doctor—a stranger—for comfort?' she demanded.

She felt her anger spiking when he paled.

'Or do you know the fear of being left alone at *nine-
teen years old* with a new infant and nobody to go to
for help or advice except a nursemaid and a few kindly
servants who'd had children of their own?'

'Isabelle—'

'No.' She held up a hand, halting him. 'We are done
here.'

'And what if I claim her anyway?'

Isabelle took a step back as the horror of his threat
hung over them. 'You promised you would never—'

'That was before you had my *child*.'

He closed the space between them again, catching
her wrists in his big hands and pulling her closer, until
she was nearly up against him.

'Don't you *dare* touch me,' she warned, braving her
own nerves to meet his furious gaze.

'Or *what*, Duchess?' he growled, his breath sawing
out of him to strike her forehead.

He was close—so close that Isabelle could feel the
rage and heat pouring off him.

Instead of being afraid, she felt a thrill shoot through her. Memories assaulted her. She could remember the matching canter of their beating hearts and the feel of his big hands stroking her skin. She could remember the weight of his body, pinning her down, grounding her to the earth as she shattered. And the way he'd cradled her gently afterwards, as if she were special, as if she were precious—precious *to him*.

Good Lord, she realised with no small amount of horror, she would give a lot to have this man kiss her again. Her eyes tracked to his lips even as her own opened on a shaky exhalation that she was helpless to prevent.

Matthew's hands flexed around her wrists, and when she dared to look up at him she saw that he was no longer angry. He was watching her expression, his hunger blatant. And instead of making her angrier, the fact that he so clearly desired her forced tears into her eyes.

Matthew released her suddenly and took a step back as the last of the fight drained from his eyes.

He sighed tiredly. 'Please don't cry.'

She wiped her face, furious with herself—furious with *him*. 'You are threatening everything that I have,' she replied, despite the cool tears trailing down her face. 'And now you dare tell me not to cry?'

'Duchess—'

'Get out of my house.'

His head snapped up at the command, but instead of the fury she'd expected all she saw in his gaze was a deep sadness punctuated by the flickering flames of his desire—desire for *her*.

He bowed ever so slightly. 'I will send terms, Duchess.'

'You would blackmail me?'

'You would think so little of me?' he countered bitterly.

And before she could issue a retort, he turned and left, closing the door softly behind him.

Chapter Eight

As Isabelle had expected, Lord Ashworth's 'terms' arrived the very next day. However, instead of the mere letter she had been expecting, the missive was accompanied by a beautiful rocking horse, with a large red bow tied around its neck, and a zoetrope.

The rocking horse was crafted from dark mahogany wood and set upon gliders that slid over a stationary base. The bridle and saddle were miniatures, made from real leather, and when Isabelle lost to temptation and touched the horse's mane and tail, she was both shocked and fascinated to find that it was real horsehair.

And that was nothing compared to the name that had been skilfully carved into the glider closest to her: *MATTHEW*.

It had once been his.

The zoetrope was beautiful too. The animation device included a cylindrical tub that looked almost like a hat box, set atop a spinning wheel-like base. A strip of images depicting a horse and rider had been placed inside, and when she turned the wheel rapidly and looked through the side slats the moving reel made it appear as if the horse and rider were galloping round and round. There was a small accompanying box that included different image strips to place in the device.

The receipt of gifts was not something that Isabelle was comfortable with for two reasons. One, she and Matthew were most certainly *not* courting. And two, the extravagance of the gifts he had sent for the children would certainly raise eyebrows should anyone discover who they'd come from. And, worse, if she returned them she knew he would simply send them back, pointing out that they were for the children—not for her.

Her theory was proved correct when she opened the letter and read:

Duchess,

I know what you're thinking—you've always wanted to be gifted a pony. Unfortunately, said equine is spoken for by another dark-haired beauty. And it would be unfair to gift one child and not the other, don't you think? Should you like to ride a real horse sometime—or, rather, any time—I would gladly accompany you.

In the more likely scenario you never want to see me again, and after our last encounter I find that I cannot fault you. I am sorry, Duchess. While it is no excuse, I was overwhelmed and behaved poorly as a result. Please forgive me.

Though I understand all your reasons for forbidding any contact with S, forgive me again when I

say that these are my terms: I want to see her, Isa-
belle. Twice a week, at a time and location conve-
niently private and safe to both of you.

   Send me a letter indicating when and where and
I will be there. If you agree to those meetings I
promise never to approach you or S in public or
otherwise interfere with her upbringing.

   While I don't know exactly how this will end, I
hope you believe me when I say that I have no de-
sire to harm you or the children. I merely want to
make up for lost time.
Yours,
M

Isabelle found herself alone with her emotions. How
could one letter so easily tear down her defences? If he
had written and demanded money, or threatened to publicly claim Sera, it almost would have been easier to deal
with than the desperate compromise he'd offered. She
could have hated him then. But the fact that Matthew
demanded nothing but the opportunity to spend time
with his child was perhaps the only argument he could
have used that would override her common sense—
because it would be absolutely reckless to allow such
meetings to occur.

But how could she deny him? Even if she wanted to,
Matthew had all the power. With only a few negligent
words he could start a rumour that would ruin not only
Isabelle, but Sera and Luke too.

With one last glance at the toys, she directed Gordon

to have them moved upstairs—the rocking horse to the nursery and the zoetrope to Luke's bedroom. Although she tried not to dwell on it, accepting the gifts felt like welcoming a Trojan Horse into her home. What anyone else might have considered innocent children's play-things were, to her, weapons of war—a war that she was already losing.

Isabelle went into the study and closed the door. She sat at the big desk and removed a crisp new sheet of paper.

She had no point of reference for what she was about to do, so she took several minutes to think over her reply before penning it.

M—

Although entirely inappropriate, the children will appreciate your gifts. Thank you.

As to your request, it would seem I have no choice but to accept. Given the unusual circum-stances, and our need for discretion, I propose that we meet here, at E Place, every Monday and Fri-day at midnight.

Although an inconvenient time, my reasoning is two-fold. S has an ingrained clock that seems to chime at the witching hour. She is always awake then, as you may remember from your last mid-night visit. Additionally, my household will be long abed and less likely to interrupt—or talk of your visits with anyone.

If that is amendable to you, I shall see you tomorrow.
D

PS Please don't knock or otherwise make your presence known by tripping over in my hall again. I will leave the servants' entrance at the back of the house unlocked and wait in the study for you to let yourself in.

With the letter written and re-read a dozen times, Isabelle sealed it inside an envelope and addressed it to the Viscount.

Before she sent it, she called Gordon into the study and bade him close the door behind him. 'Gordon…' Isabelle trailed off, unsure of how to speak to the elderly butler—especially given the topic of the conversation.

'Your Grace?' he said, concern lacing his tone.

'Gordon,' she tried again, 'I have found myself in a situation that is going to require your particular discretion.'

Gordon tipped into a bow, but the expression on his face remained completely neutral. 'I am at your service, Your Grace. I assure you that I and your entire household would never betray your confidence.' He frowned, his bushy brows almost meeting in the middle. 'Were any of the staff to talk, I would personally see to their dismissal.'

Rather overwhelmed by this passionate speech, Isabelle observed, 'I do believe that is the most I have ever heard you speak, Gordon.'

'A servant should neither be seen nor heard unless required, Your Grace.'

Isabelle's lips turned up in a small smile. 'Your standards are stricter than mine. I rather enjoy hearing you all laughing and talking amongst yourselves; it makes the house feel less lonely.'

Gordon's lips hinted at a smile for a small moment.

Encouraged by the small gesture, Isabelle forged ahead. 'I have renewed my acquaintance with a friend who has recently returned from his tour of the continent. He will be visiting with me every Monday and Friday.'

'Yes, Your Grace.'

'At midnight.'

Gordon did not hesitate. 'Would you like me to attend you and your guest personally, Your Grace?'

'No,' Isabelle replied immediately. She could barely speak to Gordon about the meetings, let alone have him witness them. 'You should take your nights to rest, Gordon. I'm merely letting you know why I shall be unlocking the servants' entrance and wandering about the house on those nights.'

'Yes, Your Grace. If you should need anything prepared ahead of time, you have only to let me know.'

'Thank you.' Isabelle cleared her throat. 'There is one other matter I wish to discuss with you.'

Gordon waited expectantly.

'On those nights I would like Seraphina's cot to be made up in my room. She shall stay with me.'

If he was surprised by her request, he didn't show it. 'And Tess?'

Isabelle considered the nursemaid. 'God knows that Tess would love two nights a week when she didn't have to wake up with Sera, Gordon. I will speak to her and make sure that she knows she's not needed.'

'Yes, Your Grace.' Gordon gave another stiff bow. Then he opened his mouth, closed it, and opened it again as he struggled with his need to add more.

'Please, speak plainly,' she told him.

'Your Grace, I would not presume... That is, I would hate to overstep...'

Isabelle waited patiently.

'Your Grace... Are you in any kind of trouble that I could assist you in resolving?'

Isabelle smiled. The butler stood a little straighter and returned to his infallible self.

'No,' she replied. 'I am not in any trouble. However, I do recognise your concern, Gordon. Your commitment to me and my family is greatly appreciated.'

'Your Grace.' He took a fortifying breath. 'I shall make the necessary arrangements. If that is all?'

'Yes, thank you.'

He bowed one last time and left the room as routinely as he'd entered, leaving Isabelle with no doubt that Gordon had been asked to do far worse in service to her late husband. She felt newly indoctrinated into a world of secrets and scandal that she'd never thought she'd be a part of.

Alone again, she slouched back in the chair, considering what she'd done. Her butler—and potentially her entire household—would now think that she was having an affair. And, worse, they would quickly surmise as to why she was letting her midnight visitor meet with her infant daughter. The servants were not idiots. If they had already suspected that she and the Duke had never consummated their marriage, they would almost certainly be able to confirm it now. Her only consolation was that her servants knew the value of discretion—and the advantage of being employed by a duke. It was a coveted position, and one she suddenly hoped they all took very seriously.

Chapter Nine

Matthew supposed that no true rogue would have felt the way he did, standing outside Everett Place in the middle of the night, staring at the small servants' entrance at the back of the house. It felt indecent. Wrong. As if he were some thief in the night—not a mere man, preparing to meet his infant daughter in secret for the first time.

Even the nerves swirling through his stomach were new and unsettling, as alive and mobile as they were weighted and heavy. It was strange, he thought, but he had not felt this tight-chested fear even when he'd secreted himself in the Marchioness's bedroom on the nights when her elderly husband had not been at home. At twenty-five, he'd barely stopped to think of anything—not impropriety, nor risk or heartbreak. He'd only thought of the woman eagerly waiting for him.

Raising his hand, he placed his palm on the door and pushed, surprised when it gave no resistance. He'd been half expecting that Isabelle wouldn't let him in after all…that maybe she'd come to her senses and bar his entry.

Yesterday, when he'd made his threat to claim Seraphina, he'd seen the Duchess's fear, and although it still shamed him to have scared her, he wouldn't have been surprised if that same fear had prompted her to renege on their compromise.

He stepped into the kitchen and immediately saw the single candle and matches that had been left there. He lit it before making his way through the glistening scullery, past the kitchen, with its faint smoky tang, and up the narrow servants' stairs.

He opened the door at the top of the stairs and turned down the corridor towards the study. The door was slightly ajar, with the faint glow of candlelight beckoning him like a moth to the flame.

Matthew took a cautious step forward, then paused as he became aware of the rapid acceleration of his heart in his chest. For someone who had only ever been superbly fit, he discovered the anxious threshing of that organ was not only surprising, but deeply terrifying. There was no doubt in his mind that this was what a man felt just before his heart simply failed and his soul took flight from this mortal coil—breathless, sick, and filled with fear of the unknown beyond.

Had he been able, he might have laughed at himself. He had faced much worse, and still he didn't think he'd ever been this afraid.

He took a moment to calm himself by taking deep breaths and reminding himself that he was meeting an infant—not walking to the front line or the gallows. Forcing purpose into his footsteps, he strode to the door. He raised his hand to knock and then, remembering the Duchess's warning for discretion, merely placed his shaking palm on the cool surface and pushed.

He wasn't sure what he had been expecting, but seeing Isabelle sitting on the floor in a simple hunter-green dress, her black hair cascading down her back, most certainly wasn't it.

'Duchess,' he murmured quietly, in case she hadn't heard his silent entry.

Isabelle turned, angling her head over her shoulder to glance at him. Her dark eyes took in the whole of him, from his un-styled hair to the tops of his freshly polished shoes.

'You came.'

'Of course.'

'You did not reply to my letter.'

She rocked forward onto her knees with a small grunt of effort, and it wasn't until she stood and affected an ungraceful turn that he realised why.

Seraphina stood in front of her. The child's little arms were stretched upwards, her hands in Isabelle's, as if she were supporting herself—or maybe as if they were supporting each other. Seraphina took two confident steps forward, her laughter-lit eyes—*his* eyes in *her* face—watching him.

He stared at her, unsure of what he was supposed to do—how he was supposed to act, or what he was supposed to say, if anything. He swallowed down the emotions—sadness, fear, awe, excitement—that knotted his throat.

She had a halo of thick, dark curls and grey eyes. She was so *small*, and yet also adorably chubby. She reminded him of a mischievous cupid, lying in wait for the perfect moment to release an arrow and wreak havoc.

Both females stood there, waiting for him to do something—*anything*, really.

'Matthew?' said Isabelle.

'Mmm?' he managed, tearing his eyes away from Seraphina to look at the Duchess.

She was watching him cautiously, almost as if she wasn't sure what to do either. But then, after a barely perceptible pause, she started walking towards him, both hands gently propelling Seraphina forward too.

It was only when they were standing directly in front of him that he managed to admit, 'I… I don't know what to do.'

Her dark eyes softened. 'You could start by introducing yourself.'

'Oh. Um…' Matthew ran one hand through his hair. 'Introduce myself…'

Changing tactics at the last moment, he lowered himself to his haunches and regarded Seraphina at her level.

The child seemed to know that this was no typical introduction. She didn't reach for him, only smiled happily and tilted her head, as if giving him time to sort his jumbled thoughts.

'Hello, Seraphina,' he managed, his voice hoarse with emotion, his heart thick with regret, and confusion, and a strange need to be known by this little person in front of him.

'Hello!' she squeaked.

Matthew, who had not been expecting a reply, let alone such an exuberant one, reared back, falling arse-first onto the carpet, his hands braced behind him.

There was a moment of perfect silence, during which he looked from the Duchess's shocked face to his daughter's. And then Seraphina started laughing, her high-pitched baby giggles filling the moment and pushing the awkwardness out.

A strange effusion of heat spread through Matthew's chest at the sound and, try as he might, he didn't think he'd ever heard anything so pure and joyous. When he chanced another glance at the Duchess he saw she was trying very hard not to laugh, but her pretty mouth trembled visibly with the urge.

'Perhaps we can try that again,' he murmured, and rearranged himself on his knees.

Matthew opened his coat and removed a small sprig of flowers from his inside pocket. He considered the three bright yellow blooms for a long moment before holding the bundle out to Seraphina.

'Daisies?' Isabelle asked as Seraphina released her hand and reached forward to take the offering, her tiny fingers closing around the stems.

Matthew shook his head. 'These are the blooms of the cinquefoil plant,' he explained. 'My sisters are obsessed with that book *Le Langage des Fleurs* by Madame Charlotte de la Tour. I had reason to peruse it once I got home last night.'

'Oh, yes. I believe we have the translated version here somewhere.' There was a brief pause before she asked, 'What does the cinquefoil signify?'

Matthew floundered for a fleeting moment, before clearing his throat and replying, 'Lasting friendship.'

His words came out tight and clipped, and he wondered if the Duchess would sense the lie.

'That's very sweet of you.'

Sweet? Could she not see that he was devastated? That his entire heart, his very life mechanism, was straining on the edge of implosion as he watched his tiny daughter wave the flowers about as if she'd been born to receive them. He was distraught…broken by the fact that Isabelle hadn't told him—hadn't planned *ever* to tell him. He was tortured, angry at the thought of what the Duchess had suffered alone, when he should have—*would have*—been there. And, perhaps most of all, he was defeated. Because even as he raged against the thought he knew that Seraphina would never truly be his—*could* never truly be his.

Because Isabelle was right. If Matthew's past did not affect Seraphina, the circumstances surrounding her birth most certainly would. It would ruin them, and the only thing he knew to be true any more was the fact that he would never harm either Seraphina or Isabelle. Not like that. Not in any way. They were his to protect. Seraphina as his child. And Isabelle at the very least as the mother of his child.

As if she'd sensed the offence she'd inadvertently caused, the Duchess added, 'I didn't mean to imply—'

'I know.' Matthew tried to meet her eyes and smile, but the attempt fell flat.

When Seraphina released her mother's hand and walked to him, the flowers outstretched in front of her, as if she were going to give them back to him, he raised his hands instinctively.

His daughter walked straight into his bracketed palms, her small ribs pressing against palms that suddenly felt too big…too clumsy. Matthew's entire body went rigid.

'What do I do?' he asked, simultaneously wanting to pick her up and hold her and yank his hands away for fear of scaring her.

He had no experience with children—of any age.

But his inexperience didn't seem to matter to Seraphina. When he didn't move, she simply turned in a plodding semi-circle and plopped into his lap, as if she had no thought to the unfamiliar man in her home, no knowledge of the danger of strangers.

'Is she always so oblivious to potential danger?' he asked, newly terrified.

God, London was one of the most dangerous cities in the world! And Seraphina was so small, so breakable. The possibilities suddenly seemed endless and terrifying.

'Are you a danger to her?' Isabelle inquired, her dark eyes lit with humour.

'No,' Matthew replied, 'but she doesn't know that.'

The Duchess laughed, and the unfamiliar sound

reached for him, unspooling some of the new tension in his chest.

'If it brings you any comfort, she's never unsupervised.'

'I have to be completely honest, Duchess. I don't think I'll ever be comfortable again.'

'It is strange, is it not? To want to protect someone you don't know at all?'

He nodded, listening to Isabelle's softly spoken words as he watched Seraphina sit on his lap and deconstruct the flowers one petal at a time.

'From the first moment I held her, I've been terrified in a way I never knew possible.'

He could imagine her holding Seraphina for the first time…

'Was it long—your labour?' he dared to ask, knowing that they had long left propriety behind them.

Isabelle still flushed a brilliant pink at the question, but instead of deferring, as he'd expected, she sat down in front of them and started rearranging the yellow petals on the carpet, as if unable to meet his eye. Her long, slender fingers enchanted him. Her hair spilled haphazardly over her shoulder, making her look like some fantastical nymph.

'Fourteen hours.'

Matthew blanched. 'Fourteen *hours*?'

Was that normal? He had no idea.

'It was terrifying,' she admitted quietly. 'I felt as if I was somehow inside and outside my body at the same time.'

'Who attended you?'

'Mary—you know my cousin Mary. And my physician, Dr Taylor.'

He ignored the twinge in his chest at the knowledge that another man had been there when he had not. 'Your mother…?'

'My mother did not come.'

There was enough said in the simple statement, enough in her unemotional tone, that Matthew didn't push for more.

'I… I wish I could have been there.' He could have held her hand and told her that everything was going to be fine. He could have talked her to distraction. He could have held Sera the moment she'd arrived…

Isabelle shook her head. 'No, you do not—trust me on this. Even *I* did not want to be there.'

He laughed, and Isabelle leaned forward conspiratorially.

'I thought poor Mary would faint away at any moment—and so did Dr Taylor. He made her sit at the side of the bed and hold my hand so that she couldn't see what was happening. She didn't say a word the entire time—only sat there, pale and silent, like a wrongly convicted prisoner in front of the judge. And then Sera came out, screaming for all of England to hear.'

Isabelle reached forward and brushed Sera's hair back from her forehead.

Seraphina leaned against his chest and yawned, making a sound that was close to 'Mary'.

'She doesn't talk much yet?' he asked.

'It depends. I feel as if she picks up a new word every day, but usually her talking is more babbling.'

As if to prove Isabelle's point, Seraphina issued a long sentence that Matthew couldn't decipher. He looked to Isabelle for translation, but she merely shook her head and laughed.

'Your guess is as good as mine.'

'Ma!' Seraphina squawked, and held out her arms in Isabelle's direction.

The Duchess moved as if to take her, and then caught herself. She looked up at Matthew. 'Do you mind?'

'No, of course not.'

She plucked Sera off his lap quickly, only coming close to him for the fraction of a second it took for her rosewater scent to fill his sinuses and flood his mind with memories. But the moment she leaned back with Sera he felt bereft. Alone.

'She usually stays up for an hour or so before I can get her down again.'

'Not your nursemaid?'

'Tess. She used to try for hours, but Sera was not very accommodating of her efforts. I think it's because I let her sleep in my room for too long after she was born— almost six months.'

'For convenience?'

'In part. I…' She hesitated.

'Tell me,' he urged, hearing the desperation in his tone And casually added, 'I want to know.'

'I couldn't bear to be separated from her. My entire body mourned the distance.'

'I understand.' He knew what it was to mourn being physically close to a particular person—albeit in an entirely different way.

Seraphina started to nod off in the Duchess's lap, her eyes blinking closed and then open again, as if she was fighting sleep even as it overtook her.

'She's losing the battle,' he commented quietly.

Isabelle looked down at Sera and smiled. 'I'm not surprised.' She placed an unconscious kiss on their child's head of curls. 'She doesn't usually have additional entertainment.' Her eyes snagged on the petals strewn about the carpet. 'I'm sorry she destroyed your gift.'

'Don't be.'

Matthew pushed himself to his feet and looked down at Isabelle and Sera. Isabelle sat sideways on one thigh, the dark red and gold carpet complementing the deep green of her dress as it pooled around her legs. She looked up at him, her eyes wide, filled with unsaid things.

Reaching down, he gently extricated Seraphina from her lap, immediately struck by the unfamiliar weight of a sleeping child in his arms. He held out a hand to help Isabelle up. The Duchess took it, her small, cool palm sliding into his fiery hot one.

Matthew tugged her to her feet and released her immediately, afraid of what he'd do if he had time to ponder the feeling of her skin on his and the small distance separating them. He gently unlatched Seraphina from his arms and passed her back to Isabelle.

'Thank you,' he said. 'I appreciate you allowing this.'

'You didn't give me much choice.'

His eyes snapped to hers, but there was no anger or judgement in her expression now, only a faint smile. 'I'm sorry, Duchess, for everything I never did for you—for both of you.'

'And I'm sorry I never told you, Matthew,' she replied, her expression painted with sorrow. 'I almost wrote a thousand times, but…'

'I understand why you didn't. My behaviour that night—'

'Was unimpeachable, all things considered.' She said the words firmly, despite the brilliant blush flooding her cheeks.

Unable to stop himself, Matthew reached out and tucked a long coil of sable hair behind her ear. Isabelle didn't move…she barely breathed.

'Goodnight, Duchess.'

'Goodnight.'

'Friday?'

She nodded once, and although he longed to brush his own palm over Sera's downy head he resisted, somehow knowing it would be too much too soon for the Duchess. Instead, he bowed once and stoically left the room.

It was only once he was back on the dark street that Matthew linked his hands behind his head and took a single deep breath in, filling his lungs with the crisp London air and releasing the anxious breathlessness he'd suffered all through his first meeting with Seraphina. The breath slowly eased the tightness in his chest, filling him with renewed hope.

He could make this work. He *would* make this work.
He had to. For Sera. But also for Isabelle.

He was in awe of her, of what she'd done, young and
alone in a world that rarely cared for either of those things.

The Duchess was…well, rather magnificent.

Isabelle waited an entire thirty seconds after Matthew
had left the room before gently placing Seraphina down
on the nearby settee and hurrying over to the large floor-
to-ceiling bookcase against the far wall of the study.

She knew she had the translated *Le Langage des
Fleurs* somewhere. The book had been all the rage when
she was younger, and she'd bought a copy for herself a
year or so ago, when she'd seen it on display in a book-
shop—only to realise that one did not need a book on
floriography if one did not receive any flowers.

Isabelle found it in minutes, tucked between a book
on English horticulture and another on modern agricul-
tural practices. She hastily flipped through page after
page, her eyes quickly scanning the text until she found
the cinquefoil plant and read the description.

*Beloved Daughter. In wet weather the leaves of this
plant contract and bend over the flower, forming,
as it were, a little tent to cover it—an apt emblem
of an affectionate mother in protecting a beloved
child.*

Isabelle, who had seen the embarrassed flush spread
over Matthew's face, had sensed that he hadn't been

entirely truthful about the flower's meaning, but she never would have expected such a compliment—for a compliment it most certainly had been.

She wondered why he hadn't been honest with her. Most men she knew—nay, most *people*—would have preened at their own thoughtfulness and inadvertently removed any genuine sentiment in doing so. But Matthew...

She supposed he had always been a contradiction to her. She'd approached him because of his tarnished reputation, and instead of the rake she'd been expecting she'd discovered a man with an immense propensity for honour. He was a man who'd told her he'd never wanted to see her again—and then been devastated when she'd adhered to his wishes. Though she supposed that had more to do with the surprise of Seraphina than with Isabelle herself. He had boxed her into a corner and issued his 'terms', giving her no choice in his introduction to Sera, yet somehow she understood that the action had been born more from his desperation than any literal threat to ruin them.

She didn't know Lord Ashworth well, but she didn't have to know him to recognise that he was not the type to expose a child—*his* child—to the world for his own petty revenge.

The knowledge brought with it a new truth. She should call an end to this madness before it got out of hand—before someone saw him sneaking into her house in the middle of the night, or Seraphina grew old enough to know him. Or, God forbid, became attached to him, only to have him devastate her when he eventually decided it was too much and abandoned her. Abandoned *them*.

For Isabelle already knew that she would not remain unaffected by Matthew either.

With a glance at the settee, to make sure that Sera was safely positioned, she walked around the desk and collapsed into the big chair.

Isabelle's own fear, and her anxiety over Matthew's effect on her, made her want to end their arrangement. But what of Seraphina? What was the best thing for her?

Isabelle leaned back in the chair as she pondered the question. She had no husband. If something happened to her, Sera would have Willa, Mary and the financial means to have a fulfilling life, but surely having one more person to love and protect her would be a good thing?

Matthew was titled and powerful. And if something *did* happen to Isabelle she felt that he *would* look after Sera.

Luke, should he be of age in such a scenario, would too.

But what if it was next year? Or the year after that? Or tomorrow? She'd leave both children alone in the world, with nobody but her solicitor with any real means to oversee them and ensure that they stayed clear of the dangers of the world.

It was a sobering thought—one that, once in her head, Isabelle couldn't ignore. She couldn't push Matthew out of Sera's life. And, although she tried not to dwell on it, it wasn't only because she was certain he would never expose them. She had recognised the awe-struck fear on his face when Sera had first gone to him. He'd said, 'I don't know what to do.' And wasn't that exactly how she'd felt when Dr Taylor had placed Seraphina in her arms for the first time? Hadn't she, in that moment, desperately wished that she'd had someone there—wished she'd had *Matthew* there, taking charge of the situation, telling her that everything was going to be fine?

'I'm probably making a huge mistake,' she said aloud.

She suspected he would be the type of father she wished she'd grown up with…the type of husband she wished she'd had the chance to marry. And she found that she didn't have what it took to deprive him of Sera—or deprive them both of him.

Chapter Ten

She had been expecting Lord Ashworth to stay completely out of her life, with the exception of his bi-weekly meetings with Seraphina, so Isabelle was shocked to see her name penned in his neat hand on a letter that arrived for her the very next evening.

She tore it open without hesitation, drawing a curious look from Mary, who sat across from her in the drawing room, embroidering a small cushion cover.

Duchess,
All of last night, when I should have been sleeping, the questions that scattered from my mind upon meeting S came back to plague me. There's so much I don't know. More even that I want to know. Forgive me for not waiting until Friday, but I am returning to this page every time a new question occurs to me. And even if you choose not to reply, I find that penning them gives me a chance to commit them to memory, so that I may ask them at another time.

Why the name S?

What was her first word?

Last night she said, 'Ma', which leads me to believe it was some variation of that...

When did she take her first steps?

Do she and Luke get on? Or is he like I was at his age—rather uninterested in his little sister?

When did she first sleep through the night?

Are you exhausted all the time?

More to come,

M

Isabelle read and re-read the letter, committing each question to memory, as Matthew said he had. There was a strange burning sensation in her chest—one that was so immense and uncomfortable that she instinctively raised a hand to press down on it.

'Izzy?'

'Mmm?' Isabelle looked up at Mary.

'What is it?'

For some inexplicable reason a hot blush climbed up Isabelle's neck. There wasn't anything personal in the letter, only questions about Seraphina, yet Isabelle didn't think she'd ever felt such an intense sense of intimacy before, and over something as simple as words on paper.

'It is a letter,' she replied finally. 'From Lord Ashworth.'

'And? What did he say?'

Mary, who had been entirely disapproving of Isabelle's decision to let Matthew meet Seraphina, but had not been able to come up with an alternative compromise, stared at the letter as if she might incinerate it with her scorn alone.

'He has questions—about Sera.'

'Questions?'

Isabelle read them aloud, deciding at the last moment not to share the final one.

'You're not going to reply, are you?' Mary asked, horrified. Before Isabelle could comment, her cousin continued, 'Isabelle, these meetings are dangerous enough. But letters—letters that anybody could intercept and read!'

'Neither of us mentions any names, Mary. And I've been destroying them after I've read them.'

'Knowing no names doesn't stop the society pages from exposing their subjects to ridicule—and names aren't going to matter when the correspondence is occurring *between your homes*!'

'You're right. I shall ask him not to write again the next time I see him.' Isabelle pushed herself to stand.

'Where are you going?' asked Mary.

Isabelle tucked the letter into her sleeve. 'To find Seraphina.'

It wasn't exactly a lie. But Isabelle felt Mary's eyes on her back as she left the room.

Inside the nursery, Sera was sitting on the rocking horse while Tess held her steady with one hand and gently moved the horse back and forth with the other. Instead of holding the little reins, Seraphina grasped the horse's mane with her tiny fingers, alternately pushing and pulling at the long hairs with each back-and-forth movement. Her contagious baby giggle filled the room with lightness and joy.

'She's found a new passion, Your Grace,' Tess said, laughing. 'Every time I take her off, she cries as if I've personally wronged her.'

Isabelle's eyes tracked Tess's hand as it pushed the toy, her fingers resting by the name carved into the glider. If the nursemaid had questions about where the toy had come from, she didn't dare ask them. Still, Isabelle fought self-consciousness.

'I've come to relieve you of your rocking duty, Tess,' she said, walking towards the rocking horse. She opened her hands and lifted Sera from the seat.

Instead of fussing, as she'd expected, Sera babbled with pleasure and reached up with one chubby hand to touch Isabelle's hair.

'Would you like me to change her so she's ready to go out, Your Grace?'

'No, thank you.' Isabelle noted the simple white dress Seraphina was wearing. 'I'm just going to write some letters in the study for now.'

Knowing that Isabelle would ring for her when she was needed, Tess started packing away Seraphina's small mountain of toys.

Isabelle carried Sera from the room and down the stairs, only pausing to reposition her daughter on her hip and mumble, 'You're getting heavy, my love.'

Time was passing indiscriminately. Soon Sera wouldn't want to be carried. Then she'd be too big to carry. Before she knew it, her daughter wouldn't need her at all—and then what was Isabelle to do with herself? She had thrown herself into motherhood with a fervour born from the need to be a better mother than her own had. She had no leisure pursuits, no particular talents that could be exercised. It was a sobering thought, really, that a title could not buy a woman everything.

Inside the study, she settled Seraphina on her lap at the desk and passed the child a piece of paper to tear to shreds as she removed a second sheet for herself.

For those few precious minutes that they sat together Isabelle found comfort in Seraphina's nearness. She could smell her daughter's familiar baby scent. She could feel the way Sera relaxed back against her, with absolute trust that she was safe and loved. It made Isabelle wonder how any mother—her own included—could bear to be deprived of that connection.

Hadn't Jemima Conway felt that first swoop of overwhelming emotion the moment Isabelle had been placed in her arms? Hadn't she been filled with the same awe and fear as Isabelle had the first time she'd held Seraphina, after labouring alone in pain for hours and hours?

All the years she'd lived in her mother's house had already supplied her with an answer. Her mother had only participated in Isabelle's upbringing on the rarest occasions, choosing instead to go about her own life and leave the child-rearing to nursemaids and governesses. Though Isabelle had seen her almost daily growing up, they had only ever spent time together during perfunctory meetings—meetings that had been scheduled and that had never lasted more than thirty minutes before Isabelle had been swept back to the nursery.

It had been the reminder of those short visits to her uninterested parents—the anticipation and excitement, and afterwards the disappointment—that had made Isabelle vow to be different. *Her* children would never question her love. They would never think that they were anything but the centre of her world.

With Sera's comforting weight on her thighs, and a simmering burn of anticipation in her chest, she began her reply to Matthew.

M,

When I was a child my father brought home an angel for the top of the Christmas tree one year. The angel had a white silk dress, a fur-lined coat, gossamer-like wings and blond ringlets that felt like real human hair. It was the most beautiful thing I'd ever seen, and when I asked my father which angel it was, he panicked and replied, 'S—'.

I don't think he even knew about the biblical six-winged angels. But the name held, and that rare gift from my father became my most treasured memory. Until S was born. So when Dr Taylor placed her in my arms it seemed only natural that she replace that happy memory.

It is only in writing this story now that I realise perhaps I wanted the reminder too. A reminder that my child must not have only one fond memory of me. A reminder of the type of parent I wanted to be.

Her first word was not, 'Ma', as you assumed. It was, 'More', and she was pointing at her half-finished blancmange at the time.

She took her first steps just a few months ago—which Mary thought rather delayed, but which I am grateful for now that she is active and impossible to keep up with.

She adores Luke. But, though he loves her, his interest seems born more from a sense of familial duty than a genuine desire to entertain her.

She has yet to sleep through the night.

Yes, I am exhausted. Although I must admit that my fatigue is purely self-inflicted, as I insist on helping the nursemaid when S won't go down and cannot stay abed myself once the sun has risen.
D

PS Given the circumstances, I would ask that any future correspondence be exchanged in person rather than via post, and that you personally destroy my letters once you have read them.

Matthew was transported by the Duchess's letter. He could imagine her, a dark-haired, serious child, asking her father who the angel was. And he could see Seraphina, covered in blancmange, demanding, 'More'. It was no stretch of the imagination to picture Sera walking for the first time—she still had the wobbly confidence of a child who was not proficient but rather practising her bipedal locomotion.

An unfamiliar elation filled his chest as he re-read the letter, and the feeling was only dampened by the last paragraph, which confirmed what he'd suspected when he'd seen the Duchess last: Isabelle was tired.

It didn't matter that she was a duchess, with countless servants to help her. Isabelle would be handling every trial in her life—including a sleepless child—herself. Matthew knew that to be true because her stubborn independence was the first thing he had recognised in her when she'd come to him that night, her mind set on taking control of her life and assuming responsibility for Luke's.

It was no wonder he'd been enraptured—the Duchess was unlike any woman he'd ever met.

Then Matthew read the postscript of her letter and, although it hurt, he tried not to let her request that he destroy her letters grate on his already stretched nerves. Her demand was fair, and her concern well-founded. And yet he still could not escape his own bitter regret and shame.

He wondered how things might have been had he never set eyes on Christine Dalmore. Had he just done one or two things differently. Had he just been a little older, a little more mature…

He knew that regret was futile.

Along with all the questions he'd drawn up about Sera the night before, his mind kept searching for a reasonable solution to their predicament—some way for him to be in Sera's life publicly and regularly, instead of behind closed doors as if he was ashamed of her.

If he were any less of a gentleman he'd force the Duchess to marry him and be done with the whole fiasco...

And then what? he asked himself.

People would talk—they always did. And even if there was no proof of Sera's heritage, everybody knew of Matthew's past. Because of that, they would take one look at Seraphina and they would assume the worst.

'My word—has somebody died?'

Matthew looked up, his frown clearing when he saw his mother standing on the other side of his desk. He'd been so deep in thought he hadn't heard the Countess enter.

'Mother,' he said and, holding out both hands, stood to embrace her.

Diana Blake, the Countess of Heather, was a tall, striking woman from whom he'd inherited his black hair and grey eyes, although his nature was closer to his father the Earl's quiet intensity. Matthew could always trust his mother to loudly cut to the heart of any matter—whether he wanted her to or not.

She returned his greeting with real affection, her eyes narrowed on his face with maternal insight and, upon observing the deep-set fatigue in his eyes, she said with concern, 'You look awful, my dear boy.'

Matthew laughed and released her hands. 'I haven't been sleeping well,' he admitted as he rounded his desk once again.

Since he'd found out about Seraphina he'd found sleep impossible. Every time he closed his eyes he saw her—*his child*.

'Would you like to tell me what has been keeping you from your sleep?' his mother asked as she took a seat in one of the chairs opposite his desk.

'No.'

She arched back, shocked by his blatant reply. 'Well, why on earth not? So long as it's not a mathematics test again… As we both know, I was more a hindrance with that than a help.'

'Because if I tell you, you will worry—and, worse, you will tell Father. Which will bring him here with a reprimand and a lecture. And I don't want to hear it.'

'Because you are in the wrong?'

'No. Because I don't feel in the least bit sorry for what I have done,' he replied immediately.

He stopped as soon as the words had left his mouth, stunned with the realisation that they were true. He could never regret that night with Isabelle—rather, he lived to remember it. Seraphina, though a surprise, was *his*, and for that alone he would cherish her.

'I merely need to find a way to bend circumstances and gain the result I want.'

He'd been thinking aloud. But the Countess considered him for a long moment before stating, 'If your intention is to dissuade me, I'm afraid you are not succeeding. You are only making me more curious.'

Matthew pressed his index finger and thumb over

his eyes. 'Mother, though I do enjoy your visits, I must ask… Why are you here?'

The Countess arched one brow. 'Do I need an excuse to visit my only son?'

'No. Of course not.' His pause was barely perceptible. 'Shall we pretend you don't have a reason, then?'

She laughed loudly. 'I don't suppose I am very subtle.'

'When you just want to visit me you send a note, inquiring after my schedule.'

He saw her eyes, so similar to his—and to Sera's—glisten with humour.

'When you want to coerce me into something I'm sure to dread, you arrive with no word or invitation so as to take me off guard.'

'You, my dear, are too much like your father.'

They both lapsed into silence as a maid hovered on the threshold of his study, a tea tray in her hands. Matthew waved her in and waited for her to place the tray down and depart before continuing the conversation.

'So?'

'Contrary to your opinion, I am not here to badger you.'

The Countess moved to pour herself tea without asking Matthew if he'd like any. She knew he hated the stuff.

'I merely wish to ask if there is anyone you'd like to invite to the masquerade ball?' She sat back in her chair. 'Invitations go out tomorrow.'

'Ah…' With everything else on his mind, Matthew

had quite forgotten about his mother's annual masquerade ball—an event that most of London wished to be invited to, but for which his mother kept to a deliberately select group of people, totalling about seventy-five guests.

'Well?'

'Leo, of course.'

'He is already coming. Your father and I saw him in St James's Square yesterday and invited him in person.'

'Lord and Lady Windhurst.'

His mother's eyebrows arched. 'I have heard *he* is a philandering nincompoop.'

'He is, most certainly.'

'Good God, Matthew!' she exclaimed as a new idea occurred to her. 'Tell me it's not Lady Windhurst who has you so *déboussolé*?'

Matthew ignored the question. 'And the Duchess of Everett and her companion Mary Lambert.'

His mother was uncharacteristically quiet as she considered him through narrowed eyes, the only sound in the room the whirr of the silver teaspoon against the teacup as she stirred her tea.

'You may speak plainly, Mother.'

She took a dainty sip, all the while watching his face. 'I am merely trying to discover which of the ladies it is that you wish to see.'

'Your imagination is running rampant.' He took a deep breath. 'If you must know, Leo is keeping an eye on Lady Windhurst. Her husband's "philandering", as you call it, is taking its toll on her.'

'Is Leo having an affair with her?'

'No. They are childhood friends.'

'Hmm…' The sound was noncommittal. 'And the other two?'

'Are Lady Windhurst's closest friends. She will attend if she knows that they are going to be there.'

'You know, Matthew, you have become a most proficient liar.' She placed her teacup down in its saucer, the little rattle sounding much too loud in the quiet room. 'I don't know whether that makes me relieved that you are now more able to protect yourself from the world, or deeply sad that you thought you had to lie in the first place.'

She stood, forcing her gloves back onto her fingers with irritated tugs. 'I will invite your friends. But heed my warning: nothing good will come from you carrying on with a married woman—as well you know.'

Matthew let the pain come, used to it after years of people referencing the affair either to tease him, as his friends did, or, as his mother did, to remind him of his past mistakes.

Though his parents had both stood by him throughout the months following the scandal, he had felt the full weight of their disappointment keenly. Looking back now, he supposed he had never let them down before. Rather, he had always strived to be a good son… to make his parents proud. He had done well at school. He hadn't drunk to excess or gambled. When he had sought female company he had done so discreetly. Even his affair with Christine had been carefully orchestrated to avoid attention—until he'd called things off and discovered she'd had other plans.

He watched his mother for a long moment as he considered leaving her to her assumptions. But he didn't. For one reason. It wasn't fair to Wilhelmina, who already had to withstand enough of society's scrutiny.

'It is not what you think, Mother,' he said.

She paused, her eyes coming up to search his face. 'And you cannot confide in me because...?'

'It is not my secret to impart.'

'You are not having an affair with the Lady, then?'

'No. Though I would remind you that, irrespective of my past mistakes, my sex life is none of your concern.'

The Countess linked her gloved hands together. She leaned forward and lowered her voice. 'One day, Matthew, you will have children. And I promise you, not a night will go by when you don't worry about them—their carnal desires and mistakes included.'

If she had only known how close she was to the truth just then, the Countess might have stayed. Instead, she turned around and disappeared through the open door, her back straight, her head held high.

Exhausted, Matthew dropped his forehead to his desk and knocked it gently against the hard wood. He knew that hindsight was useless, but that did not stop the deluge of regret.

As if living with the recurring memory of Christine's tear-streaked face and frenzied begging wasn't enough.

Now he not only had to live with the consequences of his actions, he also had to ensure that Isabelle and the children did not.

Chapter Eleven

Much to her own embarrassment, Isabelle eagerly awaited a reply from Lord Ashworth for the remainder of the week. Each time Gordon brought in the post she would casually sort through it, regret settling over her when she realised that he had adhered to her request and not written at all.

'It's your own fault,' she reminded herself aloud as she sat on the floor with Seraphina, awaiting Lord Ashworth's Friday night visit. 'You can hardly blame the man for respecting your request.'

Seraphina nodded and mumbled her agreement from her seat on the red and gold carpet.

'Your father is much too honourable,' she said and, smiling, reached out both hands to help Sera rise to stand. 'Don't you think?'

'Ya!' Seraphina laughed and kicked her little feet, forcing Isabelle's sombre mood away entirely.

Isabelle laughed as Sera strung her arms around her neck. She nestled her face against the child, breathing in her familiar scent. 'Oh, Sera. What on earth am I going to do?'

'Ya!' Sera laughed again.

'You think we should run away?' Isabelle asked.

Seraphina giggled, her high-pitched baby laugh merging with Isabelle's.

'If that isn't the perfect sight to greet a man…'

Isabelle's heart simply stopped beating for one perfect moment. She closed her eyes as Matthew's deep voice reached for her, enveloping her like an embrace. How long had he been standing there, looking at them, *listening to her*? A flush of mortification spread through her when she remembered what she'd been saying.

Seraphina suffered no such embarrassment. She peered over Isabelle's shoulder and immediately started jumping up and down when she recognised Matthew.

'Hello, beautiful girl,' Matthew said, his quiet voice filled with humour.

It was ridiculous that his greeting filled Isabelle with heat—she knew he was talking to Seraphina—but it *did*. It spread through her, starting low in her womb and climbing up through her chest to her neck.

Isabelle shifted Sera off her lap, sending her in Matthew's direction before she dared to turn fully and look up at him.

When she did, her breath caught. Matthew was not so formal tonight. His jacket was slung over one shoulder, revealing a burgundy silk waistcoat with the finest gold thread woven through it at even intervals to form a pinstripe. He'd rolled his sleeves to just below his elbows, and Isabelle's eyes immediately strayed to his large hands and powerful forearms, both dusted with a layer of dark hair. He held a sprig of purple vervain in one of those hands. His grey eyes, tired but silvered with happiness, watched as Sera toddled across the room to him.

Sera extended her arms even before she'd stopped, and Matthew immediately bent to scoop her up, his forearms flexing.

Isabelle sat on the floor and observed the exchange. Seraphina didn't hesitate to raise her hands to Matthew's face, touching his nose, his cheeks, and then his hair, as if he was a favoured toy and not a full-grown male.

'Were you having fun with your mother?' he asked, his deep voice travelling across the room even though he whispered.

Seraphina nodded and, without waiting for an invitation, reached for the flowers in Matthew's free hand. He grinned and started to pass them to her, but before her hand could close around the stem, he snatched them away, hiding them behind his back and affecting a gasp of bewildered surprise that had Sera's own eyes widening.

'Where did they go?' he asked.

Sera's little mouth hung open as she considered him, and then she leaned her entire body to one side to try and peek around his back.

Matthew grinned and glanced at Isabelle. 'She is not so easily fooled, I see.'

He removed the flowers from behind his back and held them out to Sera once again.

She immediately plopped her entire face into the blooms and gurgled. 'Smow!'

'Smell,' Isabelle corrected, looking up at Matthew. 'She wants you to smell them.'

He complied, lowering his face to the blooms as Sera had done, but keeping his laughter-lit eyes on Isabelle the entire time.

'Vervain?' she asked.

'Enchantment.'

Isabelle sensed that it was the truth, but she knew that she'd check the moment he left anyway.

Matthew turned and closed the study door behind him before carrying Sera over to where Isabelle still sat on the floor. He lowered them both down to the carpet and placed Sera on her feet.

Sera walked to Isabelle, the vervain blooms outstretched. 'Smow!'

Isabelle leaned forward and took an exaggerated inhalation.

Then Sera walked back to Matthew and leaned her entire body against his side as she waved her flowers back and forth.

'She won't bite you!' Isabelle laughed, and then, remembering a rather unfortunate incident with Mr Briggs, she amended, 'At least, I hope she won't.'

Matthew blew out a deep breath. 'It's all so new—so overwhelming.'

'I know.' Isabelle looked at them, their dark heads

bent together, and a wave of pleasure tumbled through her. Sera lowered herself to sit on Matthew's thigh. 'It would seem as though she doesn't have the same fears.'

'No. I don't suppose she does.' He raised one large palm and tentatively ran it over Sera's curls.

Sera craned her neck to smile up at him, like a puppy enjoying the attention.

But Isabelle was distracted by Matthew's large, tanned hand, too aware of the memory of those same hands stroking over her bare skin, cupping her breasts, lifting her up...

'How was your week?' he asked.

The question, and the banality of it, took her so off-guard that for a yawning stretch of time all she could do was stare at him like a simpleton.

'Good,' she said at last.

He seemed to be waiting for her to say more but, at a loss for the right words, Isabelle chose to focus on Sera instead. It was so much easier...giving herself to her children.

Matthew tried again. 'My mother says that you have "politely declined" the invitation to her ball?'

'I have.' Isabelle had been surprised by the invitation—surprised and then afraid. 'You haven't told her...?'

'No. I wouldn't make a decision like that without asking you first.' His grey eyes darkened and he raised one hand to run it through his black hair. 'But I would be lying if I said I didn't want to, Duchess. I hate pretending that she's not mine. My family... They would be shocked—' he laughed wryly '—and probably angry with me once they found out how she came to be. But they would love her.'

Her blood froze in her veins. What would his mother, the Countess of Heather, think of her if she knew the truth? If she knew that Isabelle had propositioned her son and then birthed his child?

'I would like to tell them eventually—when you're ready.' Now his laugh was mirthless. 'Grandchildren are the only thing they've talked about for years.'

'And if I am never "ready", as you call it?'

She didn't know why his answer was so important to her—but it was. Isabelle had been handed from man to man without ever having been asked what she wanted.

Matthew was kind, and he was quickly turning into one of the best men she knew—though, admittedly, she knew few. Still, that wouldn't change the fact that once his family knew about Seraphina he'd hold all the cards—including hers. As a man, he'd always have more power than her. And as Sera's father, he'd have the power to destroy her completely.

'Then I won't ever tell them,' he promised. He watched her over their daughter's dark head of hair. 'Did you ever stop to think that I would never deliberately hurt you, Duchess? Or that I would want nothing but to care for you and protect you, the mother of my child?'

She deliberately ignored the pleasure that his words evoked and replied honestly. 'No. I have never seen a man take an active interest in his children—especially his illegitimate ones. If I am wary of you, Matthew, it is because I cannot completely trust that you do not have some ulterior motive.'

'What ulterior motive could I possibly have?' he asked in exasperation. 'Sneaking in through your servants' entrance, denying Sera as my own to my family, pretending nothing ever happened between us—those are not the actions of a man who has an ulterior motive.'

He watched her closely, his eyes narrowed on her face as if she was some strange creature that he could not make sense of.

'Have you ever had a man—*any* man—in your life that you could trust? Is it only me that you are wary of?'

'No, it is not you—or not only you. My experience of men has been limited to my father, who gave me away to one of his friends—my late husband, who practically bought me—and you, who...'

Changed everything.

'Who got you pregnant and left you,' he finished quietly for her.

'No.' Isabelle shook her head. 'That's not even close to what I was going to say.'

'Duchess, you are the mother of my child. You have my word that I will never do anything to hurt you or scare you or threaten you.'

'Even if that means depriving your family of knowing Seraphina?'

'Even then. You have carried, birthed, loved and protected my child.'

When Sera looked up at him, curious at his angry tone, he softened his voice.

'I would choose your happiness over my family's knowledge of Sera every time.'

'But you don't even know me,' she argued, terrified by what he'd admitted. 'We had one night. That is all.'

Matthew's eyes snapped from his daughter's face to Isabelle's, his anger at her observation dying immediately when he saw the glazed fear in her expression. She looked so afraid.

She *was*, he realised. But he was not a threat to her; in fact, he was certain he'd cut his bleeding heart from his own chest to protect her if the need arose.

'Duchess, I don't have to know you inside out to know that you are brave and strong and kind. You showed me that the first time that we met. You show me still every time we are together.'

She merely tilted her head and frowned.

Needing to lighten the heavy mood his words had conjured, he added, 'Stubborn too.'

Instead of gasping, or looking offended, she surprised him by grinning, the wide smile wrinkling her nose adorably. 'I am terribly stubborn. It is my worst trait.'

'No. It's not your worst trait.'

Her eyes narrowed on him, her kissable lips pursed as if in thought. 'Pray, do tell—what *is* my worst trait?'

Matthew had the strongest urge to run his lips across her mouth until she smiled again. Instead, he said, 'You don't trust anyone except for Mary and Willa, and that limits your experience of the world.'

Her shoulders drooped. 'Oh…' Her eyes, so bright a

moment before, had lost their shine. 'I suppose you do know me rather well,' she observed forlornly.

'Well, it's either that or your penchant for throwing things,' he teased, hoping to return to their previous light banter.

Her smile returned, but it did not meet her eyes. 'You remember me telling you that?'

I remember everything, he thought.

But, knowing that the confession would not comfort the Duchess now, he answered, 'It is not your fault that you have had to be strong against all the weak men in your life, Duchess—and I include myself amongst them. I shouldn't have…'

Realising that he couldn't regret their night together, he did not finish the sentence.

'Mistrust is a defence mechanism,' he continued. 'And it's one that is extremely difficult to overcome. And you've had to develop yours from the age of thirteen, when your father first accepted your betrothal to a man he never should have considered. I do not judge you for being mistrustful. But I hurt knowing that I will always be included amongst the people you don't fully take into your confidence. And I am ashamed, because I know that there is nobody to blame but myself.'

He made sure to look into her eyes, so that she could see his sincerity when he finished.

'Despite my past mistakes, I would give a fortune to have your trust. And I would never break it were you to honour me with it.'

Matthew did not make promises lightly. And he had

most certainly never made such a promise to a woman before. But he hoped that Isabelle would overlook what she knew of his past to see that he told the truth—that nothing had become more important to him than Seraphina and, by default, Isabelle.

'I…'

She raised a hand to her chest, clearly bewildered. Her eyes filled with tears, and he hated that he had caused them. And then she ruined him.

'You have done nothing to earn my mistrust,' she said. 'Despite your "past mistakes"—' she used his own words to hammer home her point '—you have time and time again proved that I *can* trust you. It's *me*. I'm…so afraid. Of everything. Of *everyone*.'

She bravely met his eyes.

'I apologise for declining your mother's invitation. But I don't do well with so many people—especially those I don't know. I have been largely left on my own for most of my life, so it is overwhelming for me to be confronted with so many strangers, all of whom fawn for my attention. It terrifies me,' she whispered, her dark eyes round with anxious dread at the mere mention of a crowd. 'You were right last time—when you called me a coward.'

'I didn't mean it,' he countered, growing more ashamed by the second. 'I was hurt and angry. I don't think you are a coward. I think you are the bravest person I know.'

'No…' She sent him a wobbly smile. 'I hide behind the children.'

'Which is completely natural, considering.'

Isabelle looked at him with those big, sad eyes. 'That may be, but I would like our daughter to have a better example—to feel comfortable in her skin. Luke will go off to school soon enough, and will be indoctrinated into the world by default. But Sera…'

He wondered if she realised she'd said it—*our* daughter…

Their eyes simultaneously moved to where Seraphina had fallen fast asleep on his lap without either of them noticing. Her head was tilted slightly to one side, her little mouth ajar.

Matthew's chest expanded with a foreign emotion, one as deep as it was soothing, as he watched her tiny chest rise and fall with each peaceful breath. He knew, with absolute clarity, that he was exactly where he was supposed to be.

'I should put her down…'

Matthew was desperate to prolong his time with them, even for a few minutes. 'Let me carry her up for you.'

Isabelle opened her mouth to argue, and then just as quickly closed it. 'Thank you. She's getting too heavy for me.'

He gently untangled Sera's legs and tucked her into his side before pushing himself first to his knees, and then to his feet, his usually agile movements made cumbersome as he tried not to disturb the sleeping child.

As he followed Isabelle out of the room and they walked in silence up the dark stairs, Matthew couldn't help but watch her in front of him, her long, thick hair

falling out of its haphazard braid down over her laven-
der gown, the colours contrasting erotically.

He wanted to reach out and wrap his hand in her hair.
He wanted to crane her neck back until her lips met his.

Inside her bedroom, he deliberately avoided looking
about her private space. He kept his gaze stoically away
from the big bed in the centre of the room and placed
Seraphina in a small curtained crib. He paused only to
tuck the covers around her and brush one hand over
her downy head before quickly turning to make his escape—and almost walking into Isabelle, who had come
up behind him to see to Seraphina herself.

Her hands came up instinctively, bracing against his
chest even as his own hands reached out to grip her
upper arms and steady her.

'Oh, I'm sorr—'

'Apologies,' he said, accidentally talking over her.

Instead of releasing her, his hands tightened on her
arms, bringing her a fraction closer. Matthew's body
flared to life at her proximity, and though he dared not
move he had to actively fight his need to close the distance between them and plaster himself against her.

Isabelle did not move her hands from his chest either. She stared up at him with dark eyes, her breath
leaving her lips in a ragged exhalation that tore through
the room.

'Resisting you is the single most difficult thing I have
ever had to do,' he murmured quietly.

She swallowed. Matthew's eyes tracked the movement. He wanted to place his lips there and feel her hammering pulse reaching for him.

'Matthew, I… I don't know what the right thing to do is.'

He heard the need in her voice as she leaned against him and rested her head on his chest for a long moment. As if she needed the contact too. As if she craved him as much as he did her.

He wondered if she could hear his heart galloping, as she had that first night. And, helpless to resist, he raised one hand to cradle the back of her head. When she sighed, and relaxed more fully against him, Matthew closed his eyes and simply breathed in her rose scent.

He wished he cared for her less so he could seduce her more. Just the thought of kissing those soft lips again had him aching with arousal. But although she had come to him willingly that first time, and although she'd carried and birthed a child, Isabelle was frighteningly innocent. So, even as he felt her yielding, and even as his own body hardened in erotic contrast, Matthew summoned the last of his self-control and stepped back from her.

Isabelle exhaled shakily.

'I want you,' he told her. 'You know that to be true.' She opened her mouth, but before she could admit anything that would crush his resolve, he added, 'But I need your trust more. So, until you are certain of what you want, and can ask me for it without any doubt in your mind, I will not touch you.'

It was a promise to himself as much as it was a promise to her.

She nodded, but didn't say anything else. Matthew strode past her and paused at the door to torture himself with one last look at her. Isabelle had wrapped her arms around herself and was looking after him with such raw, honest need that his entire body tensed with regret and longing.

Still, he managed a stiff bow and, before he could change his mind, said, 'Monday, Duchess.'

Chapter Twelve

In the three weeks leading up to the Countess of Heather's infamous masquerade ball, Isabelle saw Matthew every Monday and Friday, as they'd agreed.

At first, Isabelle had been terrified that he'd be seen sneaking into her house through the servants' entrance. However, as the weeks passed, her own desire to see him, coupled with his obvious discretion, had eased the sharp edge of her fear.

Matthew never came empty-handed. He usually brought flowers—white lilacs for youth, poppies for sleep, in the hope that it would facilitate Seraphina sleeping through the night soon—and once, of all things, a pineapple.

Isabelle had been rather caught off-guard by that offering. The hostile-looking fruit, which had been rarer and more expensive than a white elephant at the beginning of the century, had become mainstream with Britain's expansion through the colonies, and it was a diversion from the usual delicate blooms. It was only once

Matthew had taken his leave that night that Isabelle had checked in the *Language of Flowers*. And there it was.

The pineapple. Its meaning: you are perfect.

Isabelle had kept the fruit for days, too enamoured of it to send it straight to the kitchen, and her fondness for it undoubtedly resulted in a few raised eyebrows amongst the servants.

In the month during which they had been communicating, Isabelle had grown not only to enjoy Matthew's company, but to *crave* it. The days between Monday and Friday had never felt so long, and the time he spent with them was always too short. And their short time together was somehow ruined, because even as she tried to enjoy it, Isabelle felt swamped with melancholy over the fact that he would be leaving so soon.

She knew that he came for Sera—she *loved* that he came for Sera—but Isabelle had started to ponder where his obligation to their daughter ended and his interest in her began. Worse, even as she knew nothing could come of him—of *them*—she wanted *something*. Only she didn't know what that something was.

But she remembered what it had been like to be with him, and in remembering she dreamed that they would find each other again. Because, sinner that she was, she still burned for him. Sometimes she even woke in the night, aching for his hands on her skin and his mouth on her breasts.

Her desire for him was nothing new. But before he'd

come to London—before he'd started visiting, before he'd almost kissed her again—she'd been able to roll over and will herself back to sleep by convincing herself that she'd never see him again. Now...

Isabelle flushed with shame when she thought about the recent pleasure she'd found in using her own fingers and her secret, lurid memories. But instead of the spreading relief she'd expected it had left her feeling rather desolate. As if she'd been saddled with a life of blancmange after a taste of the finest Parisian desserts.

And Matthew had been true to his word. Not only had he not kissed her, he had not even touched her in the most casual of ways since he'd made his promise to earn her trust. And Isabelle, who still felt like the shy, inexperienced girl who'd first gone to him, could do nothing but wish she'd been more certain, more brazen.

The thought made her grumble aloud.

'Is anything the matter, Izzy?'

Isabelle considered her cousin. Even now, at home with nobody about, Mary was perfectly made up in a light blue day gown, not a hair out of place.

'Mary, may I ask you a dreadfully personal question?'

Mary put down the book she was reading and waited in silent invitation.

Isabelle searched for the correct phrasing before settling on, 'You loved your John dearly—correct?'

Mary's gaze turned wistful almost immediately. 'Yes. Of course.'

'And you...you had a *good* marriage?'

'Yes, for the short time that we were married.' Mary

turned to face Isabelle again, her smile dying when she saw the look on Isabelle's face. 'What is this about?'

'Do you miss…? That is to say, do you think about…?' Isabelle covered her eyes with one hand, as mortified by the question as she was desperate for an answer.

'Isabelle…?'

Isabelle took a deep breath, squared her shoulders and, without quite meeting Mary's eyes, asked, 'Do you miss having *relations*? With John?'

Her friend could not have looked more shocked had a horse flown in through the window and laid a golden egg. 'I beg your pardon?'

'I asked if—'

'Oh, I heard you well enough,' Mary said hurriedly, before Isabelle could repeat herself.

Isabelle waited for what seemed an age.

Then Mary pushed herself to her feet and marched to the open door, her back ramrod-straight. She closed them into the study with an impatient snap of her wrist, took a deep breath, and then turned to face Isabelle again, her face set in an unusually stern expression.

'What on earth would prompt you to ask such a question?'

'So, you don't? Miss…*it*?'

Mary ignored Isabelle's question and asked one of her own, demanding, 'Is this about *him*?'

'Does it matter if it is?'

'Izzy!' Mary looked stunned.

'Mary,' Isabelle countered, unsure of how to breach

this new awkwardness between them, 'it's a simple yes or no question. I'm hardly asking for the sordid details.'

Mary advanced upon her, her blue skirts trailing behind her like an advancing naval gunboat's wake, her green eyes filled with panic. 'This cannot go on.'

'It was just a question—'

'It was not *just a question*—and you know it.'

Isabelle grew more embarrassed by the second. 'Forget I asked,' she said quietly.

But she couldn't help but wonder if maybe there was something wrong with her—some inner wanton, or a strumpet that whispered the devil's work through her body and made her ache for a man she should not want and could not have.

'Isabelle, you have to reach different terms with Lord Ashworth,' Mary hissed. 'He is dangerous to you. To Seraphina!'

'No.' Isabelle shook her head vehemently at that, and when Mary opened her mouth to speak, she cut off her cousin. 'As my friend, Mary, you may take liberties in speaking your mind. But I'm going to ask you to refrain from passing judgement on a man who has been nothing but a complete gentleman—to me *and* to his daughter.' She took a deep breath in an attempt to calm herself. 'Matthew has made mistakes in the past—'

'He ruined a woman! To the point where she cannot even show her face—'

'Do you think I have not thought about that?' Isabelle demanded. 'Do you think it does not plague me?'

'Izzy…'

Isabelle refused to cry, but she felt the telltale burn of tears. 'Where Sera and I are concerned, he has been *kind* and *gentle* and *protective*.'

Mary paled. 'Izzy…he blackmailed you!'

'He forced my hand in order to meet his child,' she argued immediately, knowing that there was a difference, knowing that *Matthew* was different.

Even though her experience of men had been limited, she knew Matthew was nothing like her father and the late Duke of Everett. While they had bargained and bartered over her, discussing her worth as if she were a brood mare and not a human being, Matthew had not—and with the leverage he had over her he certainly could have if he'd wished to.

'Until you take the time to actually get to know Lord Ashworth, you will not say another thing about him. You…' She shook her head. 'You don't know him, Mary.' She softened her tone. 'You don't see how he is with Sera.'

With me.

'Need I remind you that he is responsible for this mess in the first place?'

'That is categorically incorrect—and you know it,' Isabelle hurried on before Mary could argue further. 'You are so afraid of the fact that he *did* bed me that you forget I was the one who *begged* him to.'

Isabelle pushed back her chair and with one last look at her friend's pale face and stunned expression left the room.

She needed to get out of the house…perhaps go for

a walk. Yes, a walk. She could walk off her anger and her frustration and tire out the children at the same time. She needed to take her temper away from Mary, before either of them said something they would regret.

Isabelle curled her hands into fists and resisted the urge to throw down the new crystal vase on the hall table as she passed—but only barely.

Before she could change her mind, she rang for a maid and asked her to have Tess prepare Seraphina and ask Luke if he'd like to take a break from his lessons to accompany them.

Only twenty minutes later, she exited Everett Place to climb into her awaiting barouche. 'Hyde Park. Thank you, Phillip.'

'Any particular route, Your Grace?'

'If you'd please drop us at Cumberland Gate? I believe we are all in need of exercise.'

The driver bowed and waited for the footman to hand her into the barouche before resuming his seat. And then they were off, gliding through London in the early afternoon.

Isabelle leaned forward and looked out from beneath the leather canopy as they drove, her eyes tracking the sights and sounds of the city as she tried to forget her argument with Mary.

It was a beautiful day, and the weather seemed to have brought everyone out, giving her the perfect distraction. Oxford Street was bustling. Women in colourful dresses perused the shopfronts, pausing to look in the confectioner's window or enter drapers and silk shops.

Men dressed for the day's work hurried about. London was busy and thriving.

In her lap, Seraphina babbled happily and toyed with an errant strand of Isabelle's hair. In the seat across from her, Luke sat quietly, holding the small leather ball he'd brought with him.

'How are your lessons going?' she asked, trying to draw him into conversation.

Luke's green eyes found hers. He smiled and shrugged. 'Mr Watts taught me the phases of the moon by making a new picture strip for my zoetrope.'

'That sounds like fun,' Isabelle commented, unsurprised by the tutor's ingenuity.

Mr Watts, a retired vicar with a love for discovery, was undoubtedly a jewel of the St Claire household. He tried hard to make everything fun for Luke. But Mr Watts was much more than a tutor. In a house full of women and servants, he was Luke's bridge to manhood—something that Isabelle did not take lightly.

It seemed every time she turned around Luke had grown again, with each small spurt bringing big changes. Changes she had no experience in explaining. Changes she had very little knowledge about herself.

Her consolation was that Luke had Mr Watts, and that her stepson would be going off to school in two short years. Boarding school wasn't something Luke had chosen for himself; it was something Isabelle had encouraged. Because there were some things that boys needed to learn from other boys—just as girls needed to learn from other girls.

In theory, her mind corrected, as she reflected on her conversation with Mary.

Isabelle had been expecting Mary to be shy, or even embarrassed—it was, after all, an entirely inappropriate question to have asked. But she had never thought that her friend would immediately see through her. Because although Mary had been wrong in her judgement of Matthew, she had not been wrong in her judgement of Isabelle. And therein lay the problem…

Her thoughts were interrupted by the barouche coming to a gliding stop. Isabelle shifted Seraphina on her lap, welcoming the distraction of the park. While Phillip lowered the leather roof, a footman took Seraphina and then helped Isabelle out of the conveyance. Luke, ever eager, clambered down and ran ahead of them, only slowing when Isabelle called out for him to wait.

After hurried instructions to Phillip to return in an hour, Isabelle set off after Luke, adjusting her pace to Seraphina's little legs. The large footman followed discreetly behind.

She started moving south through Hyde Park, heading towards Rotten Row, keeping Luke in her line of sight and Seraphina's small hand in hers the entire time.

Like the rest of London, the park was bustling. Ladies dressed for display paraded about, hoping to be seen. Several riders trotted by. Barouches and carriages kept to South Carriage Drive, avoiding the footpaths and the dozens of pedestrians.

Isabelle ignored the stares and whispers as several people recognised her and pointed her out to their companions. She must look a fright, dressed in a simple day gown, her hair falling from its pins, her face red from being bent over while hurrying alongside Sera.

She would later blame her own shyness for the fact that she hadn't been watching Luke carefully enough. All she saw, the moment she looked up, was his leather ball careening towards a group of oblivious dark-haired ladies walking with a single man.

Luke watched in horror, frozen to the spot, as the ball flew through the air and hit the gentleman on the back of the head.

With no time to think, Isabelle hiked Seraphina up onto her hip and hurried across the green grass. 'Luke!'

He started back towards her immediately, his face flushed with shame.

As soon as Isabelle caught up with him, she whispered, 'What have I told you about throwing a ball too close to people?'

She stepped in front of him before he could reply, prepared to apologise to the gentleman the ball had hit and to defend Luke against a potential scolding from a stranger.

'I'm so sorry…' she began, looking up—only to trail off when she met a pair of rather amused grey eyes. 'It's you!' she blurted. And then, realising what she'd done, she tried to rectify it with an awkward curtsy and a mumbled, 'Lord Ashworth…'

'Your Grace.'

Matthew's deep voice whispered over her skin.

'I—' Isabelle stopped talking. Because Sera had

recognised Matthew and begun squirming, leaning her body forward, her arms outstretched to him. Isabelle instinctively refused to let her go, tightening her arms around the child instead.

When Seraphina cried out in response, kicking her feet in an embarrassing display of temper, Isabelle simply froze. Before she could think what to do—or run away, as she rather felt she might—Matthew plucked Sera from her and settled the child on his own hip.

Isabelle felt as if her shield had been taken away. All around them people seemed to stop what they were doing and watch. And if they thought it strange that her child had reached for Lord Ashworth, they must find it stranger still that Sera instantly stopped fussing the moment she was in his arms.

'No apologies necessary, Your Grace.'

After the smallest pause, in which he seemed to search Isabelle's face, Matthew glanced down at Seraphina.

'And who is this?' he asked in a perfect imitation of polite curiosity.

'My daughter,' Isabelle murmured breathlessly. 'Sera—Seraphina.'

'Hello, Seraphina.'

He greeted his daughter with the same polite smile, but Isabelle saw the warmth snaking through his eyes when he looked at her. And instead of relief that he'd lied for her, she felt the first lick of shame over the fact that he'd always have to. Yes, he had made mistakes. But the man standing in front of her deserved more—so much more than two secret meetings with his daughter a week.

'Matthew?' The eldest of the women standing behind him spoke first. 'Are you going to just stand there, or are you going to introduce us to the Duchess and her family?'

Isabelle's awkward smile tightened as she stared into the woman's familiar grey eyes. Her heart raced, forcing a hot flush of anxiety through her body.

'Forgive me, Mother.'

As if he'd read Isabelle's thoughts, Matthew leaned close.

'Relax, Duchess,' he whispered, before turning around with Seraphina still in his arms. 'Your Graces—' Matthew included Luke in his introduction '—may I introduce my mother, the Countess of Heather, and my two sisters, Lady Caroline Westmoor and Lady Eleanor Blake?'

The ladies curtsied.

Luke bowed politely.

Seraphina hiccupped, causing a round of genuine laughter that momentarily broke through the awkwardness of the moment.

Isabelle turned to her stepson. 'Luke?'

He stepped forward to face Lord Ashworth, looking sufficiently repentant. 'I am sorry for hitting you with my ball, my lord.'

Matthew smiled and gave a small nod in Luke's direction. 'If I may say so, you have a powerful arm, Your Grace.'

Luke flushed, his eyes lighting with a bashful pride that Isabelle had never seen before. 'Thank you, sir.'

'Perhaps we can leave the ladies to get acquainted and put it to good use?'

Luke's green eyes widened and he gave a stammered 'Y-yes', his nervousness at this attention from Lord Ashworth apparent.

Matthew placed Sera on the ground and gave her an elaborate bow. Raising their daughter's hand to his lips, he kissed the back of her tiny fingers.

'Lady Seraphina. It has been an honour.'

Sera laughed happily.

Overcome with emotion, Isabelle could do nothing but move forward and take Sera's hand, stopping her from walking after Matthew and Luke as they moved away to continue Luke's game.

She watched the first few throws between them before turning back to Matthew's family. 'I apologise for interrupting your walk,' she began awkwardly. 'It—'

'Oh, it is nothing, Your Grace,' Lady Eleanor Blake exclaimed immediately.

The younger lady, who appeared to be around the same age as Isabelle, was dressed in a yellow gown that complemented her black hair. Her sister, similarly attired, but in green, looked just as striking, and Isabelle couldn't help but imagine that this was what Sera might look like when she was grown-up. Tall and fair-skinned, with that striking midnight hair and those expressive storm cloud eyes. Isabelle looked more like her Italian ancestors on her mother's side—her hair dark and heavy, her skin golden, not pale, and her eyes near-black. But these ladies were pure English delicacy.

'We see our brother quite regularly,' Lady Caroline affirmed. She turned to look to where Matthew was throwing the ball with Luke. 'Though I must admit he's not usually this amiable. Is he, Nora?'

'No,' Eleanor replied matter-of-factly, her own gaze tracking where the duo played. 'He is typically quite reserved.'

'If I may ask,' the Countess said, 'how are you acquainted with my son, Your Grace?'

Isabelle turned, a reply ready on her lips. But any words she might have said died as her heart climbed up through her chest and into her throat. Because the Countess was not looking at her. She was staring intently down at Seraphina, and her eyes were wide with equal parts shock and denial.

'Through a mutual friend—Lady Windhurst,' Isabelle managed eventually. 'We were introduced at Lady Russell's ball a month ago.'

She wondered if they could all hear the blatant lie in her words.

'I see,' the Countess replied, and Isabelle thought she rather *did* see.

Noticing their mother's lapse, but perhaps not recognising its reason, both of Matthew's sisters jumped in to further the conversation. 'Are you enjoying the season thus far, Your Grace?' Eleanor asked.

After a strange glance at her mother, Caroline added,

'We love being in London, Your Grace. Don't we, Nora?'

'Please, call me Isabelle,' she replied distractedly, not realising that she hadn't answered the question.

The Countess bent closer to Seraphina and asked, 'How old are you, Seraphina?' in a tone that signalled to her nearby parent that she was the one who was meant to answer.

Isabelle tried to sound calm. 'She is eighteen months.'

'How does a walk sound, child? We are probably close to the same speed.'

The Countess held out her hands, and as Seraphina walked to her grandmother, Isabelle forced herself to let her daughter go, when every instinct was demanding that she take both children and leave.

As the Countess led the toddler down a nearby pathway, Matthew's sisters fell into talking of London and the season. They made observations about recent balls and gave compliments to their hosts, commented on particular dresses of interest that they had noticed, and asked several polite questions regarding Isabelle's own forays into society.

For anyone else, the topics would have been easy small talk. Isabelle nodded and murmured her agreement, but soon ran short of things to say. Mortified beyond reason at her inability to communicate, and desperate to make an effort with Matthew's sisters, she broke a long moment of awkward silence.

'You'll have to forgive me…' A hot blush swept through her at their patient smiles. 'I am recently out of mourning and find that my conversation skills need some practice,' she said honestly. 'With Luke and Seraphina occupying so much of my time, I've grown accustomed to talking predominantly with children.'

Both sisters leapt on the olive branch she had offered, reassuring her that it was entirely natural and that she should not concern herself, but it was only when Matthew wandered back with Luke a few minutes later that Isabelle felt any real relief.

The two were a welcome distraction as they approached, their conversation trailing off naturally once they came abreast of the group again.

Luke looked up at Isabelle. His green eyes were bright with joy, his face flushed with exertion. 'Lord Ashworth has invited us to his family's country seat this September,' he said happily. 'He's going to show me how to fish—and teach me how to hunt.'

'Oh…' she managed. 'That is very kind of him.' She knew her voice sounded too tight, making her seem displeased when in fact the offer was a thoughtful one.

'Oh, you must come!' Nora exclaimed. 'My father and brother host an annual hunting party, but their friends' wives are either too old for Caro and me to enjoy talking with, or—'

'Or non-existent,' Caroline cut in, a teasing glint in her eye. 'Matthew's friends are notoriously single.'

'And proud of it.' Nora grinned.

'They are dropping like flies, and you know it,' Matthew replied. He winked at Isabelle. 'Caro snagged one of my oldest friends from right beneath my nose.'

'I hardly *snagged* Westmoor.' Caro laughed, undeterred. She lowered her voice. 'He came quite willingly.'

Nora and Caroline laughed at Matthew's mock-horrified expression, causing Isabelle to smile too. But she was saved from having to accept or reject the spontaneous invitation by the arrival of the Countess and Seraphina.

While Sera wore a wide grin, the Countess looked grave. 'I dare say,' she observed, 'I haven't had this much exercise in an age.'

'I am told that children keep a person young,' Isabelle replied breathlessly. 'Though I have yet to confirm the hypothesis.'

Everyone laughed, their easy manner unspooling some of the nervous dread still in Isabelle's chest.

The Countess looked at her for a long moment, her eyes missing nothing. 'Forgive my impertinence, Your Grace—'

'Isabelle, please,' she corrected, but she held her breath, terrified of what the Countess might have to say.

'I did receive your apologies regarding my ball, but I do hope you will now reconsider. We shall be eagerly awaiting you.'

Isabelle expelled a long, quiet breath. If the Countess suspected anything it was clear that she would not broach the subject—at least not today. 'I will check with my companion. Perhaps we can attend for a short while.'

'And Lady Windhurst has accepted,' Nora added. 'So you won't have to suffer our company the entire night.'

'Your company is no hardship, Nora,' Isabelle replied—and she meant it.

'You only say that because you do not know her,' Matthew mock-whispered, drawing a dramatic gasp from Nora and chuckles from everybody else.

'I will gladly receive you.' Isabelle turned to the other ladies, including them in the invitation. 'Any time that is convenient for you.' Leaning down, she picked up Sera. 'Unfortunately, I don't get out as often as I should.'

'It's true,' Luke added helpfully.

Matthew's lips quirked. 'We shall have to remedy that, won't we?'

'Yes, sir!'

Isabelle couldn't help but smile. 'Perhaps another day—for now you have lessons you have to get back to.'

Luke hung his head and grumbled his acquiescence.

'Thank you.' She turned to the other women. 'All of you, for including us in your walk.'

Though she didn't say it, Isabelle had found it both unusual and lovely to see how close Matthew's family were to each other, their manner easy, their jokes teasing but light-hearted. It made her wonder about things she shouldn't.

'Thank you, Lord Ashworth,' Luke added.

Matthew bowed, treating the young boy like a peer. 'My pleasure, Your Grace. Perhaps we will see you all at the hunt this year?'

Luke nodded and looked up at Isabelle, fairly begging her to accept the invitation.

Matthew met Isabelle's gaze. 'May I walk you back

to your carriage?' he asked, saving her from having to dash Luke's hopes in front of an audience.

'Thank you, but there's no need,' she replied. 'My footman is here, and my driver should be waiting.' Isabelle tipped her head in farewell. 'Lord Ashworth…'

'Duchess.'

He bowed slightly, but not before she saw the disappointment flash in his eyes.

Isabelle turned to say goodbye to Matthew's family. 'It was lovely to meet you,' she said honestly. 'I hope to see you all again soon.'

'At my ball, perhaps?' the Countess reminded her.

Isabelle nodded, and with one last look, to make sure Luke followed, hurried back in the direction of her barouche.

Chapter Thirteen

Matthew hadn't quite believed it when he'd turned around and bent to pick up that ball, only to come face to face with the Duchess, her heavy hair falling from its pins, her face flushed with embarrassment. In that moment his mind had blanked, words had fled. He'd stood there like a mute until she'd started the conversation.

'Oh, is that Penelope Periwinkle?' Nora asked Caro now, and before he could turn to see where she was pointing both his sisters had walked off to go and talk to their friend.

His mother waited until they were both out of hearing. 'Matthew…'

He turned to find her eyes boring into him. 'Yes, Mother?'

'What have you done?'

Matthew knew what she thought without her having to make the accusation. His own mother believed he'd seduced and abandoned Isabelle. It crushed him. There was a fleeting moment of panic, when he wondered if it would always be like this—if he would always be found lacking because of an affair he'd had when he was *twenty-five*. He even considered denying it, but one look at his mother's face told him that it was too late.

'It's not what you think—'

'Do not lie to me.' She shook her head, closing her eyes in momentary frustration. 'Not about this. Not about *her*.' She placed a hand over her chest. 'I felt I was back in the past, twenty years ago, staring at my own child. Good God, she is Nora reincarnate!'

'I am not lying, Mother,' he said tightly, trying to hold on to his control. 'I'm merely telling you that I'm not entirely to blame for the circumstances.'

'You expect me to believe that?' she whispered. 'The Duchess is barely twenty years old—and she is *certainly* less responsible than you. Of that I am certain.'

'Yes, Mother,' he replied curtly, frustrated that she should instantly assume the worst of him. He lowered his voice. 'I do expect you to believe me when I say that I did *not* seduce an innocent woman and then abandon her—with a child.' His anger and hurt mingled and leached into his tone. 'You are supposed to be one of the few people who believe the best of me. If you do not, then how am I to convince anybody else?'

How am I to convince Isabelle?

'Are you denying that she is yours?' his mother demanded.

'No.' He turned back in the direction that Isabelle had gone, hoping for one last glimpse of them. 'I'm telling you that if it were my choice I would shout the fact on every street corner in London, the consequences be damned.'

The Countess reared back, clearly struck by the sincerity in his tone. Her grey eyes softened when she saw the hopeless expression on his face.

'The Duchess is afraid of the implications?' she asked.

'Sera looks too much like me,' he confirmed. 'We can't risk people questioning her legitimacy.'

'People will believe what they want to believe anyway. So long as there is no evidence to the contrary...' She paused for a beat, considering. '*Is* there any evidence to the contrary?'

Matthew laughed, hearing the same argument that he'd given Isabelle. 'No. But it's not that simple,' he replied, trying to defend Isabelle's decision. 'She has Luke's guardianship to think of too.'

'Well, look at your sisters.' She pointed to where both his sisters were now engaged in conversation with Penelope. 'They might have been looking in a mirror, and yet they're none the wiser.'

'It's not that simple, Mother.' God, he wished it was.

As if she'd only just realised she had a grandchild, the Countess, overcome by sudden excitement, changed tactic, exclaiming, 'We shall keep it a secret amongst the family, then! Matthew, I'm old. And your father! He could drop dead at any time without knowing he has a *granddaughter*!' she whispered.

'Father is in perfectly good health.'

'For *now*.'

'This is exactly why I didn't tell you,' he insisted, though he couldn't help but be relieved at her obvious excitement.

Whether his mother thought him reprehensible or not, it was clear that she would accept Seraphina. He supposed, given his own past, he hadn't been entirely sure of that. A bungled affair was one thing. But an affair *and* an illegitimate child was another thing entirely.

'I knew you would meddle.'

'Well, someone has to do *something*.'

'Mother…' Matthew took a deep breath in, exhaled, and prayed for patience. 'I know that you and Father stood by me before, even though you were ashamed of what I'd done.'

'You are my child!' she insisted. 'Of course I—'

'But I am begging you now: do not interfere.' He talked over her. 'Not with the Duchess—and not with Sera. I am dealing with it. *When* the Duchess is ready, we will let you into Sera's life. *Please*,' he fairly begged, 'let me fix this on my own. They're mine—my responsibility.'

She regarded him in silence for a long moment. 'I have just realised… She recognised you. Seraphina…'

'Yes.'

'You see her, then?'

'As often as Isabelle will allow,' he confirmed.

Which in his mind wasn't nearly enough. Not enough of Sera. And not enough of the Duchess.

Although he had tried to be the perfect gentleman, leaving as soon as Sera was asleep, not staying a minute past the necessary time, it took conscious physical effort to get his feet moving towards the door and away from them every time.

Matthew would have rather stayed. He *longed* to stay. But more than his own want to linger he wanted Isabelle to feel safe with him. He wanted her trust.

He started off in the direction his sisters had gone. But his mother didn't relent so easily. She followed at his side, her steps matching his easily in her eagerness.

'Did you know? When you left…?'

'No.'

'Oh.' That seemed to throw her. After a brief pause to consider, she hurried after him. 'So, you found out—?'

'A month ago.'

'Good God, Matthew. This is what you were talking about when I visited,' she observed. 'And she…she kept it from you all this time?'

Matthew rounded on her, pulling them both up short. 'The Duchess is not to blame, Mother. She has two children to protect.' Noticing that his voice was too loud, he forced a calm smile that was completely denied by his racing heart. 'Please,' he pleaded quietly, 'leave it be. If you start interfering, she will panic. Isabelle is terrified of how my past might harm Sera, and if you press her she will close me out for good.'

'You care for her, then?'

'She is the mother of my child,' he said gently. 'Of course I care for her.'

But the Countess would not accept half-truths so easily. 'Please, Matthew… When has that ever meant anything? No. That's not the whole of it,' she insisted, placing her hand on his arm. 'You feel something more—'

'My caring for her has to be enough,' he countered. 'For now.'

Chapter Fourteen

The day of the masquerade ball arrived in no time at all. Isabelle, who had spent the past weeks mulling on whether or not to attend, had mostly decided against it by the time the afternoon came. She knew she was far too invested in Matthew's visits than was safe—eagerly waiting for him to arrive and then desperately fighting her need to be touched by him every minute they were together.

She took a small sip of her tea, relieved when it soothed her itchy throat, and glanced at the clock on the mantel. Even if she decided to go, it was quickly approaching the hour when she wouldn't be ready in time to attend the ball anyway.

'I'll stay,' she confirmed to the empty room, ignoring the disappointment that settled within her at the decision.

There was a gentle knock on the door and Mary entered, a large box in her hands. 'Do you have a moment?'

Isabelle put down her teacup. 'Of course. You never

have to ask, Mary,' she insisted, hoping that this reminder would be enough to bridge the recent awkwardness between them.

Mary sat on the settee next to her and put the box on the table. She looked down at her folded hands for a moment, as if considering what to say. 'I am sorry, Izzy,' she stated finally. 'For my reaction to your question about…' She cleared her throat. 'About John.'

Isabelle blushed even as she tried to give a nonchalant wave of her hand. 'It is forgotten, Mary.' She took a deep breath. 'You were wrong about Lord Ashworth. But not about me.' Reaching across the space between them, she took Mary's hand in hers. 'Will you forgive me?'

Mary's fingers curled around hers. 'There is nothing to forgive.' Mary looked down at her hands again. 'Izzy, if your past is ever aired it will ruin your life— and possibly Seraphina's too. No excuses accepted. No sympathy allocated. Society will eat you alive and go back to their whores that same night.'

Isabelle stared at her cousin in shock, even as that familiar flicker of panic reared inside her at the thought of people finding out about Seraphina.

'My Lord, Mary,' she managed eventually, 'that is the most unforgiving statement I have ever heard you make.'

'I am being honest.'

'You are worried that Matthew and I shall be found out?'

'I am,' she conceded. 'But I understand that you have

thought it through extensively—more so than I have. And I do want you to be happy. It's the very reason I pushed you back into society in the first place—and yet it took you defending Lord Ashworth for me to realise that just because he isn't who I was expecting for you, it doesn't mean that he isn't right for you.'

'Mary, you are getting ahead of yourself.'

'Perhaps…'

Her cousin smiled in a gentle, knowing way that forced a tight fist of fear into Isabelle's stomach.

'But if you're going to do this—see Lord Ashworth and let him be in Seraphina's life—I will not stop you. In fact, I will do everything I can to help ensure that you are not caught.'

'Why?' Isabelle asked. 'I know you aren't fond of the idea.'

'I've had time to think about it,' Mary replied. 'And after some consideration I see that you have two options. The first is that you and Lord Ashworth court openly. People may talk, but so long as everything is above board they will never be able to substantiate the rumours surrounding Seraphina.'

Isabelle ignored the glimmer of excitement at the thought. 'And do you think we should—court openly?'

'Do you plan on marrying him?'

'No.'

The reply came instantly. Isabelle supposed she hadn't considered that courtship must end in one of two ways. And although she hated only seeing Matthew twice a week, she was not ready for another marriage—of that she was sure.

'I have come to care about Matthew, even in the short time he has been back in London. And I've always... *wanted* him. But I... I can't think seriously about marriage.'

The very idea of giving up her independence to another man—even Matthew, whom she was slowly learning to trust—made her chest tighten with panic, for she remembered all too well what it was to be trapped in a marriage she did not want and had not chosen for herself.

'As a widow—and a duchess—you have freedom, Izzy,' Mary affirmed. 'Most of which you would relinquish to your husband were you to marry again.'

Isabelle knew that as keenly as Mary did. 'And my other option?'

'Have an affair,' Mary replied, the bluntness in her tone belied by the embarrassed lowering of her eyes.

'An *affair*?'

'You clearly have an...*affinity* for Lord Ashworth,' Mary said with a small shake of her head. 'An affair would allow you to explore that without compromising your freedom. You are a widow.' Mary shrugged. 'Even if you were discovered there would only be a minor scandal, and then people would move on. But—'

'The children,' Isabelle finished.

Mary nodded. 'Even if society did not care, Gareth St Claire certainly would if he thought he could use it against you...'

Mary didn't have to say any more. Isabelle understood the risk she'd be taking.

'I will help you with whatever you decide, Izzy. Widows take lovers all the time. It's only dangerous to you because of Sera's likeness to Matthew. And if you truly do not want to get married again, I see no reason for you to go the rest of your life…' she cleared her throat, as if searching for the right word, before settling on '…unsatisfied.'

At the same time Isabelle said, 'Alone.'

They looked at one another—and immediately started laughing.

'I dare say your father would have something to say about my position as your companion should he ever learn of this,' Mary teased.

Isabelle tapped the box between them, desperately hoping to change the subject before Mary could mingle any more topics as awkward as ruination, carnal desires and her father. 'What is in here? My curiosity is aflame.'

'It came for you a moment ago.'

Mary reached forward and prised the lid off the box to reveal a beautiful black mask covered in lace and adorned with a spray of black feathers, and tiny paste diamonds on one side.

Isabelle's resolve softened immediately. 'From Matthew?'

'I'm assuming so. There was no note. Just two boxes— one with your name on and one with mine.' Mary smiled. 'It was nice of him to remember me.'

'He is thoughtful,' Isabelle said. 'Do you know he brings Sera flowers every time he visits?'

'I do,' Mary replied. 'Although I thought they were for you.'

No, the flowers were definitely for Seraphina. *Weren't they?* Still…

'Mary…' Isabelle looked at her cousin, knowing that she didn't need permission, but wanting it all the same.

'Promise me you'll be careful' was all Mary said.

'I promise.'

Isabelle's heart stuttered in her chest when the immensity of her decision dawned on her. She reached into the box to remove the mask. It was light in her hands. The lace was impossibly delicate. And when she turned it around to fit it over her face, she saw that the inside was comfortably padded and lined with silk.

Mary reached over to pull the black ribbon around Isabelle's head and fasten it. 'We'll have to get Meg to pin the ribbon in your hair.'

Isabelle raised her fingers to touch the mask. 'How does it look?'

'Beautiful. Although it does not even begin to hide your identity.' Mary adjusted the mask slightly. 'Your hair gives you away—so be cautious.'

Losing herself in her excitement, Isabelle flung her arms around Mary.

Mary laughed.

'Thank you, Mary. For…everything.'

'You're welcome.'

'I just want to be *with* him. He makes me feel…' Isabelle waved her hands, searching for the right word. '*Excited*. Happy. And, though it shames me to admit it, Sera is not all of it…'

Mary nodded, perhaps not understanding Isabelle's infatuation, but not doubting it either. 'What you asked me…the other day…'

Isabelle tried to defer. 'You do not have to—'

'I miss it every day,' Mary said quietly, though her eyes remained dry. 'And that is my curse—to always want what I have had and lost and will never find again.'

'I'm sorry, Mary. I wouldn't have asked…'

'I know.' Mary cleared her throat. With one final maternal pat on Isabelle's hand, she rose from the settee. 'We should go and change if we're going to attend.'

Isabelle took a deep, fortifying breath. 'Yes,' she replied firmly. 'Yes, we should.'

'You came.'

Matthew's rather blunt observation caused a few raised eyebrows in proximity to where he was standing by the door, bowing over the Duchess's gloved hand, as the guests behind them waited patiently to be greeted.

He didn't care.

The Duchess was a vision, dressed in a silk emerald gown that bared the smooth skin of her slender shoulders and emphasised the shape of her narrow waist and hips. Her mass of hair had been expertly lifted and pinned in place. Other than the black mask he'd sent her, she wore no other adornment.

His mother greeted the Duchess enthusiastically. 'Your Grace. Welcome!'

A few curious murmurs travelled through the assembled crowd. He saw Isabelle's spine stiffen perceptibly at the sound, but she lifted her chin, as if bracing herself against the attention.

She curtsied gracefully. 'Lord Ashworth. Countess. May I introduce my cousin, Mrs Mary Lambert?'

The Countess and Mary exchanged pleasantries. 'Your Grace, Mrs Lambert—please allow my son to escort you inside.'

Matthew barely refrained from rolling his eyes at his mother's public favouritism, but he did not delay in leading Isabelle and Mary into the ballroom and away from the curious crowd.

'Please forgive my mother,' he murmured as soon as they were alone, 'she is eager to know you.'

Even with her mask on, Matthew saw the questions in Isabelle's eyes. But after the briefest hesitation she stopped to look out over his mother's ballroom, which had been decorated decadently for the evening with colourful silk bows, huge profusions of flowers and strategically placed oil lamps.

'Your mother has outdone herself, Lord Ashworth.'

The comment was issued politely, and with good intentions—Matthew hated it. At least when they were alone with Sera the Duchess didn't waste time on small talk.

'She will undoubtedly enjoy your praise,' he said, trying to remain coolly polite. 'Though Caro and Nora have been working tirelessly alongside her to ensure the evening's success.'

Isabelle smiled at that. 'How are your sisters?'

Mary, who had been watching this polite back and forth between them, interrupted before he could reply.

'Excuse me. I am going to go and talk with Lady Windhurst.'

She walked off before either of them could reply, disappearing into the crowded room like a sparrow to its flock.

Matthew turned back to find Isabelle smiling at him. 'I believe that is Mary's way of telling me that I have no need of a chaperone.'

'Perhaps that's for the best,' he teased, 'considering what I know of Mary's chaperoning.'

Isabelle lowered her head shyly, but Matthew saw the smile on her lips. His heart ticked impatiently in his chest, reminding him that his time with her tonight was limited.

'Would you dance with me, Duchess?'

He didn't really want to dance, but he needed her in his arms, as close to him as possible, and dancing was the only way he could guarantee that without breaking his promise and carrying her off to some dark corner of the house.

She looked to where couples were lining up for a quadrille, and when she met his eyes again he saw that she was unsure. 'Matthew…'

'You do not wish to dance with me?' he said for her, seeing the look in her eyes.

'No—'

'Oh?'

'It's only that I do not wish…'

'You do not wish…?' he repeated, holding his breath against her reply.

'I do not wish to share you,' she said quietly—so quietly that Matthew found himself leaning forward to hear her. 'In fact, I would rather leave here altogether and be alone…with you.' She took a deep breath. 'That is to say…' She closed her eyes as a flush of embarrassment rose up her chest and neck. 'Oh, God…'

'Duchess…'

Matthew paused again, falling silent as a couple walked past them. He tried to make sense of her words, running them over and over in his head. And even though there was no mistaking the desperate need pouring off her, for it mirrored his own, he had to ask.

'Are you saying that you…?'

Isabelle looked at him in silence for so long that he thought he might have imagined it.

But then she nodded, just one small dip of her head, and whispered, 'Yes. I want…you.'

Chapter Fifteen

They stayed an hour to avoid comment, but after they'd each made polite small talk with their acquaintances, and danced a single dance together, Isabelle feigned a headache and took her leave.

The Countess of Heather, in her concern, kindly offered her own carriage, so that Isabelle could get home safely and Mary could remain at the ball. And so, less than ten minutes after she'd first said she was feeling indisposed, Isabelle was off, moving through the dark streets of London in the Earl's smart black conveyance.

For minutes, the motion of the carriage seemed to wind her nerves tighter and tighter, each turn of the massive wheels reminding her of what she was risking. This wasn't simply wearing breeches at home or sitting on the floor with her child. This was the stuff of ruin.

'What *are* you doing, Isabelle?' she murmured to herself, overcome with panic.

Alone in the carriage now, she wasn't sure of the wild spirit that had possessed her. She'd only seen Matthew, standing in the hall, dressed in formal black. She'd seen the look in his eyes when he'd greeted her, and in that single moment in time she'd known with absolute certainty that she could not deny him any longer. As he'd escorted her through his parents' house Mary's suggestion had run in circles through her head until the words had simply spilled from her mouth—and not eloquently at all.

But now, with distance, she couldn't help but panic. 'This is a terrible idea,' she said aloud. 'People will find out. And you will be cast out of society.' Leaning forward, she rested her masked face in her hands. 'And you will have nobody to blame but yourself.'

'And me, technically.'

Isabelle gasped and sat up in her seat at the sound of Matthew's voice. She had been so consumed with her thoughts that she hadn't felt the carriage slowing once it had turned the first corner, nor heard the door quietly opening.

Matthew stepped into the carriage, his large body forcing her to move backwards to make space for him.

He closed them in and sat down as the carriage started on its way again. His eyes found Isabelle's immediately, and softened when he read the fear on her face. 'You are afraid?'

'Not of you,' she insisted. 'I want you. I've thought about this for…for weeks.' It was a lie, of course. She had thought of him for far longer than a few weeks. 'But the situation is…*risqué*.'

'To say the least.'

He didn't approach her, as she'd expected—didn't reach out and touch her as she wished he would.

'Isabelle,' he started, his deep voice gliding over her, 'if you are uncertain of me in any way—'

'No.' She shook her head vehemently. 'It's not that. Though I know of your past, I am certain that you would never deliberately hurt me. I've watched you with Seraphina, Matthew. I see the way you look at her—as if you're shocked and terrified and halfway in love already. And I know you'd never do anything that could harm her. In fact, I have never been more certain of anything…'

She had also seen the way Matthew looked at *her*, but Isabelle did not dare bring it up. And as she sat across from him she wondered what it would be like to touch him again, to have him touch *her* again. Her entire being ached to be touched by him again.

'Would you like me to tell you about Christine—the Marchioness?'

Isabelle hated her own insecurity…hated that it mattered to her. But after a long pause, she nodded.

He tried to smile. Isabelle saw the attempt, and she saw what it cost him, and she hated that she had caused him even a moment's pain.

'I want you to understand that an affair, especially one that I intend to be long-term, is no small commitment for me either,' he said.

'I know.'

He tipped his head gravely, but he did not meet her eyes as he started to explain.

'Christine and I began our affair with the mutual understanding that it would one day end. We liked each other. We were...*compatible*. But she was married, and I was an heir who would one day have to take a bride of my own. I was young and arrogant. I thought there would be no consequences for two adults who enjoyed each other's company.'

'Her husband was older, if I remember correctly?'

'She was twenty-two and he sixty-four when they married,' Matthew replied. 'When we started the affair I was twenty-five. She was thirty. For a year, we saw each other when it was convenient for both of us. And, as immoral as it was to have an affair with a married woman, I was not with anyone else while I was with her.'

He was quiet for a long moment, the only sound the roll of the carriage wheels on the cobbled streets.

'For a long time—*months*—I didn't know that she had developed stronger feelings for me. I should have. Looking back now, I can see that the signs were all there. The moment I realised her affections ran deeper than mine, I ended things. It seemed like the right thing to do. I knew I would never feel the same way. I liked her. I cared for her. But...'

'You did not love her?'

'No. And even now I cannot take blame for that. But I can accept responsibility for how poorly I handled everything afterwards.'

Matthew shifted, moving closer, as if he wanted her to see the truth on his face.

'I assumed that because she was married she would

not cause a scene. I was young and immature. I ignored her attempts to write to me. I refused to admit her when she tried to visit. And then, after a few weeks, she…'

Isabelle saw the words stick in his throat as the memory rose.

'She came to your club?'

He exhaled a forceful breath, and although she knew he wasn't conscious of doing it, his hand found the back of his neck and pulled.

'I still see her in my sleep sometimes,' he whispered. 'She was…frenzied. Mad… Crying and begging me to take her back in front of a half-dozen people.'

Isabelle's heart went out to the Marchioness—but also to Matthew. She could see what it had done to him. Moreover, she could see the genuine shame pouring from him.

'What did you do?'

She knew the answer before he replied. Matthew's eyes spilled anguish and self-loathing.

'I walked away. I left her there for her husband to come and collect her.'

Isabelle took a steadying breath and, placing one hand on his muscular thigh, braced herself against him so that she could manoeuvre herself and her skirts closer to him in the confines of the carriage.

When she would have sat down next to him, Matthew tugged her, overbalancing her so that she toppled into his lap instead.

'Duchess…' He sighed when she did not move to get off him. His muscles slowly relaxed beneath her.

'I have made mistakes. But I would never let anybody hurt you or the children,' he said.

She could hear the certainty in his voice.

She *believed* him.

'I know.' She shifted so that she could meet his eyes when she said, 'Thank you for telling me—about Christine. I'm sorry. For both of you. But I… I don't want to pretend that knowing the truth of it would have made a difference. I would have come with you anyway.'

'Irrespective, I promise that I will do everything in my power to keep our secrets safe.' His arms caged her, holding her securely on his lap. 'They are my secrets too, Duchess. But you need to be sure that I am what you want, because…'

'Because?'

'Because if I step inside your house I'm not leaving until morning.' His voice lowered. 'I am going to keep you in bed for hours, debauching you in ways that you could not have imagined.'

The warning should have terrified her. She was no inamorata. She was a twenty-year-old widow who had been bedded just once in her life. She should have demanded that he drive her home and then refused to see him ever again. And yet that very fact made her bold. For she had tasted what it was to be loved by this man, and she so desperately wanted to be loved by him again.

Summoning the fragments of her courage, she replied, 'We are decided, then.'

Her tone did not come out sounding confident, like

his. It wavered, sounding meek and uncertain. Inexperienced…

Matthew tensed. 'Are we?'

'Yes,' Isabelle managed breathlessly.

She reached up to yank the mask off, suddenly feeling hot and flustered with the fabric over her face.

'No.' He caught her hand in his. 'I want you naked in bed with nothing but that mask on.'

Isabelle slowly lowered her hands. 'You…?'

She couldn't even repeat the words. But a hot flush of awareness seeped through her as they trailed through her thoughts, and the word 'naked' coming from the beautiful man beneath her compounded her nerves.

Did he know what carrying a child did to a woman's body? Was he expecting her to look the same? Isabelle was not a vain woman; however, her eyesight was perfectly fine. She felt the physical differences in herself as viscerally as she had felt Seraphina growing inside her. And although she was still gawkishly slender, motherhood had left its mark on her body.

'Matthew, I'm not…'

He waited patiently, his eyes focused on her face.

'That is to say, I'm no longer…' She took a deep breath. 'Having a child has…' She closed her eyes, mortified at her inability to say the words.

'You are trying to tell me that your body is different from what I remember?' he offered quietly.

'Yes.'

She hadn't realised that she had turned her face away

from him until he tipped her chin up. 'Isabelle, look at me.'

He yanked off his own mask then, and Isabelle wasn't sure if it was so he could see her better or if he wanted her to see his face when he spoke.

'You carried and birthed my child. For that alone, your body is something I will always cherish and adore.'

'You are saying that because you have yet to see it,' she pointed out matter-of-factly.

Matthew made a sound deep in the back of his throat. It threaded through Isabelle, soothing her nerves with desire. She felt him already...the hard length of him pressing into her right thigh even through her layers of clothing.

'You feel me, Duchess?'

Isabelle nodded shyly, and resisted the urge to slide over him so that he was positioned closer to her aching centre. The memories came, and with them anticipation. It heated her blood with lust, so that her body throbbed intimately and her breasts ached.

'We have yet to do anything. We have not kissed, nor removed a scrap of clothing, and still my body yearns for yours. The mere *thought* of you is enough to get me hard as iron. These last weeks in your company... so close to you and yet unable to touch you... It has been the worst kind of torture—a hell specifically designed for me.'

One large hand moved to cradle her face.

'In the last month I have found my own release with nothing but my hand and the thought of you.'

'You *have*?'

The image his confession evoked was… Well, she supposed it was lurid and improper—and exceptionally erotic.

Matthew released her face to nip playfully at her ear. 'I have thought of you naked beneath me and on top of me. I have thought of you swollen with my child, your breasts heavy in my hands. I have thought of you in every way you could possibly imagine.'

Isabelle swallowed as slick heat gathered between her thighs. 'You have thought of me with child?'

'If I had been there…'

He sighed, and although she didn't think he was conscious of doing it, he placed one large palm on her corseted stomach.

'I would have worshipped you.'

The admission brought with it an unfamiliar pang of loss. She had hated being pregnant, her body limited and clumsy, her feet painfully swollen. But Matthew's words made her wonder what it would have been like to have had him there with her, whispering delicious confessions in her ear, making her feel beautiful and desired despite her waddling gait and aching back.

'Forgive me,' she whispered, suddenly sad. 'I am sorry I never wrote to you. I didn't know you then. I thought I was doing what any man would have wanted…'

'There's nothing to forgive.' His arms wrapped around her again, holding her close. 'I have revisited every scenario over this last month,' he admitted, 'and there was no way we could have been together without scandal. You did what you had to: you protected your children. You protected *my* child. And you did it largely alone. Do not apologise for it,' he repeated.

'I wish I'd had you with me,' Isabelle offered. 'I think I would not have been so afraid if I'd had you by my side.'

'You have me now,' Matthew promised.

'And that is enough,' she told him, her tone leaving no room for doubt.

'It is everything,' he corrected and, raising his palm to her masked face again, guided her lips to his.

The kiss was soft and sweet and filled with longing. It was as if they both needed the delayed moment of contact to finally relax into being together again.

Isabelle's lips were so soft under his. Her rose scent wrapped around him like the familiar smell of home after a long journey. Her gloved hands found his face, her thumbs stroking over his jaw in a caress that was loving and familiar, as if she had done it a thousand times before.

Matthew held her close, using both hands to steady her on his legs, and when she sighed, opening her lips for him, he slid his tongue into her warm, wet mouth and took her, gently stroking her, encouraging her to take her own pleasure in return.

And she did. Isabelle's tongue eagerly sought his, taking his gentle caresses and turning them into something deliciously sinful. Her innocent eagerness drove her to be bold. He felt her hands shift from his face to his neck, as if she would bring him closer still. She pressed her body against his in a completely unconscious plea.

Matthew broke the kiss to trail his lips over her bare shoulders, down to the dip in the bodice of her gown where her chest heaved with every in-out breath. He ran his tongue gently over the faint swell of her breasts above her bodice, not stopping until she was writhing in his arms.

'Matthew…' she moaned.

His name on her lips tore him in two. His aching cock became painfully hard, a testament to the years in which he had imagined this very moment.

'You are my every fantasy come to life, Duchess.'

He dipped one hand into her bodice, freeing her breast to his gaze. Her rosy nipple was pebbled with desire, straining up towards him as if begging to be tasted. Several faint white lines that had not been there before ran from her nipples outwards. He trailed his finger over one.

Isabelle instinctively raised a hand to cover these remnant signs of how much her breasts had grown during pregnancy, but Matthew caught her hand in his and held it. Leaning down, he followed the path his finger had trailed with his tongue.

'These lines, Duchess… They drive me wild.'

Matthew smiled to himself, vowing that he would be the last man ever to see her like this. He swirled his tongue around her peaked nipple once before sucking it into his mouth.

'Oh…' Isabelle moaned.

He released her. 'Do you like that, Duchess?'

She shuddered and buried her face in his neck. 'God, Matthew,' she panted. 'I feel as though I'm going to burst into flame. I… My body is so hot.'

'Where do you ache, love?'

She breathed heavily into his neck, refusing to answer.

Undeterred, Matthew slid his free hand beneath her heavy dress and chemise, moving up her stockinged leg to her drawers.

He cupped her over the fabric. 'Here? Is it here where you ache for me?'

'Yes…' she groaned in reply, and pressed herself boldly into his hand. 'Please, Matthew. It's been so long.'

Her plea broke him. Did she know how many times he had imagined losing himself in her again?

'In a minute,' he said gently, feeling the carriage slow. 'We're about to stop.'

He gently lifted her bodice, covering her, and when the carriage stopped had to ask, 'Isabelle, are you certain this is what you want?'

She didn't reply. Instead, she raised her hand and opened the carriage door before the footman reached it, telling him everything he needed to know.

'I'll go around the back.'

He nodded to the footman and waited inside the carriage as Isabelle was escorted to her own front door.

Though it was nearing ten o'clock at night, Matthew

knew, perhaps more keenly than Isabelle herself, that only one person had to witness a scandal for news of it to spread like a forest fire. He understood the risk she was taking. And his past experience had taught him that the risk would always be far greater for a woman than any man. Perhaps if he had stopped to think about that at twenty-five he would have been more careful, more sensitive to Christine's deepening emotions and his inability to reciprocate them. He might have spared them both a lifetime of pain and regret.

So he waited now. And when the carriage had dropped him at a darkened corner of the street, he navigated his way to the back of the house and used the familiar servants' entrance without a blush of shame.

He made his way through the house to the hall, where Isabelle stood with her elderly butler, Gordon.

'If you could send up some water for a bath,' she was saying to him.

'Yes, Your Grace.' Gordon took Matthew's coat and gloves from him and then bowed, passing Isabelle a lit candle before leaving them alone together.

'It is shocking how blasé he is about all this,' she commented.

'He undoubtedly did far worse for the Duke while he was alive,' Matthew replied, knowing that Isabelle, for all her freedom, was still relatively naive.

'It doesn't worry you?' she asked seriously as she walked towards the study. 'That people will know…?'

Matthew followed, closing the study door behind him. 'Being in service to a duke is no laughing matter. I'd wager that not a single person in your household would risk their position without a serious financial incentive to do so.'

'I know you're right,' she murmured as she placed the candle on the desk, casting the room in a warm, sensual glow. 'It just feels dangerous…'

Isabelle walked to the whisky decanter on the sideboard and poured two drinks. She handed one to Matthew before taking a small, fortifying sip from her own glass.

He looked at her then, noticing the way her eyes lowered shyly and the way she curled the glass against her chest, as if she were an anxious warrior holding a shield to her breast before a battle.

'Why are you nervous?' he asked gently. 'We have been here before.'

'I know,' she replied breathlessly. 'It's silly. It's just… Well, then there was no…no choice. I needed a favour—and you provided it. But now it's come down to choosing what I want and taking it for myself…' She took a deep breath. 'I guess it seems more… I don't know, really. Just *more*.'

That she wanted him—*trusted* him—enough to be with him was no small thing, especially considering he'd told her about Christine. She humbled him.

'If there was a promise I could make to erase your nerves I would make it in a heartbeat. My discretion—it is already yours. My fidelity—you have it from this moment on.'

'You do not have to promise me your fidelity.'

'Yes, I do,' he insisted, and it was no hardship. It was important to him that she knew him to be capable of faithfulness. 'Duchess…' Matthew closed the distance between them, coming to stand close enough that Isabelle had to tip her head back to meet his eyes. 'As long as we're together, there's nobody else—for either of us.'

Isabelle cleared her throat daintily. 'I… That is to say, there has been no one before.'

'Nobody?' He dared to ask what he'd only assumed before.

'Only you.'

The admission raged through him, sending fire to his veins. He groaned and closed his eyes against the torrent of heat. He fought to regain control, trying his best to calm his body. After a long moment he opened his eyes and found her watching him, a faint smile on her lips.

Unable to wait any longer, he took her glass from her and placed it on a nearby table with his. 'I should reward you.'

'*Reward* me?'

'For not letting anybody else touch what is mine,' he clarified.

Isabelle's mouth dropped open at his possessiveness, but Matthew didn't let that stop him.

'Would you like that, Duchess?'

She nodded slowly, as if she were a little stunned by her own admission.

'Tell me.'

'I would like that,' she said, and he saw her swallow deeply against her nerves.

'And what reward would you like?'

He led her to the settee and waited for her to sit.

'I… I suppose I don't know.'

Matthew saw her self-consciousness and quickly changed tactics—wanting her to be comfortable, wanting her to be wanton, wanting her to take her pleasure from him.

'Why don't we start, and you can tell me as we go?'

And with that he knelt on the floor in front of her and lifted her skirts.

Chapter Sixteen

Matthew ran his hands up her stockinged calves, his big palms stroking and kneading as he moved slowly higher. 'What about this, Duchess?' he asked, his voice sinfully low. 'Do you like this?'

Frozen with equal parts nervousness and anticipation, Isabelle was helpless to do anything but nod.

When no response came, Matthew looked up at her from his position on the floor. His grey eyes, dark with lust, studied her face. 'Talk to me.' His hands moved higher, settling on her upper thighs over the fabric of her drawers. 'Tell me where you want me.'

Isabelle remembered those skilful fingers parting her most private flesh and stroking deep inside her, but she found that she could not make the request—could not beg him to touch her *there*.

'I want you everywhere,' she murmured.

Matthew smiled knowingly, but he did not laugh at her shy avoidance. He watched her masked face as he slid one hand through the slit in her drawers, finding her bare thigh. His fingers trailed over her, leaving a fire of sensation in their wake.

'Do you want me here, Duchess?' he asked, keeping his hand on her, mere inches away from where she ached for him.

'No…' she found the courage to say.

'Hmm…' Matthew's hand slid to her inner thigh, edging an inch closer. 'Here?'

Isabelle shook her head and held her breath as he finally stroked over the damp, downy patch between her legs.

He didn't ask again, but Isabelle sighed, 'Yes…' as his thumb ran up and down her seam, threading molten pleasure through her entire body.

'Hold your skirts, Duchess,' he whispered, bunching the fabric of her gown around her waist. 'I want to taste you,' he said, placing his thumb on the small knot of nerves at her apex. 'Here.'

Isabelle froze at the scandalous words, even as her body involuntarily shuddered with the pleasure his touch there wrought. 'Is that…*done*?' she asked, shocked. 'We did not…'

Matthew groaned as he slid a single finger into her. 'We didn't have time for a lot of what I'm going to show you, Duchess.'

Isabelle's head fell back against the settee as pleasure coursed through her, seeming to be concentrated in the spot that he claimed. Her muscles relaxed and her legs fell open in invitation as he thrust deeper inside her, his finger sliding against a particularly pleasurable point each time he withdrew.

Matthew shifted suddenly, leaving her aching and empty. But before she could object, he'd lifted her legs and strung them over his shoulders. He tugged her forward, exposing her to his gaze.

Isabelle should have been horrified, but instead she brazenly gathered her skirts with both hands, as he'd instructed, too desperate for him to touch her again to be coy. From her position on the settee she watched as his dark head lowered, disappearing beneath the mound of her skirts. There was a small, heavy moment when he didn't touch her at all, and the anticipation made her moan in frustration. But then he was spreading her with both thumbs...opening her folds.

Isabelle held her breath.

Matthew cursed. 'You're so wet for me,' he whispered.

And then he curled his tongue through her heat.

Isabelle's hips rose off the settee as her body followed the unusual wet touch. She cried out, digging her heeled slippers into his back to try and find purchase against the impossible sensations raging through her.

Matthew's husky chuckle grazed her inner thigh. 'Did you like that, Duchess?'

'Again,' Isabelle replied, shifting her hips forward. 'Please, Matthew.'

Her request was all it took for his control to snap. With a few deft tugs and several curses he divested her of her shoes and drawers and then settled back between her thighs, his mouth finding her instantly, his lips and tongue winding ecstasy through her as he alternately lapped and suckled.

'Your smell was made for me, Duchess,' he murmured. 'I could stay here for hours…tasting you.' He slid his finger back inside her, thrusting the digit in and out as he leaned forward and tortured her with his mouth.

'Matthew!'

Isabelle panted as her pleasure crested, eradicating her remaining embarrassment. Her body began to draw in, contracting around his finger in time with her ragged breaths.

'Matthew…' she moaned again, while her mind and her body screamed that this was so much more than she remembered.

'Relax, Duchess. Let go,' he whispered, and inserted a second finger inside her channel, stretching her wide.

Isabelle shattered on a loud moan that she would be embarrassed by later. Her body tensed, her back arched and her legs closed around his head, instinctively keeping him with her as the orgasm rippled through her again and again.

His tongue slowed, helping her to ride out the waves of sensation.

Isabelle's thighs trembled. Her breaths strained against the tight cinch of her corset.

Matthew slowly slid his fingers out of her. He kissed each of her thighs before lowering her feet back to the floor and righting her skirts.

His face was flushed. His eyes gleamed with a strange male pride that brought a smile to Isabelle's lips.

'You don't have to look so pleased with yourself,' she pointed out shyly.

'Duchess…' he shook his head, as if searching for the right words '…it pleases me to pleasure you.'

He stood, and Isabelle's eyes widened when she saw the heavy protrusion in his trousers. That same low ache started again between her thighs. She had the strangest urge to reach out and touch him. Her hand even hovered in front of her for a moment—before she realised where they were.

'We should go upstairs,' she said. 'I don't know what time Mary will be home, but I'd rather she didn't walk into the study while we're…'

'In the act?' Matthew offered.

'Yes.' She walked to the desk to pick up the candle, pausing to pick up her drawers and slide her slippers back onto her feet.

When she turned round, Matthew was watching her, his eyes warm with emotion, his person uncharacteristically dishevelled. He looked at her as nobody else had before—as if she was the sun and the moon somehow wrapped in one.

'You are exquisite.'

His words caused a strange sensation in her chest… something that felt like pleasure and panic vying for the upper hand.

'You make me feel…different,' she said, admitting

more than she'd planned to. 'As if I'm not alone.' She flushed. 'That must sound silly—'

'No,' he said instantly. 'You make me remember what the point of all this is.'

She frowned, not quite sure what he was saying.

'Life, Duchess. You make me realise what the point of life is. When you're with the right person, at the right time, life changes from an aimless wandering into a *terrifying* adventure. Everything is amplified. The highs are higher…the lows so much lower.' He expelled a huge, shaky breath. 'When I'm with you, I know with absolute certainty that I'm exactly where I'm supposed to be.'

His words hit her like a runaway horse, galloping through her and leaving fear in their wake. She had been expecting him to say something funny or light-hearted; instead, he had decimated her with his answer.

Because wasn't that exactly how she felt too?

Wasn't that why she was risking so much to be with him?

She opened her mouth to say something, but no words came.

Matthew came to her. He nipped her bottom lip.

'Don't panic.' He held out his hand, waiting until she slid her fingers through his. 'I won't ever ask for more than you're prepared to give,' he said, and led her out of the study.

As he guided her up the stairs to her bedroom, Isabelle had the terrible realisation that he wouldn't have to. It was already too late. She would have given him anything—she already had.

* * *

He'd said too much. Matthew knew it the moment the words left his mouth, and yet he could not regret them. It was true. From the moment he had found out about Seraphina he had discovered new purpose.

He was consumed by them—by Sera's quick smile and her instant acceptance of him, by Isabelle's shy, mistrustful approach when it came to him, and her ferocious stubbornness when it came to their daughter's well-being.

He wanted them, he realised with alarm. And not in the way he'd thought—because of a gentleman's honour-bound duty to take his role in their circumstances. He wanted them to be his because suddenly he couldn't bear the thought that they might not be. He wanted them because the idea of being *without* them brought physical panic to his chest. And because he was hopelessly besotted—with both of them.

The truth settled low in the pit of his stomach. Loving Seraphina came naturally. Loving Isabelle was a frightening revelation. Because the things he cherished most about her—her bravery, courage and independence—would be the very things that kept them apart.

Isabelle would be fine without him. She had no need for him. She was a wealthy widow, a duchess. She could live her entire life in the safety of her title, with no need to marry again. In fact, he couldn't think of a single reason why she would *want* to marry again.

Love, perhaps?

The thought left him oddly unhinged. Irrespective of

how deeply he searched, he could not see enough within himself for her ever to come to love him. Everything that made him eligible—his title, his money, his family name—were things that Isabelle did not need. And the only other thing he was known for was scandal.

'Matthew?'

'Mmm?' He looked up to see her standing outside her bedroom.

'Are you all right?'

'Yes. I'm…happy.'

And he was. He told himself that just being with her again was enough. It had to be. And if one day she realised she needed more than what he had…what he *was*… Matthew supposed he'd deal with that then.

Isabelle opened her bedroom door. Though he had been in her bedroom several times, to put Seraphina in her crib, he had deliberately avoided looking around or staying longer than he needed. Now Matthew took the time to study the room. There were few pastels and frills, and none of the delicate, spindly furniture uphol-stered in floral print that he'd come to expect in any feminine domain. Instead, Isabelle's mahogany furni-ture was heavy and sturdy, the rug on the floor a deep red that contrasted with her white bedding.

Her entire domain was just like her: as luxurious as it was practical.

Isabelle stood only a few feet away, resplendent in her emerald gown and mask. She had appeared like some fantastical fairy, promising him ruin, and Matthew was helpless but to take every minute that she offered.

'Matthew,' she said quietly, 'I have to take this mask off. My face is itching.'

He closed the distance between them. 'May I help you?' he asked, one hand reaching up and hovering by her face, waiting for permission.

'Please.' She angled her head to one side. 'Meg has pinned it into my hair, so you're going to have to undo everything.'

Pleasure rumbled through his chest and caught in his throat. He started pulling at the dozens of pins in her coiffure. Her heavy locks slid between his fingers, the silky tresses falling by degrees as he worked to free her. With each long coil of ebony hair that fell, Matthew's lust grew.

'You are so beautiful,' he whispered reverently, running a particularly long strand between his fingers.

Isabelle shifted her head slightly so that she could see him. 'You make me feel beautiful,' she said.

Matthew lost all words as he slid the last of the pins from her hair and un-wove the mask's ribbon. He turned her gently to face him and lifted the mask from her face, untangling the last few strands of her hair as he removed it.

He moved to throw it down, but Isabelle saw the movement and reached out, catching his hand in hers. 'Wait!'

He froze.

She gently tugged the mask from him and, once he'd relinquished it, turned to place it gently on a table. 'I want to keep it—to remember.'

He knew what she meant—that she wanted to remember this night with him, not necessarily the ball—and knowing it soothed some of his panic. He traced the angry splotches that the mask had left beneath her eyes.

'I will buy you more—some that do not do this to you.'

Isabelle laughed. 'I blame Meg's expert fastening rather than the quality of the mask—'

Her breath caught as he smoothed her skin with both thumbs, his fingers gently cradling her head. Her eyes fluttered closed with pleasure.

'Do you like that, Duchess?' he asked, reminding her of their earlier game.

Her eyes opened and she nodded. But instead of letting him lead, she turned her back to him and asked, 'Will you help me out of this dress?'

'With pleasure.'

Matthew wasted no time. He deftly unwound the ribbons at her back and then unbuttoned the gown to expose her corset and chemise. Instead of stepping out of her skirts, Isabelle raised her arms and ducked, forcing him to lift the heavy dress over her head.

He held the garment in both hands as he took his fill of her, standing in the centre of the room wearing nothing but a corset, a chemise and stockings, her long black hair trailing down to her hips.

She blushed and lowered her gaze, and although her corset laced at the front, the Duchess did not move to take it off.

Reminded of her inexperience, Matthew vowed to be

gentle, to give her pleasure and to show her how much power she had.

He draped the dress over a nearby chair and went to her. Taking her hands in his, he placed them on his chest and then reached for the hooks that ran down the front of her corset. 'May I?'

'Yes.'

He made quick work of the structural garment, too aware of Isabelle's self-consciousness to linger as he would have liked. As soon as it was off, leaving her in only a chemise and stockings, he took her hand and led her to the big bed in the centre of the room. He didn't lift her onto the pillowed top; he reached for the hem of her chemise and raised it over her head, taking it off.

He dropped the garment on the floor, and before she could cover her nakedness, Matthew wrapped his arms around her and pulled her into his chest. 'Do not be shy. Not with me. I assure you…you are more beautiful to me than any woman I could imagine.'

She did not reply, but he felt her nod against his chest.

Matthew released her and took a step back, desperate to see her, desperate to touch her.

She tensed at his perusal, then softened slowly as she watched him watching her. He was giving everything away—he knew he was. And he didn't care. He wanted her to know what she did to him.

'Matthew, I…'

'Tell me,' he urged.

'I don't want another baby…' She flushed and lowered her eyes. 'I'm…'

He waited patiently for her to continue. Isabelle in the candle-glow was divine: her golden skin flushed with awareness, contrasting with her long, jet hair and the small thatch between her thighs. Her breasts were small and rose-tipped, her nipples pebbled for him. Her waist was tiny. The front of her stomach was no longer flat, but beautifully curved where it had housed his child. Those same faint lines that he'd traced on her breasts climbed up her sides like roots that had once nurtured.

Sensing that she couldn't finish voicing what she'd wanted to say, he knelt in front of her and placed his lips against her bare stomach, before resting his forehead against the same spot.

'I will be more careful going forward,' he promised. 'I won't put you in that position again, Duchess.'

He felt her body yield as she relaxed. They stayed like that for a long moment… Matthew on his knees in front of her, and Isabelle sifting his hair through her fingers.

'Matthew…?'

He rested his chin on her stomach and looked up into her beautiful eyes.

She brushed his hair back from his forehead. 'I don't regret you.' She frowned. 'Do you know, now that I think on it, I never have? Even when I first realised I was pregnant… I never regretted that night. Even when I thought I would never see you again… I knew that I would cherish the memory of you, of the short time we had together.'

Matthew exhaled a deep breath at her confession, knowing that it was more than he could ever have hoped for. He stayed on his knees, his head against her stomach, loving how far they'd come in such a short time and yet lamenting their impossible situation. For impossible it was. Even if Isabelle chose him, they could never be together. Not openly—and not if they were going to protect Seraphina.

He rose slowly to his feet. Cradling her face with one hand, he kissed her gently. 'I have never regretted you either. Not for a single moment.'

Isabelle smiled and, rising up on her toes, returned his kiss. She slid her tongue boldly into his mouth. Her anxious hands fumbled with the buttons at his waistband. Desperate to press his naked flesh against hers, he broke the kiss and hurried to help her, stripping off his clothes in no time at all while Isabelle removed her stockings, clambered onto the bed and slid beneath the covers.

Leaving his own garments in a pile on the floor, Matthew followed. He climbed between the sheets and reached across the mattress to pull her to him.

She laughed loudly and gazed up at him, her dark eyes bright and happy.

Matthew levered himself up onto one elbow so that he could watch her as he trailed his fingers from her collarbone down to her breast. He circled her nipple, teasing the bud into tightening, before he bent down and sucked it into his mouth.

Isabelle moaned and pressed her chest upwards in offering. Her hands found his hair and tugged, as if she would bring him closer still. And when he used his teeth to nip her gently, before moving to worship her other breast, she panted his name.

His hand brushed over her stomach as his mouth worked on her breasts, moving slowly lower and lower until it found her soft, wet centre. He slid his fingers between her seam, stroking them up and down over her damp inner flesh without penetrating her. Her smell... that unique scent of salt and sin and sex...reached for him.

Isabelle's hands floundered before finding his head again, her fingers sliding through his hair and gripping it as if she needed something to hold on to. Her breaths came fast and irregularly, so unused was she to her mingled excitement and urgency.

'Matthew, please...' she moaned when he pressed his thumb against her.

'Please what, Duchess?'

She blushed, but she did not cower. She flattened her chest against his and reached one hand down between them to find his iron-hard length. She gripped him firmly and Matthew closed his eyes, steeling himself against the urge to thrust against her hand.

She brought her lips to his ear. 'Please take me,' she pleaded. 'I need you...inside...'

'Shh, my love...' he whispered, trying to calm her urgency.

He rolled them both so that he was on top of her, supporting his substantially larger weight with his elbows. His cock came to rest on top of that triangle of hair—close, but not close enough for Isabelle.

She shifted her hips, trying to angle herself to take him, and Matthew obliged, guiding the swollen head of his cock to her entrance and gently easing into her.

He stopped when she tensed against the intrusion, and with a quiet 'Relax, Duchess…' lowered his head to suckle her nipple into his mouth.

Isabelle's body slowly yielded. Matthew felt her inner muscles loosen, making it easier for him to press deeper. Her thighs dropped to either side even as her feet pressed into the mattress, and she pushed against him, taking him in all the way.

He cursed quietly as her tight, wet heat enveloped him. He held still for a long moment as he tried to regain control. 'Does it hurt?' he asked, his voice hoarse as he steeled himself against the urge to thrust.

'No. I feel…fulfilled…'

She sighed and contracted her inner muscles, causing him to groan and drop his forehead to her chest.

'Matthew?' she asked, her hands finding his hair again. 'Are you quite well?'

Matthew grinned. He nudged his hips slightly, sinking further into her heat. 'I am perfect,' he replied, and began to move.

He braced himself, his elbows by her head, conscious of his weight, and the movement brought them eye to eye. Isabelle was flushed, her huge eyes dark with lust. Her skin was aflame beneath his. She raised her palm to his face and guided his lips down to hers as he moved inside her.

The kiss tore through him. Matthew was lost to her…

to her softness and her smell and the quiet little sounds she made. And when he felt her body tightening, drawing him in, he lowered one hand between them to touch her.

Isabelle's moans grew louder as she closed her eyes against the pleasure.

'Look at me, Duchess,' he demanded. He wanted to watch as she unravelled beneath him.

She opened her eyes and struggled to focus on his face. Her panted breaths brushed against his neck as her body cinched around him. 'Matthew…'

'I know.'

'I can't…' she panted.

'You can,' he promised, increasing the speed of his thrusts. Leaning down, he brought his lips close to her ear. 'Be a good girl.'

She moaned at his words.

'Take your reward,' he rasped as his own body drew inwards, preparing for release. 'Come on my cock, Duchess,' he demanded.

Whether it was his demand or his foul language that she found appealing didn't matter. Isabelle exploded, her body rising off the bed, her loud cry pealing through the room. Her body gripped him mercilessly, and it took every ounce of willpower he had to pull out of her in time. He caught his cock in one hand, and with two quick pumps and a loud groan spilled onto Isabelle's stomach, marking her with his seed.

He collapsed onto the bed beside her, his chest heaving, but when Isabelle tried to move, he stopped her with one heavy hand. 'No.'

'No?' She arched one brow.

'I need one minute,' he said, and buried his face in her rose-scented pillow as he regained his breath.

Chapter Seventeen

Isabelle looked at the beautiful man beside her, his muscular back golden in the candlelight, his shaggy black hair falling over his forehead. Her eyes traced the side of his face from one arched dark brow to his straight nose and sinfully full lips.

She supposed he didn't have the classic handsomeness so valued by the *ton*. Matthew was unfashionably large, with shoulders rivalling any dockworker's, and his rakishly long hair was borderline indecent.

Still, he was quite perfect in Isabelle's eyes.

He cracked one eye open as if he sensed her gaze. He sighed. 'Duchess…'

She smiled at the way he made it a sensual endearment, at the way he murmured it as if he had no adequate words to describe what they'd done.

'You didn't spend yourself inside me that time,' she remarked with a blush, remembering the way he had withdrawn from her, his eyes closed, his throat working on a deep growl, his stomach muscles tensed as he stroked himself to completion.

'Most men are able to pull out before—to prevent the chance of a child,' he told her.

'Oh, but…'

He slowly levered himself up onto his elbows, his shoulders and arms flexing with the movement. 'I was planning to that night…' he told her.

He pushed off the bed, walked around to her side and lifted her easily into his arms. He carried her through to the dressing room and lowered her gently into the bath, even though the water the maid had brought up was now lukewarm.

'That night you came to me, I wasn't going to… But then I was inside you, and—' he shook his head incredulously '—I lost control. There's no excuse. It should not have happened. It had never happened to me before. And although I cannot regret Seraphina, I am sorry that my actions took that choice from you. It was not my intention.'

Isabelle believed him. 'I knew the risk I was taking,' she said quietly, thinking of all the ways that night might have gone differently. They could have stopped before… He could have withdrawn…

But instead of filling her with regret, the thought terrified her.

If things had gone differently, she would not have had Sera. She may not ever have had a child *at all*.

She stilled as a new thought assaulted her. She might never have seen Matthew again.

Confused by the punch of terror that swept through her at the thought, Isabelle began to panic. She thought of her wedding to the Duke and the terrifying weeks after. She thought of Luke and of Sera. And she thought of Matthew's scandal. Not, as everyone else did, of what he'd done, but rather how it had followed him through life, haunting him.

If the same thing were to happen to Seraphina because of *them*…

'Matthew?'

'Duchess?'

'I want…'

Perhaps sensing her fear, he raised a hand and placed it on her face, turning her gaze to his. 'You can always be honest with me, Isabelle.'

But she could not.

Isabelle smiled despite her inner struggle. *I should take him while I have him*, she thought. Because, despite what he'd said about his fidelity, Matthew was an heir. He would be an earl one day, and he would want heirs of his own to continue his family's legacy. But tonight…

Matthew was on his knees, his muscular forearms pressed against the rolled lip of the tub. She scooted forward, making space for him behind her.

'I want you to come in here with me,' she dared to say.

He pushed himself up to stand, his powerful body rising above her like some marble statue, all corded sleek muscle covered with the black hair that marked him as a man in his prime.

Isabelle tried her very best to be dignified, only sneaking a quick glance at his manhood as it came into view, but Matthew caught the discreet peek.

He held his arms out to his sides, comfortable with his nakedness. 'Look all you want, Duchess.'

His words spread liquid fire through her. Before she could overthink it she turned to look at him, taking her time as she ran her gaze over the golden skin, taut over wide, muscular shoulders, down to his tensed abdominals and the straining length of him. He was beautiful... raw power. He was thick...harder than he had been moments before.

Isabelle's stomach dropped low. 'You are...' She waved in the general direction of his crotch. *'Again?'*

Matthew gave himself one long stroke, his fingers cinching at his base and sliding upward. 'It would seem my body will not stop wanting you, Duchess.'

And with that he climbed into the tub behind her and sat down, his long legs bracketing either side of her.

When Isabelle didn't move, he reached for her, pulling her back against his chest so that she could feel the hard weight of him at her lower back. She thought it odd that something so uncomfortable should also be so comforting, so familiar.

Matthew's hands ran through the water beside her, lifting it so that he could gently rinse the signs of their lovemaking from her. When she was wet and gleaming, he reached for the cake of soap on a nearby stool, lathering it in his hands until his palms were slippery with suds.

Isabelle stared as he worked, fascinated by his broad

palms and strong fingers as they travelled to her chest and began to knead and massage her sensitised breasts.

Her head fell back against his chest, allowing him more room for his ministrations.

Matthew made that now familiar pleased sound deep in the back of his throat as his fingers tugged gently at her aching nipples. Isabelle moaned wantonly as sensation after sensation rolled through her.

He trailed kisses down the side of her neck as one large hand lowered between her legs, his fingers expertly parting her to his touch and the warm water.

Isabelle couldn't help but open her eyes and look down. She watched…embarrassed, heated and utterly wanton…as his index and middle fingers slid over her inner flesh.

'Matth—'

Whatever she had been about to say died on her lips as a knock sounded on the door.

Isabelle was moving in seconds, pushing up from the water and climbing out of the tub before Matthew had even realised that someone was outside. He moved to get out too, but Isabelle held one hand out, stopping him.

'Wait here.'

She waited for him to nod, before hurriedly wrapping a strip of linen around herself and hurrying through to her bedroom. She threw her nightgown over the towel, took a deep breath to try and calm her racing heart, then reached out and opened the door.

Tess stood outside, holding Sera. The child was red

in the face, her eyes wet with tears, her little hands scrunched up angrily.

The nursemaid bobbed a quick curtsey. 'Excuse me, Your Grace. I saw the light...'

'What is—?'

Before she could finish her question, Tess started crying too. 'Something's wrong! She's burning up and she won't stop crying.'

'It's all right, Tess.'

Isabelle reached for Seraphina, alarm coursing through her when the baby's hot skin touched hers. Warmed by the bath as she was, *she* should have been far hotter to the touch than Sera.

Keeping her voice calm, despite her panic, she said, 'Wake Gordon. Have a footman send for Dr Taylor immediately. If the doctor's out, have him keep looking until he finds another.'

'Yes, Your Grace.' Tess turned to fulfil the request.

'And Tess!' Isabelle called. 'Bring up some cold water. Ice too—if we have it.'

Tess didn't waste time replying. She hurried off.

Isabelle closed her bedroom door. As if sensing her mother's worry, Seraphina started crying again—first quietly, and then with loud wails that echoed in the small room.

'What's wrong?'

She turned from the door to find Matthew, already dressed in his trousers and shirt, sans waistcoat and shoes.

'I don't know. She has a fever...'

She lifted Seraphina away from her body, noting that everywhere Sera's bare skin had been pressed to hers was already sticky with the baby's sweat.

'God, Matthew. She's so hot.'

He came forward instantly, placing one huge palm on Seraphina's forehead. 'How long has she been like this?' he asked.

His voice was devoid of emotion, but when she looked up at him she saw the sliver of fear in his eyes before he managed to bank it down.

'I don't know.' Isabelle searched her mind. 'She seemed fine this morning. And with the ball, I didn't… Oh, God…'

'Don't. Don't do that, Duchess.' Matthew held out his hands. 'May I?'

At a loss as to what to do, Isabelle complied, passing Sera to him.

Seraphina's wails turned into quiet sobs the moment she was in her father's arms. The child looked at Matthew for a long moment before plonking her head against his neck and taking a deep, shuddering breath. She fisted her little hand in his shirt, as if she wanted to be as close to him as possible.

Matthew crooned to her. 'Hello, beautiful,' he whispered, and kissed her cheek. When Seraphina started crying loudly again, he brushed his hand over her head. 'Shh… You're going to be well, darling.'

Isabelle's own eyes flooded with tears at the sight of them. Seraphina, unwell and feverish, and Matthew, so calm and reassuring. This, she realised as she watched him take charge, was how it was supposed to be. Not father and daughter seeing each other twice a week, for the hour Sera stayed awake, with Isabelle and Matthew sneaking about as if they were both ashamed of what they'd done, when really neither of them was in the least.

Matthew rocked gently, comforting Sera even as his free hand lifted the tiny white nightdress.

Isabelle was watching his face, and she knew the moment he looked down at Seraphina's back that something was terribly wrong.

'Matthew…'

He turned then, angling Sera's back in her direction and showing her the angry red splotches spreading over the toddler's skin.

Isabelle's heart simply stopped beating. Fear, new in its intensity, sank through her to her very bones. And when she looked into Matthew's eyes she saw the same fear reflected there.

'Measles.'

Chapter Eighteen

Isabelle paled, one slender hand coming up to cover her mouth. Her enormous eyes had turned glossy with tears, and even though she didn't speak, Matthew could see her thoughts running rampant.

'It's a common enough, disease, Duchess,' he said quietly, refusing to acknowledge his own fear. 'She'll be fine.'

His words, although true, left so much unsaid. Measles was particularly dangerous to small children, whose little bodies often succumbed to secondary symptoms, like fever or pneumonia. There was so much that could go wrong, and in one as young as Seraphina those potential risks were twofold.

But his words seemed to be enough to pull Isabelle from her panic. Matthew watched as she slowly straightened her spine, her hands hurriedly wiping away the tears running down her cheeks.

'Yes,' she said firmly, 'she will be.'

'The doctor?'

'He's coming.'

Matthew could feel Seraphina's little body burning against his, her skin so hot that he felt overheated just by his proximity to her. And yet for some absurd reason he couldn't bear to put her down.

'Is he any good?' he asked.

'Dr Taylor?'

He nodded. 'Our family doctor is elderly, but he's been with us almost twenty years…' His mind raced with thoughts of everything he could do, and before Isabelle could reply, he added, 'I'll send for him anyway.'

'Dr Taylor is young, but he has not let us down yet. From what I understand, his services are quite sought-after.'

Matthew shifted his weight from one foot to the other, not stopping his rocking as he attempted to comfort Sera. 'How long will he take to get here?'

Isabelle smiled briefly. 'I have only just sent for him—maybe an hour…'

'That's not soon enough.' Matthew suddenly shifted, passing Sera to Isabelle. 'Here—take her.'

As soon as Sera was out of his arms her cries grew louder, and it took every ounce of willpower that he had to keep moving, to put his waistcoat on without reaching out to comfort her.

'I'm going to fetch my mother to stay with us until the doctors get here.'

'Matthew, the ball… Your mother can't just leave— not without raising suspicions.'

He looked across the room at her. In that moment he

knew he would have done anything to protect her from the days to come.

She turned to kiss Seraphina's red cheek, where the rash was already becoming visible, and Matthew forced a half-hearted smile in an attempt not to scare her further.

'My mother nursed me and Caro through it when we caught it at the same time. She's more equipped than we are. Quite frankly, I'm calling in all the reinforcements we have. My sisters are perfectly able to act as hostesses for the rest of the evening.'

'What will the Countess say? About Seraphina?'

Matthew heard the dread in Isabelle's voice and braced himself against it when he admitted, 'She already knows. When she saw Sera at Hyde Park…'

But Isabelle did not seem surprised, as he'd expected. 'I assumed as much.' She rocked back and forth unconsciously, trying to calm Sera. 'Was she angry with me?'

'No. She was shocked. Then ecstatic. And she immediately started scheming—it took everything I had to convince her to stay out of it.'

He watched his words sink in, watched Isabelle's brows dip together in confusion.

'Why would she be angry with *you*?' he asked gently, trying to understand.

'Well, for starters, maybe she thought I was a strumpet who'd had my way with you. And I'm sure that discovering her first grandchild is illegitimate probably came as a huge shock.'

Matthew couldn't help but laugh quietly. 'I assure

you that my mother's first inclination was to immediately assume that *I* was entirely to blame.'

Her dark eyes met his. 'Because of the Marchioness?'

Swamped with regret, all he could do was nod and tug on his boots. He still felt that familiar nausea low in his stomach when he remembered Christine's fevered panic and frantic voice as she'd begged him to take her back. But for the first time, instead of bitter anger towards her, he also felt understanding—and a deep, deep shame for his role in her heartbreak.

Because if Isabelle cut him out of her life, he realised, he would probably feel as frantic, as hopeless, as lost as Christine had. And it was the strangest thing to realise that love could be as much of a curse for some as a blessing for others.

'Matthew…' Isabelle waited for him to look at her. 'Even though you were involved in a scandal, you've only ever been a gentleman to us.' She smiled gently. 'And the Marchioness scandal was the reason you came to be on our list.'

That gave Matthew the courage to say, 'It was a mistake—or I used to think it was, until just now. Because if it had not happened you would not have come to me, and for that alone I can no longer regret it. But my mother—and everyone else—has used it to measure my every action for years. When she found out about Sera, she thought that I had ruined you.'

'It is strange, is it not, how the people who are supposed to know us best often don't know us at all?'

Matthew shook his head vehemently. 'Don't forgive

me my sins, Duchess. I was to blame for the Marchioness's scandal.'

'Yes, but only as much as she was,' Isabelle insisted.

Seraphina rested her head against Isabelle's collarbone, and Isabelle responded by rubbing her cheek against their daughter's head.

'And in this you are only as much to blame—less so, even—as I am.'

He opened his mouth to argue, to remind her of her innocence, but she wouldn't have it. She spoke over him.

'Do not take that away from me, Matthew. The decision to go to you was mine to make—and I *did* make it. It took an immense amount of courage, but I would make it again if I were given the choice to go back— I would make the same decision every time. I went to you expecting a rake, and I found…you. And you are honourable and loving and kind.'

'No.' Matthew kept his voice low, so as not to alarm Sera, who had finally settled into a restless silence. 'You did come to me, Duchess. But I was not honourable in the least. I wanted you from the moment you spoke to me—before I even saw your face. And even if I had sent you home that night I would have found my way back to you eventually. I would have been powerless to resist you. Do not paint me a gentleman.'

'Fine. But then do not paint me an innocent either. It was *I* who came for *you*, my lord.'

He felt something shift inside him at her words—as if some part of himself that he'd closed off long ago had been released, filling him with an immensity of emotion that nearly overwhelmed him.

He knew, perhaps more than Isabelle, that society had been far harder in its judgement of Christine than of him, but for the first time he accepted that Christine herself had been an equal and eager participant in the affair—and the primary cause of the ensuing scandal. The difference between her and Isabelle was that Isabelle not only made her own decisions, she also accepted the consequences of them. She was truly independent.

Isabelle ran her hand over Sera's head, leaving it on her forehead for a few seconds. 'I can't tell if her fever's getting worse or if I've simply adjusted to her temperature.'

The reminder snapped Matthew from his reminiscing. 'We're going to have to establish a schedule… have someone always monitoring her fever and her other symptoms over the next few days.'

He was mostly talking to himself as he planned.

'Leo has had it—he had it while we were at school.' He paused to look at her. 'He will be discreet, Duchess. But it is your decision to make.'

Isabelle didn't even reply, knowing that she'd take all the help she could get when it came to the health of her child.

'And Willa,' Isabelle said. 'I know she's had it. She'll come, if Windhurst allows it.'

'I'll speak to her if she's still at the ball.'

A new and terrible thought occurred to Matthew. His

gaze snapped to Isabelle, and he knew the truth by the stubborn glint in her eyes before he even asked.

'And you?'

'Will it make you feel better if I lie?' she asked, her body growing rigid.

'Duchess…'

'Matthew, you could bodily remove me from this room and have me shipped to India and I would still slit the throats of my captors and come straight back.' She stared at him, daring him to argue. 'I am an adult, capable of making my own decisions.' When he still didn't reply, too consumed by the thought of both his girls being ill, she added, 'If you even try, I will never forgive you.'

'Duchess…'

'It's probably too late anyway,' she added. 'If the rash is showing already it's too late for me to leave—and you know it.'

Infuriated, helpless, and raging with inadequacy, he paced the room. 'And what of me?' he demanded. 'Am I to stand idly by while you are both ill?'

His very heart flailed at the thought.

'No.' Her mouth turned up in a tired smile. 'I hardly expect you to be idle, Matthew.'

He groaned his frustration. 'Duchess…'

'I need you here,' she said softly, but with not a hint of acquiescence in her voice. 'Matthew, I *want* you here. But if you try to come between me and Seraphina, I will have you removed from my house.'

His eyes snapped to hers even as he paced like a

caged animal. But even though he was angry—no, *infuriated* by her—his chest swelled with a strange pride that was equally born from love and admiration.

God, she was magnificent. So strong-willed and brave.

'Fine. Have it your way,' he acquiesced. 'But if you become ill, I'll...'

'You'll what?' She smiled gently.

Matthew couldn't help the exhausted laugh that rumbled out of his throat. 'I will be exceptionally angry with you.'

Instead of laughing, or jesting, Isabelle came to him, tucking herself and Sera against his chest.

'Thank you,' she whispered. 'It makes me feel safer knowing you're here.'

Her words made Matthew feel equal parts happy and devastated. For as much as he craved her confidence in him, he knew that there was nothing he could do to help. Measles was a waiting game—and Sera's tiny little heart, the one he could feel pounding angrily against his own chest now, as Isabelle held their child between them, was the clock.

'I've got to go. I'll be back with my mother and the doctor soon.' He kissed Sera's head of curls.

'What do I do?'

'Try to cool her down.'

'Tess is bringing ice.'

'Once she's brought it, have her wake the rest of the servants. Send anyone who hasn't had it before home until it passes—we'll pay for their leave.'

'You don't think it's too late?'

'I don't know…but it would be impossible to know everyone who's had contact with her recently.'

'Matthew…?'

'What is it, Duchess?'

'If they are already unwell and they leave…'

He cursed. 'They will take the disease home with them.'

'We have the resources to care for anyone who becomes ill here. At their homes they might not have that—and, worse, they might infect their own families.'

'What do you want to do?' he asked.

'We give them the choice but encourage them to stay here. I know Mary and Tess have definitely had it. They can conduct any outside business until the rest of us know that it has passed.'

'It's your household, Duchess.'

She tilted her chin up. 'I value your opinion.'

'I hate it that you must risk keeping ill people in proximity to you,' he said honestly. 'But we cannot let the servants face this alone—especially if they contracted the disease here.'

'Perhaps we shall be exceedingly lucky and everyone has had it already?' she suggested, her overly bright tone carrying a false humour that he tried to smile at.

Matthew was less optimistic. 'And Luke?'

'He had it as a young child—I was not permitted to see him or tend to him.'

'Well, that's something.'

Leaning down, he took her mouth in one last fierce

kiss, pouring everything—all his love and terror and frustration—into it. And then he pulled back, knowing that if he didn't leave soon he'd be too afraid to leave at all.

'I'll be back soon, Isabelle.'

'We'll be waiting,' she replied as he let himself out into the corridor and, without looking back, ran for the stairs.

Diana Blake, the Countess of Heather, arrived before anyone else—including Dr Taylor. The Countess's elaborate gown and coiffure told Isabelle that she had come straight from the ball, pausing only to remove her mask.

'Your Grace.' The older woman dipped into a hasty curtsey in the hall.

Isabelle reached for the woman's hands, halting her mid-rise. 'Please,' she begged. 'No honorifics. Not any more.'

She flushed, unable to say more.

'Isabelle, then.' The Countess smiled kindly and bypassed any further awkwardness by asking, 'How is Seraphina?'

'She is sleeping; her nursemaid is keeping her cool while I check on my servants.' Isabelle blinked back the burn of self-pitying tears. 'Six of them have not had measles before. Four of them are already showing symptoms.'

The Countess did not seem concerned. She plucked her gloves from her hands in a businesslike fashion and passed them to Gordon, who was hovering nearby.

'Let me see Seraphina first. Then we shall have the servants' beds moved into the same room—it will be easier to tend them in one place. They should rest until the doctor has been to see them and given us further instructions.'

Her confident manner instantly put Isabelle at ease. 'May I have a room prepared for you?' she asked.

'Yes, please.' The Countess turned to Gordon. 'Your name?'

'Gordon, my lady.'

'Gordon,' the Countess repeated, committing the name to memory. 'I have three footmen with me who have all had the measles before. They are here to help. I expect you are able to instruct them to go where you need them?'

Gordon's chest puffed out ever so slightly. 'Yes, my lady. I will see that they're settled.' He bowed. 'Thank you.'

The Countess smiled as Gordon walked away. 'What a dignified fellow.'

She took a deep breath and started up the stairs, leaving Isabelle to follow or be left behind in her own house.

'My son tells me that you have not had the disease yet?'

'No,' Isabelle replied honestly, omitting the fact that her throat had been scratchy for days and, although she had put Seraphina down over thirty minutes earlier, she now felt as if she were heating from the inside out.

'And you will risk yourself to tend Seraphina even though Matthew and I will be here?'

'Definitely.'

Diana Blake did not scold her; instead, she nodded matter-of-factly. 'Very well, then.'

Isabelle wasn't quite sure how she was supposed to react to this powerful woman now marching up her stairs as if she owned the house. The Countess seemed strangely unfazed by the scandalous circumstances, and her calm indifference confused Isabelle to no end.

It was only when they came to her bedroom door that she dared to ask, 'You do not have any questions for me?'

The Countess paused, one hand raised to the handle. 'Oh, I am *aflame* with curiosity,' she admitted, one brow raised in the same haughty gesture Isabelle had seen Matthew replicate. 'But I have the strangest feeling we're going to have a long time to get to know one another.'

'It's not what you think—'

'It rarely is.'

Needing to defend Matthew against his mother's assumption that he'd ruined her, she started trying to explain. 'Matthew… He…he helped me to protect my title so that I could keep the guardianship of my stepson. He did not know me before I approached him. He—at least in my mind—is free from judgement.'

'Yes…' the Countess drawled. 'I'm sure he found *helping* you a great difficulty.'

Isabelle couldn't help but smile, even as she lowered her eyes, mortified by the conversation.

'Perhaps not a *great* difficulty,' she said. 'But he did

refuse me at first—until I threatened to go to someone else.'

Diana Blake's eyes widened at that. 'You…?'

'I had a list.'

'A *list*?' The Countess paused. 'Well, when this is all over I definitely want to hear that story.' She leaned forward conspiratorially. 'Matthew is being very close-lipped about the entire situation.'

'He is a good man.'

'He is in love with you,' the Countess countered bluntly. 'He may not realise it yet, but I know my son rather too well. Seeing him watching you in the park that day…' She shook her head, a wistful smile on her lips. 'It made me remember what it is to be young and in love.'

The words slammed through Isabelle. 'No,' she said, denying it to herself as much as to the Countess. 'He is merely concerned for Seraphina.'

The Countess reached out and clasped Isabelle's hand. 'Don't fret, child. How about we call it a problem for us to solve another day?'

Isabelle nodded eagerly, grateful for the compromise.

'Now, let me see my granddaughter,' she demanded, and opened the door herself.

As the Countess set about quietly feeling Seraphina's temperature and asking Tess questions about her symptoms, Isabelle couldn't help but ponder the Countess's words.

Though he had not said it specifically, Matthew had admitted enough for her to understand that he cared.

Moreover, he had *shown* her. His every action was a promise to protect her—not, as she'd once feared, to possess her or control her.

To no advantage to himself, he had kept his word and not told anyone about Seraphina. And he had promised her his fidelity. And, although the neglected little girl she had once been would have been too afraid to believe that a man like Matthew could love her, the woman she had become desperately wanted to.

Because as she watched Matthew's mother tend their child…as she thought about him out looking for his own family doctor and calling their friends to assist them… she finally understood what marriage should be like.

It was not a trade—a young woman's flesh for the hope of healthy offspring—but a partnership. Marriage was having someone to share the burden when everything fell apart. Marriage was having someone step in and help when you didn't know what to do. And it worked both ways, with each supporting the other. Marriage was a constant when the world was not—or at least it *should* be.

Isabelle fleetingly wished that things could be different—that she and Matthew could be together openly without the potential for scandal. Still, knowing that such thinking was futile, and that neither she nor Matthew would jeopardise Sera's standing in the world, she pushed it from her mind and refocused her attention on what needed to be done.

Chapter Nineteen

By the time Matthew got back to Everett Place with Leo, whom he had fetched from their club with a request for help and a promise to explain everything as soon as possible, Dr Taylor was in Isabelle's bedroom, holding a stethoscope against Seraphina's chest as the child slept. Isabelle stood nearby with his mother, Mary and Willa, all of whom had left the ball immediately upon hearing the news.

Dr Taylor looked up when Matthew entered the room, but did not comment as he moved to stand by Isabelle's side.

'Sorry I took so long,' he whispered, just for her. 'I had to track down Leo at the club.'

'He is here?'

'I have left him in the drawing room for now.'

'And your doctor?' she asked.

'He is away. Travelling for—'

'She is in the worst of it now,' Dr Taylor interrupted quietly, trying not to wake Sera.

The doctor was a small, thin man with a youthful

face that almost looked too young to shave, but when he spoke he did so in a calm, practical manner that put some of Matthew's unease at bay.

'As difficult as it is going to be, try to keep her as cool as possible until the fever passes. It should only be a day or two, but in one as young as Seraphina fever can be extremely dangerous. Try to wake her every two hours, to drink some milk or water. If she can eat, that's good, but she may not feel like it.'

'Is there nothing else we can do?' Matthew asked, feeling helpless and frustrated.

'At this point keeping her hydrated and combating the fever are crucial. If need be, bathe her in cold water every few hours, but ensure that she is dried well and changed into clean, dry clothes each time. I can leave an iodine solution for the worst of the rash to reduce itching.'

'So, that is it?' Matthew ran his hand through his hair. 'We just wait and hope she gets better?'

'Matthew…' Isabelle linked her fingers through his, and he felt her hot palm sliding against his cooler one. 'The doctor is doing everything he can.'

'There is an outbreak,' Dr Taylor added. 'I will be with many other patients—probably for weeks—but I will come back to check on her every morning and evening, Your Grace.' Then he bowed in Matthew's direction. 'My lord, your daughter is healthy and strong. Her chances are good.'

Matthew didn't even try to deny his claim to Sera. If their physical similarities weren't enough, then the fact that he was seemingly losing his mind in her sickroom most assuredly was.

'Dr Taylor—'

Matthew braced himself for Isabelle's denial—waited for her to deny that he was Sera's father.

'May I offer you some refreshment? Maybe something to take with you if you're going to be out all night?'

Dr Taylor bowed. 'Thank you, Your Grace. I would appreciate that.'

Isabelle nodded, but it was Mary who quickly left the room to see that something was prepared for the doctor.

'My lord?' The young man started putting his stethoscope back into his bag. 'If I may offer one last word of advice?'

Matthew nodded once.

'Should you need a second opinion, then, please, seek one. But do not let any doctor give her an emetic or prescribe bloodletting. There is new scientific evidence that neither method works for measles, and in one as young as Seraphina they could cause irreparable damage by stressing her body further. She is too small to attempt such practices.'

'You are awfully young to be so confident,' Matthew observed.

Dr Taylor did not seem offended. Instead, he smiled, as if he knew exactly how good he was. 'If any doctor insists on either, ask him how many of his patients have succumbed to measles.' He snapped the top of his medical bag closed. 'In my ten years of practice I have not

yet lost any patient to this particular disease.' He started
for the door, Isabelle following. 'And I'll be damned if
my first is going to be a duchess's daughter.'

'Thank you for coming so quickly, Dr Taylor,' Isabelle said at the door. 'And for your discretion, as always.'

Perhaps Matthew should be more concerned, but he
knew that secrecy was not an insignificant part of the
doctor's profession in his treatment of members of high
society.

'I'll check on your staff before I leave,' said the doctor.

'I will show you downstairs.' Willa moved to escort
him.

'Thank you, Lady Windhurst.' Dr Taylor paused one
last time before leaving. 'Your Grace, if I may be so
bold... You should be resting and hydrating too.'

The door clicked shut behind him, leaving them momentarily alone with the Countess.

Isabelle exhaled deeply and turned to rest her back
against the door. Her eyes were tired, the worry in them
clear. Her typically straight posture was rounded, as if
she were carrying an immense weight. Her hair had been
loosely braided, leaving several long strands to escape.
They were plastered to her face, and although he had
not looked closely before, while he'd been focused on
Sera's diagnosis, his eyes narrowed on the telltale red-
ness spreading around her eyes and up her neck.

'You are unwell.'

She nodded tiredly. 'I thought it was from the mask,'

she said. 'But it's the measles rash.' She shook her head. 'I've had a scratchy throat for days and I didn't—'

Matthew swore. He went to her, covering the space between them in two large steps. His hands moved to her face, tilting her chin up so that he could see the rash even as he gauged the severity of her fever with his touch.

'I am fine,' Isabelle insisted.

'The doctor checked her before you arrived, Matthew,' his mother said from her position by Seraphina's crib.

He didn't know what to say. He had no idea how to express the crippling fear that suddenly consumed him.

Isabelle caught his wrists, holding his hands against her fevered cheeks. 'I'm going to be fine. But Sera… Matthew, I need you…'

'Tell me what to do,' he begged.

Isabelle looked to his mother. 'I think it's time we woke her up and tried to get her to take some milk. Maybe a cold bath?'

The Countess nodded her confirmation and walked to the corner of the room to the bell-pull as if it were her own house.

'The doctor knew?' his mother asked. 'That Matthew is Seraphina's father?'

Matthew glanced at his mother in surprise. He had assumed that the doctor had put two and two together— not that he had known all along.

Isabelle took one look at his face and started laughing, her tired chuckles forcing tears to her eyes. 'Well, I had to curse *someone* during my labour,' she said. 'It hardly

seemed fair to the poor Duke, given that he was dead—
and not responsible for my condition in the first place.'

Matthew smiled, despite his fatigue and worry. His
mother laughed. And even though they all knew it was
going to be a long few days in Everett Place, the brief
flash of humour seemed to breathe a moment of calm,
of hope.

But the moment ended too soon—the second his
mother leaned into the crib and picked up Seraphina.

Sera opened her eyes, scrunched her little fists together and let out a loud, self-pitying wail. 'Oh, I know,
child,' his mother crooned. 'You must feel horrid.'

Seraphina screamed louder in response and Matthew
itched to go to her, to take her in his arms and rock her
back to sleep. He resisted. Despite her infallible appearance, he knew his mother needed to be useful or she'd
go mad with worry—they had that in common.

So he went to Isabelle instead, taking her hand in his
and leading her to the bed they'd vacated only hours
before. 'You need to rest. My mother and I will look
after Seraphina.'

Isabelle's glazed eyes widened as he turned her and
started undoing the buttons down the back of her simple
gown. 'Matthew—'

'She knows we've had a child,' he teased gently. 'She
hardly thinks we did it with our clothes on.'

His mother laughed quietly as she continued to comfort Seraphina, but she turned her back, giving them
some privacy.

Isabelle didn't try to stop him as he stripped off her

dress, leaving her only in her thin chemise, and while he turned away to lay the gown over a nearby chair she climbed into her bed. By the time he was back at her side, she had closed her eyes.

'I'm so tired,' she murmured.

'Sleep, my love. We'll wake you if there's any change with Sera.'

He covered her with the comforter just as four maids carried in buckets of icy water to pour into the tub. The moment they left, he used the ice block and some strips of fabric to keep Isabelle cool, alternately pressing a cold one to her forehead and rinsing and wringing out the one he'd used previously. In only minutes, she was fast asleep.

Mary knocked quietly and entered the room. 'Willa and Leo have left,' she said. 'I didn't think there was any point in us all being up at the same time. They are going to return in the morning, to help where they can.' She placed her hand on Isabelle's cheek. 'She's not as hot as Sera…'

'I think she's as exhausted as she is unwell,' Matthew said. 'It's been a stressful month for her—and that's without her being up every night with Sera. We should let her sleep.'

'Matthew,' his mother interrupted, 'why don't you leave Mary to cool Isabelle while you help me with Sera's bath?'

He looked to Mary.

'I can manage, my lord.'

'Matthew? Please,' said his mother.

Mary nodded, her eyes fixed intently on his face. 'I was wrong about you,' she said. 'But I had no reason to believe you loved them.'

Matthew opened his mouth, the denial coming instinctively, if not truthfully, but Mary only patted his hand in a gesture that was surprisingly maternal for a woman so young.

'I'm sorry for thinking ill of you. I shall endeavour to be more supportive.'

He exhaled tiredly, sensing that there was no point in pretending that he did not love them when everybody clearly saw how he felt.

'As long as you continue to care for my girls, I don't mind if you don't like me.'

'Nonetheless, it is a beneficial side benefit.' Mary waved him away with a small flick of her fingers. 'Go and see to your daughter, my lord. I shall stay with Izzy.'

Matthew rose off the bed and walked to where his mother held a sobbing Seraphina. The moment she saw him approach Sera unstuck her face from the Countess's neck and held out both arms to him.

'Hello, my princess.' He took her familiar weight, felt his own panic settle slightly once she was in his arms. He kissed her fever-flushed face. 'Do you feel terrible, darling?' he crooned, lowering his voice for her.

'Ya!' Sera cried and nodded, her lower lip wobbling.

He rubbed her back for a long moment, rocking from side to side in a rhythm that was as instinctual as eating or sleeping. 'You're going to be fine…'

'Matthew?'

He looked up to find both his mother and Mary Lambert staring at him, their faces showing equal surprise. 'Yes?'

'We need to get her into the cold bath.'

A shiver ran through his own body at the thought of the chilly water. Still, he shifted Sera to his hip and took off his shoes, then passed her back to his mother for a moment, so that he could remove his jacket and waistcoat.

He walked through to the dressing room with Seraphina and gently lowered her into the tub. The moment she felt the cold water she started screaming, her little hands reaching for him as she tensed her chubby legs and tried to lever herself out of the uncomfortable situation.

'I know… I know, beautiful…'

Seraphina didn't calm—if anything, she screamed louder. Unsure of what to do, or how to help her, Matthew supported her tiny back with one hand and climbed, fully dressed, into the frigid water with her.

Seraphina's shock at this untoward situation stopped her screams. She watched him, her sad grey eyes huge in her face, as he spread his trousered legs either side of her, making sure she was stable in the slippery bathtub.

His own breath came out in a stuttering exhalation as his body grew acclimatised to the cold.

'This is bloody awful, isn't it?' he asked as the water soaked through the layers of his clothes.

Seraphina nodded and reached for his leg in reply, her discomfort momentarily forgotten by this strange turn of events. While she was distracted, he cupped the cold water in his palms and let it fall down her nightdress, where he knew her skin was angry with red splotches. She shivered like a wet cat and turned to look up at him, her face set in an expression of horrified betrayal.

'Sorry, my love,' he murmured, not quite able to hide his grin.

'Try splashing,' his mother commented from the door, holding a towel in her hands.

Matthew obliged, using one large palm to splash water in Seraphina's direction, turning the uncomfortably cold bath into a game that had the child squealing with delight—and leaving the dressing room in a puddle of water.

They played for only a few minutes, alternately splashing one another and laughing, but once Sera started shivering with cold, Matthew picked her up and handed her to his mother, who was waiting nearby with the towel.

She wrapped Seraphina in it, leaving a corner of fabric loose to rub over his daughter's downy head. Matthew stood up in the tub. He was soaked through, his clothes dripping with what seemed like buckets of water.

'I'll have Mary find some clothes for you until one of the footmen can go to the house and fetch fresh garments.' His mother turned to leave, only pausing to add, 'You know, despite your past mistakes I've always been proud of you, Matthew. You are a remarkable son.'

Surprised by the compliment, Matthew simply replied, 'Thank you, Mother.'

'I am sorry for the way I reacted when I first saw Seraphina. To assume that you were entirely to blame was unfair of me. Regardless, I've never been prouder of you than I am now. Having a remarkable son is easy—in fact, I'm sure most women think their sons are remarkable, even when they are not. But knowing that I have raised a man who has turned into a remarkable father... Well, if this wasn't all so secretive, I would find myself rather braggadocious about my own parenting abilities.'

Unable to contain his amusement, Matthew raised a single brow. 'Should I say congratulations?'

His mother laughed, making Seraphina giggle too. 'One day he will know how I feel,' she told Sera, and exited the room, her granddaughter in her arms.

Chapter Twenty

True to his word, Dr Taylor came back every morning and evening to check on the household, only staying long enough to update his care instructions and leave additional iodine solutions before hurrying off to the other affected London families in his care.

Willa and Leo came each morning too, and stayed all through the day to help with Sera and the servants, so that the others could rest and try to recuperate for the long night ahead.

While Isabelle slept on and off through her raging fever, Matthew, his mother and Mary, with help from Meg, Tess and Gordon, took turns tending to their eight patients.

On the third morning the doctor took one look at Matthew and Isabelle—the former sitting in a chair by the bed, the latter propped upright on a mountain of pillows—and declared, 'You both need to sleep. Seraphina will be fine without you for a few hours.' Dr Taylor merely raised one sardonic brow when they both nodded tiredly and asked, 'And how are my patients this morning?'

'We bathed Sera three times last night.'

Matthew, who had got into the tub each time with his daughter over the past three nights, had been as miserable as she had by their last soaking. Just the thought of it now had a shiver of dread passing through his entire body.

'The last time was just after midnight. By then her fever seemed to have subsided, so we let her sleep through the rest of the night.'

Dr Taylor chafed his hands together, warming them, and then bent over the crib where Seraphina was fast asleep. He placed his hand on her forehead. 'Her fever has broken. That's good; she's through the worst of it.' He placed his stethoscope against her tiny chest, falling quiet as he listened to her heartbeat. 'She is going to be fine.'

Isabelle closed her eyes in relief. Although he wasn't sure she was aware of having done it, Matthew felt her hand seek his on the bed and hold on.

Matthew returned the squeeze, too relieved to do anything except ask, 'So that's it?'

'Continue to monitor her. Let her sleep as much as she can. When she wakes make sure she stays hydrated and eats. The rash will last another seven to ten days. It will look unsightly,' he warned, 'but it won't do her any harm so long as you keep her clean and apply the iodine to reduce irritation. Try not to let her scratch, and keep her indoors until the rash has gone.'

Dr Taylor approached the bed.

'If I may examine you, Your Grace?'

Isabelle smiled tiredly at him. 'Of course, Dr Taylor,' she replied, her words punctuated by a hacking cough that Matthew felt in his own chest.

The doctor asked her to lean forward, and once she'd complied, placed the stethoscope on her back. He kept his expression neutral, but Matthew was watching the doctor's face, and he saw the man's eyes dampen.

'What is it?' he asked.

Dr Taylor ignored him. 'Your Grace, when did the cough start?'

'Early this morning,' Matthew replied for her.

He'd been lying next to her, listening to her ragged breathing the entire night, so he knew exactly when she'd started coughing—that was why he'd propped her on the pillows.

'Why?'

'There is fluid in your lungs, Your Grace,' Dr Taylor replied, and gently leaned Isabelle back onto the pillows.

Isabelle did not seem surprised at all. She nodded and closed her eyes. 'I do feel rather the worse for wear.' She inhaled a deep breath once she'd finished talking, as if even that short sentence had exhausted her.

'What does that mean?' Matthew demanded, growing increasingly frustrated.

'The Duchess has pneumonia,' the doctor stated blandly.

'No!' The word was out of his mouth before he could think.

'I assure you, my lord—'

'How is that possible?' he asked, his voice rising in his fear. 'She was feeling better just yesterday!'

'It's a common secondary symptom of the measles disease. Your Grace…?' Dr Taylor cleared his throat. 'This will get a lot worse before it gets better.'

'I understand,' Isabelle replied calmly.

Matthew pushed back his chair and stood, unable to sit still, unable to keep silent while they talked as if nothing was the matter. He paced to the window, stopped, turned, and then paced to the other side of the room.

'Matthew?'

He raised one hand to the back of his neck, pulling it down as if he might relieve his fear if he only placed enough pressure there.

'Matthew!' Isabelle rasped again.

He took one deep breath to try and calm himself and turned to face her. 'Duchess?'

'You need to have Mary fetch Mr Briggs—my solicitor.'

He frowned. 'No.' He shook his head. 'We're not even close to having to think about…'

He couldn't even say the word—couldn't even think about Isabelle without any life in her.

Isabelle looked to the doctor.

He shrugged. 'You are young and strong. There is no reason that you shouldn't live through this.' The doctor paused, his eyes finding Matthew's. 'But—'

'Don't!' Matthew said immediately.

'Healthier people have succumbed,' the doctor said gravely. 'One third of all patients who catch a contagious disease die—not from the illness itself, but from pneumonia. My lord, it is never too early to have one's affairs in order.'

'Matthew,' Isabelle wheezed, clearly growing agitated, 'if I die, Luke and Seraphina will be left as wards of the Chancery Court. I can't let that happen…'

Matthew's blood chilled at the thought.

'We need to have Briggs organise everything—even if it's just a precaution.' Isabelle drew in a deep breath that rattled through her chest. 'I should have done it before, only… I've never been sick—not seriously. But I of all people should know how quickly…' She didn't finish the sentence.

Matthew was torn between wanting to deny the possibility that Isabelle would succumb and doing what he knew was best for Luke and Sera. His soul rebelled at the idea of the Duchess gone, her chest unmoving, her beautiful big eyes blank, her smile silent. She was *his*, goddammit. She couldn't leave now that he'd finally found her again.

'I'll ask Mary to send for him.'

Matthew left the room before either Isabelle or the doctor could see how much this diagnosis had affected him. He needed to be strong for Isabelle, for the children, but the moment he was alone outside the bedroom he slumped against the wall and closed his eyes.

Just for a moment, he thought, exhausted from the last few minutes—from the last few days.

Last night he'd finally thought that things were turning to the good. He'd felt Seraphina's fever receding each time he'd checked on her, and he'd sensed she was out of the worst of it. But this… Isabelle catching lung fever… This was something he had not expected and was not prepared for.

'Matthew?'

He opened his eyes to find his mother standing further down the corridor with Luke at her side. Both of them were watching him cautiously, as if they knew he would not be collapsed against the wall for any small reason.

He tried to smile. 'You can send word to Father that Seraphina will be fine,' he stated, knowing that his father and his sisters had been confused by the turn of events even as they had been worried about the Duchess and her family.

His mother nodded, but, sensing his dread, did not smile. 'And Isabelle?' she asked.

Matthew's eyes flickered to Luke as he wondered what to do. The boy was nine. He was old enough to do so many things, but Matthew had no idea how honest he should be with him—if at all. There was nothing either of them could do for Isabelle except wait, and it seemed futile to have the boy worrying.

'She is not feeling very well, but she's strong,' he said, settling on a deliberate half-truth that somehow still felt like a lie.

Luke nodded, his relief obvious. 'May I see them?'

'Of course.' Matthew reached out a hand and gave Luke's shoulder a reassuring squeeze. 'Your sister is sleeping, but Izzy is awake. She is with the doctor.'

Matthew waited until Luke had knocked on the door and entered before turning back to his mother. Unlike Luke, whose childish faith made him believe what Matthew had told him, his mother looked drawn and pale.

'What is it?' she asked.

'Pneumonia.'

She inhaled a sharp breath. 'What does the doctor say?'

'It is going to get worse before it gets better.'

He closed his eyes and pinched the bridge of his nose with his thumb and forefinger, staving off what felt like the unfamiliar burn of tears.

'Isabelle has asked for her solicitor to...' He couldn't finish the sentence.

He didn't have to, either. His mother came to him.

She placed her palm on his cheek. 'Preparing for the worst is what any good mother would do, Matthew. It does not mean that she has any intention of dying.'

'I don't know what to do,' he countered restlessly. 'I feel so useless.'

'Sometimes there is nothing you can do except love a person and be with them.' She slowly lowered her hand, glancing towards the closed door of the bedroom. 'Have you told her how you feel?'

He shook his head. 'She's not ready to hear it.'

'Matthew, if you do not tell her and something happens, you will regret it for ever. It's important to tell people that you cherish them when you have the chance.' Her grey eyes, so similar to his, tracked his face. 'Why are you so afraid? It's not like you...'

'I've never had *cause* to be afraid before,' he said honestly. 'I never even knew this type of fear existed before this week.' He unconsciously raised his fisted hand to rub it over his aching heart. 'I haven't been able to sleep for the constant need to look into Sera's crib and count her tiny breaths, or stare at Isabelle's chest as it rises and falls. I feel like a madman. If anything were to happen to either of them...' he said, and shook his head suddenly, rebelling at even the thought of everything that could go wrong. 'No. I can't even consider it.'

Feeling panicked by the possibility, and by what Isabelle had asked him to do, he turned and walked blindly away from the Countess without further explanation.

Despite Matthew's insistence, Isabelle absolutely refused to see her solicitor in her bedchamber. She would not lie abed while she discussed the future of her children with Mr Briggs, irrespective of how comfortable she felt with the man.

'You are aging me, Duchess,' Matthew murmured as he helped her down the stairs, one arm around her waist to support her.

Isabelle laughed—and regretted the action immediately when she started coughing. Pain lanced through her chest with each expulsion of air, and although she'd just washed, using a basin and a cloth, sweat dampened her back and chest with the small exercise.

She paused halfway down the stairs to take a break, exhausted from the coughing jag.

Matthew grunted and then, without a word, leaned down and picked her up.

'Matthew…' She sighed tiredly. 'I'm perfectly capable of walking.'

'I like carrying you,' he countered, stealing any further argument from her. He tightened his arms slightly. 'I like the way you fit perfectly against me.'

At a loss for what to say, Isabelle merely rested her head on his shoulder as he carried her to the study.

Gordon opened the door for them, revealing Leo, Willa, Mary, the Countess and Mr Briggs. And as Matthew carried her gently to the settee, Isabelle tried her best not to flush with mortification at the scene she was creating.

But any awkwardness over the situation did not have time to grow as Wilhelmina exclaimed, 'Good God, Izzy! You look positively awful!'

Leo snorted.

Mary smiled and shook her head.

'I must be honest,' Isabelle rasped as Matthew placed her down, 'I have felt better.'

She wheezed, and the sound sawed through the room, adding a gravitas to her voice that she wished could have been avoided.

Matthew sat down next to her, and it was Isabelle who took his hand in hers, needing to be the one to acknowledge what it was they were doing. He looked at her for a long moment, but it was only once she nodded that he turned back to the room and began.

'Thank you all for coming…'

As if sensing that this was no ordinary occasion, everyone hurried to find a seat. Mr Briggs sat down opposite Isabelle, giving her his full attention. He was a tall, thin man, with kind eyes and a wide smile that instantly eased some of the sick dread collecting in her stomach.

'Your Grace,' he began, 'I am so sorry to hear that you have been ill.'

'I have pneumonia,' Isabelle said matter-of-factly. 'And while I am certain that I will be fine, it has made me realise that my affairs are not in order, Mr Briggs.'

'Hogwash!' Willa exclaimed. 'You have years to mull over any dreary business.'

Willa opened her mouth to say more, but before she could Leo gently placed his hand over hers and shook his head, stopping her.

Isabelle replied gently, 'Willa, it's just a precaution. I have no intention of dying. But we cannot ignore the possibility.' She turned back to the solicitor. 'Mr Briggs?'

Simon Briggs stood immediately, bowing for the second time. 'Your Grace… If I may use your desk?'

Isabelle nodded, and the solicitor took his leather case to the large surface.

'You have only to tell me what you would like and I shall draft a document within a day and have it returned for your signature tomorrow.'

'Today,' Isabelle insisted tiredly. 'I will sign the draft today—just in case.'

Briggs nodded cautiously. 'Very well.' He removed a paper and pen from his case. 'Whenever you are ready.'

'It's simple, really. I have only three requests. Upon my *eventual* death, I transfer full guardianship rights of my daughter, Seraphina, to Lord Ashworth and his family.'

'That may be difficult, Your Grace. As a woman, you cannot assign guardianship in your will—'

Isabelle smiled at the solicitor, taking any sting out of her next words. 'He is her father.'

Briggs's eyes rounded with surprise. 'I see.'

'It is not what you think, Mr Briggs…' Isabelle began.

'It is not my concern, Your Grace. My loyalty lies with the Dukedom, to the current Duke of Everett, and to you, as the person whom I believe cares for him most in the world. The rest…' he leaned forward, lowering his voice '…is perhaps best kept confidential.'

Isabelle nodded, but the man's loyalty had brought the burn of tears to her eyes. 'Mr Briggs, if I am not here to look after Luke, I would like you to approach the Chancery Court and request to serve as his guardian. Gareth St Claire surely could not intervene if Luke was legally bound to the executor of the Dukedom. While I cannot legally assign his guardianship, I would like you to include this as my wish, so that the Chancery may consider it above granting guardianship to a stranger.'

'Your Grace…' Briggs shook his head.

'I trust you to do your best by my children, Mr Briggs, as you have done by the Dukedom these past twenty-two years.'

'I am honoured, Your Grace. Truly,' the elderly man insisted. 'However, as only a father can name guardians in a will, perhaps I could make a few suggestions?'

'Please do.'

'Common law states that the next closest relative who cannot inherit should be named guardian.' His astute gaze landed on her hand, which remained linked with Matthew's.

'So, Gareth St Claire, next in line for the Dukedom after Luke, cannot become Luke's guardian,' Isabelle confirmed, remembering when she and Matthew had first discussed the possibility two years ago.

'He cannot,' the solicitor confirmed. 'However, the next closest relatives—'

'My parents?' Isabelle shook her head, thinking back not only on her own lonely childhood, but on her parents' complete lack of interest in Luke and Seraphina. To them, children were not to be seen or heard until they could behave and converse like adults. 'They wouldn't be my first choi—'

Mr Briggs smoothly took over. 'But if you were to remarry, Your Grace, your *husband* would be the most likely candidate to petition for guardianship.'

The room became eerily quiet. Nobody talked as his implication sank in. Isabelle's mind raced, her thoughts a jumbled mix of confused longing and calm realisation.

'Mr Briggs, are you saying that were I to remarry, upon my death, my husband would likely become guardian not only to Seraphina, but Luke as well?'

Briggs nodded. 'Given that they would to all appearances be his stepchildren, and not his blood relatives, he would still have to petition, Your Grace. But with your express wishes and my recommendation, and considering the children's welfare, it would be a logical approval. Lord Ashworth's family estate is notoriously lucrative. Unlike any other guardian, he would have no financial motive for tampering with the Duke's estate. Coupled with the fact that I manage the Duke's finances separately…it would be difficult for the Chancery to deny that Lord Ashworth would be the best candidate for guardianship—at least until the Duke turns fourteen and may choose his guardian himself.'

As if aware of the enormity of what he was suggesting, Briggs added, 'I understand that the timing is a concern, Your Grace. But if you could arrange a special licence in the next few days—'

'Hours,' the Countess of Heather interjected. 'The Earl plays bridge with William… I mean, the archbishop. We could have a licence within hours.'

'And if you *wanted* to remarry, of course,' Briggs continued, 'it would be one way to keep the children together in the unlikely event of your death.'

'We have some concerns.' It was Matthew who spoke now. 'About how our marriage would affect Seraphina. Her resemblance to me is not insignificant.'

Isabelle's heart clenched with fear at the reminder, and yet for the first time she also felt a conflicting warmth spreading over the fear, taking the edge of panic away. Because as she watched Matthew talking to Mr Briggs, trying to find a solution to their predicament, she understood that he would do everything within his power to protect the children, even if that meant denying Seraphina as his own.

'Undoubtedly.' Mr Briggs nodded. 'However, to my way of thinking your options are twofold. You could do as the Duchess suggests, and guarantee a separate legal guardian for each child, or alternatively you could try to keep them together. Of course in the first instance, and in the unlikely event of the Duchess's death, people would assume they knew why Seraphina had been left in your legal care and Luke had not, my lord. My suggestion may result in the same rumours, but the children would most likely be kept together and raised in your care.'

'To clarify: you are saying that, either way, we are not going to avoid a scandal.' Isabelle spoke the words nobody else seemed to want to, and although her voice was clear and calm, her heart pounded with fury.

To be ruined was to be a social pariah. Despite being legally perceived as the Duke's daughter, Seraphina would never escape the whispers. Her peers would use it against her. Many suitors would not even consider her. Sera would grow up in a shame that should not be hers to carry.

Isabelle wondered how it was that a child—*any* child, completely innocent in its circumstances—could be condemned for the way they had been brought into the world? Sera was cherished and loved. She would grow up to be good and kind. She should not have to suffer because of the manner in which she had been conceived.

Mr Briggs's nod was barely perceptible. 'There will be some whispers, undoubtedly. However, so long as the rumours could not be substantiated, and along with my recommendation, they would bear little influence with the Chancery Court.'

'Do we have any other options?' Matthew asked. 'Any way to protect Sera?'

'None that I can think of, given the uncertainty of the Duchess's health and the urgency with which we must act.'

'Are we all forgetting that this may be entirely unnecessary?' Willa interjected.

'I cannot have things undecided and risk leaving the children unprotected,' Isabelle countered immediately.

The fever she could feel raging through her body made her decision easy. She knew that she must decide, and decide soon. And she believed in the deepest corner of her heart that Matthew would do right by both children should she succumb.

Although she had tried to do the right thing by Sera, although she had denied Matthew and his right to claim his daughter, Fate had intervened, and it was Fate that had decided the consequences they all must live with. For consequences there would be.

Moreover, Isabelle *wanted* to be his.

Swallowing the fear that brought tears to her eyes, she turned to face the man who had become integral to her family in such a short period of time. 'Matthew?'

'Yes,' he said immediately.

Keeping their hands linked, he moved to kneel in front of her. His intense grey eyes bored into hers, and in them she could see her own need, conflict and confusion reflected.

'Isabelle, I've been yours for a long time,' he said. 'And although this isn't how I imagined it, and although I would rather cut my heart out than see you or the children hurt, I can't pretend to be anything but over-joyed that you'll be mine. Marry me—and not just for me. Marry me for our children.' He sighed deeply, his grey eyes filled with emotion. 'Marry me because you *want* to.'

Isabelle heard both her friends' wistful sighs, but she did not turn to look at them. She didn't need anybody else's advice on this one decision. She knew what she wanted. She knew what was right. Right for her and for the children. Moreover, she knew that Matthew, who had lived with his own scandal for years, was willingly subjecting himself to society's judgement once again— for them. And his certainty solidified her own.

'Yes,' she said, her voice hoarse with fever and emotion.

Her words spurred a flurry of activity into the room. The Countess of Heather clapped her hands excitedly. 'I'll see to it immediately,' she said. She paused on her way to the door to ask, 'Isabelle? You don't mind if I organise things for tonight—here? And invite the rest of the family?'

Isabelle shook her head, her eyes finding Matthew's. 'I don't mind.'

He smiled up at her from his position, kneeling on the floor. 'Isabelle…' He shook his head as if he were undone, as if he had no words.

'I trust you,' she said simply.

But her heart leapt in her chest at this half-truth, because trust was the least of it. If she had struggled to admit her love for him before, she had been forced to confront it while she'd watched him care for her family. She loved him, this man who had time and time again been with her when he didn't have to—but wanted to. This man whom she might have for one day, one week, one lifetime…

'I am sorry that it has happened this way.' His thumbs stroked over the backs of her hands. 'I wanted you to choose me on your own—not because you had no choice. But even so, and even with the scandal, I cannot be anything but overjoyed.'

The statement brought a raspy chuckle to Isabelle's throat. 'I don't doubt it,' she said.

And in that moment, in that still second of time when what they were doing sank in, she felt the same happiness spread through her own heart.

'It is strange,' she whispered, just for his ears, 'that I am the happiest I have ever been when I am also the closest to death I have ever come.'

'Don't,' he insisted vehemently. 'Don't say that.'

Mr Briggs cleared his throat, breaking the tender moment. 'Was that all, Your Grace?' he asked. 'I should get this document drawn up.'

'No, I have one more request,' she said.

Matthew hauled himself up onto the settee next to her.

Isabelle looked across the room to her two best friends. 'Should I die, I would like my personal funds distributed thus. One thousand pounds to each of my servants, irrespective of their rank, two thousand pounds each to my butler, Gordon, my maid, Meg, and my nursemaid, Tess. And the remainder to be split equally between my two closest friends: Mary Lambert and Wilhelmina Windhurst.'

'That can be arranged, Your—'

'I refuse.' This absurd statement came from Wilhelmina, of course. 'I don't want your money, Isabelle!' her friend exclaimed. 'I want your company for many years to come.'

'It's just—'

'Yes, we know,' Willa drawled. 'Just a *precaution*.'

'You two have been my best friends. You have supported me even when your own lives were far from ideal. I'll have no use of my money when I'm dead, and Matthew will make sure that the children are taken care of. This is important to me, Willa.'

'Drat!' Willa replied, her tears spilling over for the first time. 'I don't suppose we have a choice but to keep you alive, then?'

'You will stay tonight? I would like you to be here.' Isabelle turned to Mary. 'Both of you.'

'Of course,' Willa stated.

Mary could not voice her consent through the tears in her eyes, but she nodded her promise anyway.

And now their business was concluded there was nothing for Isabelle to do but rest—and wait to be married.

Chapter Twenty-One

By the time evening came, Isabelle could barely talk for fear of falling into one of the coughing fits that left her short of breath and gasping for air. Her entire body was ablaze. Every time she stood too fast the blood in her head seemed to rush to her feet, leaving her light-headed and weak.

She was feeling worse. And even though she was aware that she should be in bed, resting, she was too anxious to complete her wedding to relax. She could not rest until she knew the children would be taken care of.

Isabelle sat patiently next to Willa as Mary put the finishing touches to her hair, adding a single red rose to the simple chignon that Isabelle had insisted upon, given the simple ceremony—and the fact that she would be back in her bed almost as soon as it was over.

'Are you positive this is what you want?' Mary asked quietly, her eyes finding Isabelle's as she moved around the dressing table to speak to her.

Willa and Mary were both watching her face, their worry amplified by their twin looks of concern.

'I'm certain,' she replied, and her voiced was laced with wonder. 'This whole time…even when I didn't know him… I missed him. I thought about him every day for the years that he was gone. Every time I looked at Sera, or got lonely…' She released a wheezing laugh. 'I know it's impossible to love someone after meeting them only once…but I don't think it's impossible to *want* to love someone you've only ever met once. And once was enough for me to know that Matthew was the type of man I wished I had married—the type of man I would want to love. I think I can be afraid—afraid of marriage and of losing my independence—while still recognising that he is what I need to be happy.'

'And love?' Mary asked quietly.

'I do love him.' Isabelle admitted it aloud for the first time. 'He's the only man who's ever adhered to my wishes, who's treated me as an intelligent woman who knows her own mind, instead of someone to be purchased and shelved—and he didn't have to. He's an impossibly good father to Seraphina. And although he hasn't had as much time with Luke, I know in my heart that he would only ever treat both children equally. He makes me feel safe—as if I don't have to worry about everything myself because I trust that he'll be there to share the burden.'

Willa cleared her throat. 'Um… I beg your pardon?'

Isabelle wheezed again as her laugh climbed free. 'It's different. You two…' She took her friends' hands, one in each of hers, and looked at them in turn. 'You two have become so much more than friends. You're the sisters I never had.'

Willa sniffled.

Mary dabbed daintily at her eyes.

'If I die, will you promise to help him?' she asked shakily, knowing it was a momentous burden he would be taking on.

When tears burned her eyes at the thought of losing them, of never seeing the children grow up, of never experiencing life with Matthew by her side, she let them fall unashamedly.

'Matthew has his family, but the children know you. They will need you. Especially Sera... You two know how devastating even a single rumour can be, and now...'

She did not have to finish the sentence. They all knew that the whispers had started already.

Mary replied, 'Of course,' without hesitation. She knew what it was to fear the worst and have those fears realised.

Willa shrugged. 'If it makes you feel better. However, I do not anticipate needing to. You shall be fine.'

'Yes, she will.'

They all turned to see Matthew. He was standing on the threshold, dressed smartly in contrast to Isabelle's well-worn hunter-green day gown, which was the only dress she could bear to have against her feverish skin. His hair was contrastingly dishevelled, as if he had been running his hands through it constantly. His grey eyes were dark with fatigue and worry.

Isabelle tried to smile, but she couldn't quite bank down the overwhelming fear that this might be it—this could be the end of everything she'd only just found. Her lips wobbled with the realisation.

Matthew looked to Mary and Willa. 'May I have a moment?' he asked. 'I will help her down.'

'I don't see why not,' Willa said. 'It's not as if we've adhered to a single tradition anyway.' She paused in front of Matthew and pulled him into a spontaneous hug. 'We're glad to have you, you know.'

Matthew smiled and returned the hug. 'I am glad to be had, Willa.'

Mary followed Willa out of the room, and although she did not hug Matthew, as Willa had done, Isabelle saw the kind smile she shared with him.

The door closed, leaving them alone together. If she'd thought she would be nervous, Isabelle was surprised to find that she was perfectly calm. Content. She looked at Matthew for a long time, taking in the broad shoulders that had held so much the past few days, and the strong hands that had reached out to help without being asked.

He came to her, lifting her easily off the chair and carrying her to the bed before sitting down with her on his lap.

'How are you feeling?' he asked, his hand rising to feel her face. He hissed out a breath before she could reply, the moment he touched her bare skin.

'The fever is coming on in full force now,' she stated, knowing that lying was futile. 'We need to hurry. You already have a blotchy bride; it won't do to have a sweaty one too.'

He didn't argue or try to deny it. And he didn't shrug away from her clammy skin either. 'Okay. But first…' He shifted slightly, making space between them so that he could reach into his jacket pocket. 'There is a tradition in my family,' he began as he pulled out a velvet ring box, 'that the first son receives this ring from the Countess of Heather for his bride.'

He opened the box to reveal a halo ring. A large oval ruby was centred atop the band, surrounded by ten tiny European-cut diamonds that gave the ring the appearance of a flower. It was beautiful.

'It is your mother's?' Isabelle asked uncertainly.

'It *was* my mother's,' he corrected. 'Now it is yours. Until, one day, Luke asks you for it.'

Isabelle understood what he was promising her—that he would treat Luke as his own though they would never share a name or a title. 'The Countess—'

'Has her wedding band,' he said, 'and she has given us her blessing.'

He slid the ring onto her finger.

Isabelle swallowed down the dry lump in her throat and raised her hand between them so that they could both look at the ring. It was slightly too large on Isabelle's finger, but she didn't care.

'Thank you,' she whispered and, placing her hand on his cheek, guided his mouth to hers for a quick kiss. 'I love it.'

'But not nearly as much as you love me,' he said, his

arms tightening around her as if he was expecting her to run away at the declaration.

Isabelle tensed on his lap. 'You heard?'

He nodded, his grey eyes dark with emotion. 'I did.'

'I was hoping to tell you in person…' She began to explain, embarrassed that he had heard her tell her two friends how much she loved him before she'd had the chance to tell him herself.

Matthew rested his forehead against hers for a moment. 'How about I go first?'

She nodded.

'After the scandal with Christine, I avoided even the most casual of attachments. I was too afraid to trust myself, let alone anyone else. Until you, Duchess… I've thought about you every day since that night you came to me, sometimes even dreaming of you, so that I would wake in the night, yearning for you. I was with one other woman between you then and you now and it felt wrong—so wrong that I promised myself I would find my way back to you, even if only to prove that it was all a figment of my imagination.'

Isabelle pulled back to look at his face, surprised by the confession.

'I extended my tour so the end of it would coincide with your mourning ending, because I knew that once I was on British soil again I would not be able to resist seeking you out.'

Isabelle was struck speechless by the confession. She stared at him, her heart pounding in her chest.

'I was lucky enough to run into Willa, who invited

me to Lady Russell's ball, but even in the days before then I was seeking out our mutual acquaintances—who are surprisingly few—in the hope of an official introduction.'

'Matthew…' She didn't know where to begin.

'I wanted you before I found out about Sera. But from the moment I realised she was my daughter, I knew I would wait a lifetime to make you—all three of you— mine.'

He touched the ruby ring with one finger.

'Duchess, you're going to get through this, and then we're going to have a lifetime together. But I want you to know before we get married that I love you. I have for a while. At least since you threatened to kick me out of your house—the first time. And I would have waited for you.' He kissed her forehead gently. 'I would have waited for ever for you.'

Isabelle closed her eyes, basking in the certainty of his love. 'I've been so afraid for so long,' she whispered, her fingers rising to stroke his face. 'I was afraid of being a widow and afraid of being remarried…afraid of being a mother…afraid of… Well, *everything*. And then you came back. And instead of exposing me or blackmailing me, as I expected, you took some of my burden and stepped into a role you didn't ask for. You put our daughter first. If I wasn't already in love with you as a man, I would love you for being the father that you've become.'

She pulled back so that he could see her eyes when she continued.

'You understand that the fact that I'm leaving my children to your care is all the proof you'll ever need? They have been my entire world for a very long time. If I did not love you with my whole heart, I would not entrust them to you.'

'I know, Duchess. They're mine now too,' he said. 'And if it eases your mind at all,' he said, laughing suddenly, surprising her, 'I have asked Luke for his permission to marry you.'

'Oh…' Isabelle sighed.

'He did not let me off lightly,' he added, grinning. 'He asked me why I wanted to marry you, and then, after I'd convinced him I loved you, he made me promise that I would never let you leave him and Seraphina.' Matthew's deep voice settled over the room. 'He went as far as to insist I move to Everett Place if I could not afford a house big enough for the entire family.'

Isabelle shook her head sadly, even as she smiled at Luke's demands. 'He's always been afraid of being left behind,' she observed. 'It's part of the reason I didn't run from marrying the Duke. I couldn't leave Luke— not when he was so clearly an afterthought for everyone else.'

'Not any more,' Matthew promised, and took her mouth, sealing the vow with a fierce kiss.

Isabelle melted against him, sank into him, drawing from his strength as she deepened the kiss, making it last as long as possible while she still could. She didn't want this moment to end—didn't want to face what she could feel blazing through her.

She groaned when Matthew broke the kiss to nuzzle her neck. His breath came as rapidly as hers as he trailed his lips across her feverish skin. 'Christ, Duchess… Your skin is aflame.'

Isabelle didn't reply. Instead, she pushed herself off his lap, self-conscious of the sweat that was starting to seep through her clothes, and held out one clammy hand for his.

'Shall we?'

Matthew took it and raised it to his lips. 'Yes.'

By the time he'd placed Isabelle on her feet by the study door, she was glistening with sweat.

'You should be in bed,' he commented.

'The clergyman is hardly going to let you marry someone who cannot get out of her sickbed,' she replied quietly, smiling despite her fatigue.

Her humour did nothing to calm Matthew, who pushed open the study door to find his family, friends and an unfamiliar clergyman his mother had undoubtedly bribed and browbeaten to be there waiting patiently inside for their arrival.

His sisters sat on the settee, with a splotchy red Seraphina between them, acting as if they hadn't discovered they had a niece only hours before. His father and mother were watching the scene, looking somehow smug despite the scandalous circumstances. Willa and Mary were fussing over an enormous flower arrangement that looked eerily familiar, and Leo stood by the fireplace with Caro's husband, Michael Westmoor, talking animatedly with Luke.

All activity stopped as he and Isabelle walked into the room, their hands clasped together. Instead of happy chatter, he heard the room fall quiet. Matthew tensed against it, knowing what they saw: Isabelle was not well—and she was getting worse by the minute.

His mother, thankfully, broke the moment, coming forward with his father in tow. 'We'll save introductions for later,' she said, cutting off the Earl, who had opened his mouth to formally introduce himself. With an impatient wave of her hand and a quick wink in Isabelle's direction, his mother called the clergyman forward.

The ceremony was blessedly quick, with none of the typical prayers or sermonising. Matthew and Isabelle exchanged vows along with the rings that Matthew had given Luke for safekeeping earlier in the day, and even though it was not customary, he couldn't resist kissing his bride the moment they were pronounced husband and wife.

For such a small group, their friends and family raised a significant racket when Matthew gently cupped Isabelle's fevered face in his hands and placed his lips on hers. They clapped and cheered loudly, while Willa released a shrill whistle that had Leo covering his ears despite his grin.

Gordon passed around glasses of champagne, but it was only once the vicar's registry had been signed by both he and Isabelle, and the clergyman had left, that Matthew called for everyone's attention.

He picked up Seraphina from the settee and waited for all eyes to turn to him before starting. 'Thank you all for being here…'

He passed a glass of champagne to Isabelle, before reaching for his own, unconsciously moving it out of Sera's reach when she tried to make a grab for it from her position on his hip.

'We understand that this wedding did not occur under ideal circumstances, but Isabelle and I are grateful to each of you for your love and support. Luke?' He called his new stepson to where they stood. 'Thank you for allowing me the honour of making Izzy my wife. I promise that I will love and cherish all three of you until my dying breath.'

Luke smiled shyly, but Matthew didn't press him to say anything, sensing that the boy was rather overwhelmed by all the attention. Instead, he turned to Isabelle, and the emotions on his face were clear for everyone to see.

'As soon as *my wife*—' he exaggerated the words, drawing another round of laughter from their guests and a blush from Isabelle '—is well, we will celebrate properly. But until then…' He held up his glass. 'Please raise your glasses to Isabelle, the Duchess of Everett and Viscountess Ashworth.'

'To Isabelle!' everyone parroted, and sipped their champagne.

Matthew couldn't resist leaning down to kiss Isabelle again, only pausing when Sera reached up and tapped his face, wanting his attention. He released his wife with a small laugh and turned to give his daughter his attention.

'So impatient,' he said, and placed a kiss on Sera's lips when she pursed them in demand for one.

'No fever?'

He looked down into Isabelle's glazed eyes, his heart softening when he saw the worry in them. 'No, Duchess. She is fine. Worry about yourself now; we're all here to look after Sera.'

The group slowly disbanded, forming clusters of twos and threes around the room as they ate, drank and celebrated the hurried nuptials.

Matthew watched Isabelle closely, and when she grew paler, her breath coming in painful-sounding rattles, he lifted her in his arms and without a single word carried her from the room.

He knew she was truly ill when she did not object, only nestled against him as he carried her up the stairs to her bedroom.

He gently sat her on the edge of the bed as he removed her shoes, stockings and dress. He tried not to show his worry when the dress came away damp in his hands, or when he saw the aggressive red splotches spreading over her beautiful skin. But when she suffered a coughing fit that left her doubled over and gasping for breath, Matthew's blood ran cold with fear.

The past three days had already weakened her considerably, turning her naturally slender frame alarmingly thin. Though her rash was not as bad as Seraphina's, it was still scattered over Isabelle's face and neck, before disappearing beneath her chemise.

Matthew tried not to think about the looming night ahead, focusing instead on each minute that Isabelle remained cognizant.

He propped her against her pillows, leaving the clean bedcovers off her entirely. 'Can you try and drink something, my love?' he asked. 'Dr Taylor should be here soon.'

Isabelle nodded tiredly, but she did not open her eyes again. She managed to drink a half-glass of water before falling asleep, and by the time the doctor arrived, thirty minutes later, she would not wake up at all.

Chapter Twenty-Two

Isabelle slept for three days, not waking when the doctor came to check on her nor when Matthew tried to lever her up to pour some broth down her throat. She tossed and turned, often mumbling nonsensically and clutching the bed-linen agitatedly in her hands. Her breathing was laboured, as if she were running for her life even in her dreams. Her skin, once so golden and healthy, had paled, with her face taking on a blue tinge that put the fear of God into Matthew's very soul. Sweat poured off her small frame, dampening the sheets every few hours as the fever raged through her.

Matthew was helpless to do anything except try to cool her, and cradle her in his arms while his mother, Mary and the maids changed her sheets, talking to her when everyone else retired for a few hours of rest.

Almost seventy hours into her fever dream, Matthew still sat in a chair by Isabelle's bed, watching her chest rise and fall with each breath, despite his itchy, tired eyes and bone-weary body. He counted her breaths, collecting each one with equal parts gratitude and dread.

In another chair in the corner of the room, the doctor dozed. He had come to check on Isabelle earlier in the night and, seeing her condition, had promptly decided to stay and tend her himself—and it was that decision that had confirmed Matthew's worst fear: Isabelle was fading.

There was a gentle knock on the door, and when whoever stood outside did not immediately enter, Matthew pushed himself to his feet and went to open it. He was surprised to find the nursemaid, Tess, standing outside, with Seraphina in her arms and Luke at her side.

Both children were dressed in their nightshirts, reminding him that it was nearing midnight and that they were supposed to be in bed—though they were wide awake.

'Forgive me, my lord,' Tess began, curtseying awkwardly under her burden. 'His Grace wanted to see the Duchess, and I could not dissuade him…'

Matthew's eyes sought Luke. The boy stood at Tess's side, trying to see past Matthew's large frame to where Isabelle slept.

Matthew stepped aside immediately, making space for Luke to come into the room. 'Thank you, Tess.' He held out his arms for Sera, sighing deeply when his daughter's familiar weight was transferred to him. 'I'll make sure they get to bed.'

'My lord?' she queried, as if preparing to argue.

'Sleep, Tess. There's no point in us both being awake.'

Matthew sat down again by Isabelle's bed, with

Seraphina cuddled against his chest and Luke hovering at the bedside, unsure of himself or what to do.

'Will she die?' the boy asked quietly.

Matthew's head snapped up at the question. The young Duke's green eyes were wide with fear and brimming with tears—tears that the child immediately tried to knuckle away.

'Luke,' Matthew said softly, 'come here.'

Luke walked around the bed to stand in front of Matthew, his entire body rigid with uncertainty.

Matthew raised one hand and placed it on Luke's bony shoulder, forcing the young Duke to meet his gaze. If he had thought that lying to the boy to protect him had been difficult, then telling him the truth in order to prepare him was ten times more so.

'I don't know,' he said honestly after a long moment. 'Izzy is very sick.'

Luke's tears started falling more rapidly, his lips wobbling even as he fought to stay composed.

'But we're doing everything that we can to make her better.' Matthew nodded in the doctor's direction. 'The doctor is staying nearby in case we need him.' He gave the boy's shoulder a squeeze.

Luke nodded and lowered his eyes. His voice, when he spoke, was quiet and full of dread. 'I'm sorry I hit you with my ball,' the child whispered.

Matthew, who had always thought the boy's aim truer than anyone else had imagined, smiled tiredly. 'That's of no matter. I know that you love Izzy, Luke. And that you were protecting her and your sister.'

'She's not my sister.'

Matthew drew back in surprise, frowning. 'Who told you that?'

'I'm not a baby,' Luke said, growing petulant. 'People think I am—but I know things! I know that my father forced Izzy to marry him, and that she never wanted to. She married him because she didn't want to leave *me*. And I know that you come and visit Sera at night—'

'Luke, I have never thought you a baby.' Realising that the Duke knew far more than he'd ever have guessed, Matthew looked into the boy's eyes.

'Everybody treats me like I'm one.'

Matthew nodded seriously. 'We don't mean to. I think it's just because we don't have any experience,' he admitted. 'Both me and Izzy, we... We're learning as we go.' Matthew searched for the right words through his exhaustion. 'Luke, you are a remarkably clever young man—nobody doubts that. And you're clever enough to know that blood doesn't make a family. Izzy is not your mother—she is your stepmother—and yet you love her as if she *were* your mother.'

'I love Sera too,' the boy said. 'But I know she's not my sister.'

'Okay. But you have to love her and protect her as if she were your sister,' Matthew said. 'Because that's what we do. We love and protect the people in our family—even if we don't share their blood.'

Luke straightened his thin shoulders. 'I know.'

'And I need your help.' Matthew ran his palm over Sera's head. 'Because I don't know what I'm doing.'

It felt strange to admit his biggest fear to someone so young, but Matthew knew that it was important for Luke to understand that some fears did not subside, no matter how grown-up you were.

The Duke seemed surprised by the admission. He considered Matthew in silence for a long moment, before nodding. 'I will help,' he said. 'But if Izzy dies, you cannot take Seraphina away.'

'I can,' Matthew countered. 'But I will take you with me too.' He watched the emotions flit over Luke's face—fear, then realisation, and along with it hope and finally, relief—and he promised himself that this boy would never feel anything but entirely wanted, completely belonging.

Luke looked at him, then nodded. 'I suppose if my solicitor says it's fine, then I *could* come with you.'

Matthew bit his cheek to stop himself from grinning. Behind him, the doctor's subtle throat-clearing told him that the man was fighting the urge to laugh too. But Matthew smiled at Luke and finished their serious discussion by saying, 'But for now, we're going to focus on getting Izzy better.'

'Yes.' Luke nodded, and turned back to face the bed, his shoulders rounding with a very adult fear when he saw Isabelle, so small in the centre of the large bed. 'Can I sit next to her?'

'Of course.'

Luke climbed onto the bed and lay down next to Isabelle, making sure not to jostle her. He kept his back to Matthew and Sera, but Matthew saw the way Luke linked his fingers with Isabelle's, holding her hand even though she did not return the pressure.

Luke was asleep in minutes, his body only slightly smaller than Isabelle's. Keeping Seraphina against his chest as she dozed, Matthew pushed himself to stand and went to fetch one of the clean blankets that was lying in wait for the next bed-change rotation. Using one arm, he unfolded the blanket and draped it over Luke, pausing only to sigh tiredly and run one hand through the boy's hair.

'You seem to be going through a baptism by fire,' the doctor commented.

'You have children?' asked Matthew.

'Two,' Dr Taylor confirmed.

'Please…' Matthew laughed tiredly '…tell me it gets easier.'

Samuel Taylor tucked his hands into his pockets and smiled. 'Each age has it challenges. Although this—this sickness,' he clarified, 'is always difficult, irrespective of what age a child is.' He paused for a moment. Then, 'If I may say so, my lord, you are doing rather well, all things considered. I dare say you will be fine.'

Even though Matthew did not have the doctor's confidence, he did not have the energy to argue. Instead, he said, 'Thank you, Doctor,' and sat back down with Seraphina to wait.

Matthew woke with a start to someone shaking him roughly. He came to immediately, his eyes finding the bed for fear that Isabelle had worsened. She was fast asleep, her chest rising and falling evenly, but Luke was awake and watching her face in silence.

'Matthew!'

He turned to find Mary at his side, her green eyes wild with panic. 'He's here—Gareth St Claire. He's demanding to speak with Isabelle. Something about the wedding…'

Exhausted from the long battle with measles and pneumonia, frustrated by his own helplessness, and furious at the gall of the bastard, showing up now of all times, Matthew slowly stood, ready for a fight.

He gently extricated Seraphina from where she slept against his chest and, walking around the bed, placed his daughter on Isabelle's other side. 'Could you watch her?' he asked the doctor. 'I'll send her nursemaid up in a minute.'

Dr Taylor nodded.

'What are you going to do?' Mary whispered fervently.

'Get rid of the bastard,' Matthew replied. 'Once and for all.'

'Should I call the solicitor?'

'No.' He tipped his shoulders arrogantly, considered the question again, and then corrected himself. 'Only if I kill the man.'

Mary paled. 'Matthew…'

He marched for the door without replying, too angry to modulate his mood, too enraged even to attempt to be rational. Gareth St Claire had been a thorn in Isabelle's side for long enough. Well, not any more.

He descended the stairs two at a time, his heavy foot-fall echoing through the cavernous hall of Everett Place.

At the bottom of the stairs stood Gordon, barring Gareth St Claire's entry to the house. The old butler's back was straight, his hands fisted at his sides as he went head to head with the unwelcome guest.

'Her Grace is ill,' the butler was saying. 'You may come back when she is recovered—'

'Who are *you* to talk to *me* like that?' Gareth St Claire demanded.

The man had the same small, round frame and blue eyes as Matthew remembered the late Duke having. His clothes were finely tailored. His hair neatly trimmed. But his manner was rotten to the core.

Before the butler could reply, Matthew took a deep breath to regulate his fury, and said, 'Gordon runs this household on behalf of the Duke and my wife, the Duchess of Everett.'

His statement, and the ice-cold tone with which he had delivered it, travelled down the stairs and through the hall, causing both men to turn and peer up at him.

Before either could move, Matthew continued, 'And who, might I ask, are *you*, storming into a house that is not yours when half its inhabitants are in their sickbeds?'

'I am Gareth St Claire!' he replied, puffing out his chest like a peacock.

It was a pity, though, that Matthew was on the hunt. 'I'm sorry—*who*?'

'The late Duke of Everett's cousin,' Mr St Claire

clarified, the first hint of a blush working its way up his neck.

'Ah, so you are Luke's *second* cousin?' Matthew calmed his voice, affecting surprise. 'Apologies... Had I known we were receiving distant relations I would have been more prepared.' He turned to Gordon, who stood completely still, awaiting instruction. 'Gordon, please have some tea brought into the study for me and Mr St Claire.'

'My lord.' Gordon bowed and left to complete his task, his head held high.

Matthew led the way to the study, knowing that Gareth St Claire would follow without prompting. Once they were inside he sat down at the late Duke's desk and, resting his elbows on the surface, steepled his fingers and waited for the man to speak.

'I have heard that you and Isabelle are married?' Gareth began, wasting no time at all.

'You have heard correctly.'

'This entire situation reeks of scandal,' he wheezed, dropping his significant girth into a nearby chair. 'First, Isabelle is conveniently with child, only weeks after my cousin died—'

'I think you will find that she was with child while he was still alive,' Matthew drawled. His eyes snapped to Gareth's face, and he purposely let his rage show. 'Unless... I do beg your pardon,' he said, keeping his voice contrastingly devoid of emotion. 'Are you implying that the Duchess—my wife—miraculously fell pregnant at eighteen years of age by someone else in the mere two weeks she was married to your cousin?'

Gareth had the grace to blush. 'No. Not at all. I am prepared to admit that the child—'

'Seraphina.'

'Yes… That *Seraphina* was a happy coincidence. But the situation surrounding Isabelle's illness and your urgent marriage, on the other hand, is questionable.'

'In what way?' Matthew held up one hand, halting the man from replying as he added, 'And before you answer that, consider your situation, *cousin*. You are in the Duke's house, accusing his stepmother, the Duchess of Everett, and his stepfather, the Viscount Ashworth, future *Earl* of Heather, of…?' He stopped abruptly. Frowned. 'I apologise… What are you accusing us of, exactly?'

'The situation—'

'A love-match between a widowed duchess and a titled peer?'

'It was rather hasty…'

'What reason had we to wait?' Matthew countered. 'The Duchess has had one white wedding and did not care for another, and *I* certainly did not want one.'

'But—'

'Your coming here, at a time when my wife is *bedridden*, not to congratulate her on her wedding or to check how your young cousins are faring in the wake of the measles epidemic… Well, it shows your true colours, *Mr* St Claire.'

Gareth huffed out an indignant breath. 'Well, I never—'

'You are a vile, greedy man who would suck the life out of a woman and her children like a leech at the first opportunity.' Matthew leaned forward in his chair, lowering his voice ominously when he added, 'Let me be perfectly clear when I say that the Duke of Everett has the full support of the Heather earldom.'

'And that of Lord Russell and Lord Windhurst,' said Willa.

'And that of Lord Westmoor,' Caro added, fortifying Willa's statement.

Matthew looked up to see Willa and Mary standing in the doorway. His father, mother and two sisters were standing behind them, forming a small but mighty army.

Gareth St Claire balked, his face whitening with rage.

'While my family, and my *connections*, span continents,' Matthew continued, 'you—a middling country squire—would dare to insult my *wife* and her children. Your own cousin's progeny,' he added, though it burned to deny Seraphina.

'I did not mean to cause offence…' Gareth St Claire started backtracking immediately. 'I only thought that, g-given the hasty nuptials, it was my familial obligation to e-ensure that Isabelle was not being taken advantage of.'

'Mr St Claire, given that you have met my wife, I find it difficult to believe that you would ever think her capable of being taken advantage of.' Matthew paused, letting the silence build. 'No. The only reason you come here at such a time is that you believe the situation might be extorted to suit your own base needs.' He leaned back in the Duke's chair. 'Let me assure you, I have married the Duchess because I love her, and because every second I was apart from her was torture. I married her *quickly* because once I found her I wanted no possibility of giving her any time to discover how completely above me she is in every way.'

Gareth mumbled a nonsensical reply to that.

'If there is nothing else, I believe I should be getting back to my wife now.' Matthew pushed his chair back and rounded the desk, only pausing to wait for Gareth to catch up so that he could show the man out—for good.

As soon as the aggrieved relative was on the outside steps, Matthew closed the door in his face and leaned his back against it.

His friends and family crowded into the hall, watching him in stunned silence like a crowd watching a mercurial tiger at the zoo.

Matthew felt mad with fatigue and worry and anger. He raked his hands through his hair.

'Good lad!' His father raised his fist in victory.

'Hear, hear!' Willa seconded.

'*That's* going to come back and bite me on the arse,' Matthew muttered, unable to feel quite as triumphant as the others.

'It's doubtful,' his father stated. 'Bullies are notorious for only advancing when they perceive an easy target.'

'If the rumours break, and a scandal—'

'Matthew.' His mother cut him off. 'Whatever comes

now is unavoidable.' When he didn't reply, she advanced, her brows raised. 'You knew that this would happen when you married Isabelle. You have dealt with it to the best of your ability. And now it is done—at least for the time being. So? Do you regret your decision?'

'No. Never.'

'Well, then.' She stepped past him and started climbing the stairs, essentially ending the conversation.

The Earl clapped him on the shoulder. 'If and when, my boy… We'll worry about it if and when we have to. For now, show me where I can find a drink.'

'Mary, could you show my family to the parlour?' he asked, even knowing that his wife's friend had had only as much sleep as him the last few weeks. 'I have to get back to Isabelle.'

'Of course.'

'We shall regale you with our scintillating company,' Willa added, opening her arms and ushering his father and his sisters towards the parlour like a mother hen with her chicks.

'Consider me regaled already,' he heard his father say, before they all disappeared into the room, the door clicking shut behind them.

Left alone in the hall, Matthew exhaled a deep breath and turned to face the stairs. Climbing them seemed momentous in his exhaustion, each small step some great feat of energy instead of a minor impediment. Still, he climbed them, placing one foot in front of the other as he made his way back to his wife's bedside.

Despite his mother's blasé attitude, and his father's

confidence that Gareth was too much of a coward to cause a stir, Matthew could not quite stem his foreboding. But he would protect Luke indefinitely. Of course he would.

And now Gareth knew that.

Still, his mother was right about one thing: there was nothing else he could do for now.

Matthew was so lost in thought that he didn't recognise the happy chatter for an entire five seconds after he'd walked into Isabelle's bedchamber. It came to him by degrees—the sound of Luke's laughter, his mother's tired chuckle…

And there, through them all, he heard Isabelle rasp, 'There he is.'

Chapter Twenty-Three

Isabelle opened her eyes slowly, wincing when her head pounded in protest. She tried to swallow, her dry throat fighting her efforts.

The first thing she saw was a familiar pair of green eyes. Luke was lying next to her, his head on her wrist, looking up at her as if he wasn't quite sure that she was really awake.

'Luke…' she murmured.

'Izzy?' His reply was whispered through tears.

'What's wrong?' she asked, confused.

Why was Luke sleeping in her bed? And where were Seraphina and Matthew?

'I thought you were going to die,' Luke said, sniffling.

Alarmed by the declaration, Isabelle croaked, 'What?'

'Try to stay calm, Your Grace.'

She tipped her head forward to find the source of the voice and saw Dr Taylor standing at the foot of the bed. The doctor smiled at her and walked to her side.

'What happened?' she asked. 'The last thing I remember is…the wedding.' She turned to look at the doctor. 'I *did* get married?'

'Yes. Congratulations, Your Grace.'

'Lord Ashworth asked my permission,' Luke stated seriously.

Isabelle remembered Matthew telling her that quite clearly now. 'Yes, I know.' She lifted her hand from under him and ran it through Luke's hair, alarmed by how much effort the small gesture took out of her. 'Thank you.'

'He said he loves you.'

'He loves *us*,' Isabelle amended, knowing it to be true.

'May I examine you, Your Grace?' Dr Taylor asked. 'I should be on my way soon.'

Isabelle nodded her consent, and the doctor helped her lean forward so that he could place his stethoscope on her back. The only sound in the room as he examined her were her own laboured breaths.

After a long moment, he said, 'There is still fluid in your lungs…though that is to be expected.'

'I feel better,' Isabelle said, not wanting to alarm Luke. 'Tired. But better.'

'Your Grace…' the doctor's voice was grave '…though your fever has broken, the pneumonia will persist for weeks—*months*. It is of the utmost importance that you do not overtax or exert yourself until your lungs fully recover. If you do, you run the risk of regressing.'

Isabelle nodded. 'I will be careful.'

Dr Taylor strung his stethoscope around his neck and looked at her for a long moment. 'I will give instructions to your husband too. Although God knows the man will not let you raise a finger for years to come.'

The words 'your husband' echoed through her head. Isabelle wheezed in pain as a laugh climbed from deep in her chest. 'He has been here?'

'He has never left. The man hasn't slept in three days—'

'Three days?'

'You were very ill, Your Grace,' the doctor replied gravely. 'Lord Ashworth is going to be very relieved to see you awake.'

'Where is he?'

'I believe there was a…situation that needed to be resolved.'

'My cousin came,' Luke clarified, his nose wrinkling with displeasure. The boy leaned forward, green eyes twinkling. 'I heard Lord Ashworth tell Mary to call Mr Briggs should he kill him.' Luke started laughing, his boyish giggle filling the room.

'He…?' Isabelle looked to Dr Taylor for confirmation.

'I wouldn't worry about it, Your Grace. I believe Lord Ashworth was jesting.' Dr Taylor turned to Luke and winked, adding, 'Probably,' causing the boy to dissolve into another round of laughter.

Isabelle tried not to laugh, not wanting to encourage Luke's questionable behaviour, but her lips threatened a smile anyway. 'I suppose I shall need to be updated in full once I'm up and dressed.'

'I recommend another week—maybe two—of bed-rest,' Dr Taylor countered severely.

'But—'

Isabelle's argument was cut off by a loud exclamation at the door. She turned to see the Countess of Heather standing on the threshold. 'Isabelle!' the Countess exclaimed. 'You're awake!' She marched across to the bed and felt Isabelle's face with her hand. 'The fever has broken?'

'Yes,' Dr Taylor replied.

Isabelle, stunned by the genuine display of affection, sat completely still.

The Countess lowered herself to sit on the bed, not bothering to rearrange her skirts before taking both Isabelle's hands in hers. 'You scared us to death, child.'

Isabelle didn't know what to say, overwhelmed by the glossy tears in the older woman's eyes.

The Countess didn't seem to mind. She laughed happily and, without releasing Isabelle's hands, turned to the doctor. 'Thank you so much, Doctor. We were all quite sick with worry.'

Isabelle heard the truth in the words and it settled through her entire body, filling her with warmth. In that moment she felt a connection with the Countess that she had never felt with her own mother. Because here was a woman who loved her children as much as Isabelle did—who understood what it was to constantly worry and fret over their health and happiness and, by default, the health and happiness of their chosen partners.

'Thank you, Countess. For staying.'

The Countess waved her hand in a nonchalant gesture. 'We are one family now, my girl. You couldn't get rid of us if you tried—though Lord knows Matthew is probably going to need a few weeks alone with you to recover from the scare.'

'Where is he?' Isabelle asked. 'And Gareth…?' The words died on her lips as Matthew's large frame filled the doorway, to be immediately replaced with, 'There he is.'

Matthew didn't move or speak. He didn't even appear to be breathing. He stared at her as if he wasn't sure whether or not he was hallucinating.

Isabelle took in his dishevelled appearance. His eyes were dark with fatigue. His face looked gaunt, as if he had not slept or eaten in days. His hair fell past the collar of his shirt, and Isabelle's fingers itched to run through the unruly mass.

The Countess was the first to speak. She rose to stand and held out one hand towards Luke. 'Perhaps we should give them a moment.'

Luke went willingly, not even pausing to look back as he started chatting to the Countess.

Dr Taylor, bag in hand, paused by Matthew's side on his way out. 'She must stay in bed for a week. Maybe longer. I will come every few days to check on her. My instructions remain the same. She must rest and try to resume regular eating and drinking as soon as possible.

Warm broth will help soothe her throat. Use the euca-
lyptus and camphor salve twice daily. Keep her warm,
dry and well rested.'

Matthew nodded, but his eyes never left Isabelle.

'It is important that she does not strain herself. Any
exertion could cause her to regress.'

'I'll make sure she rests,' Matthew affirmed. He
reached out his hand for the doctor's. 'Thank you, Dr
Taylor.'

Dr Taylor returned the handshake and left the room.

Matthew came to her immediately, sitting on the edge
of her bed when all she wanted was to be in his arms.
'Isabelle...'

She looked up into his eyes, saw the worry and relief
and love there, and marvelled at it. 'Matthew.'

Needing the contact, she reached out and touched
his face.

He bowed his head and, raising both his hands,
pressed her palm hard against his flushed cheek, as if
he was afraid she would disappear at any moment. His
breath came in one huge shuddering sigh.

'I—I thought you were going to...'

Isabelle's heart swelled with love. Leaving her hand
in his, she moved inelegantly from beneath the covers
and slid onto his lap, nestling against him as his arms
wrapped around her.

'I would never leave you willingly,' she said, meaning every word. She would fight for this man. Not just
for herself, but for Luke and Sera too. 'I love you, Matthew.'

He buried his face against her neck, even as his arms tightened around her. 'Christ, Isabelle, I love you so much.'

A ragged sob tore from his chest, shocking Isabelle into silence. Unsure of what to say, but wanting to comfort him, she ran her hand repetitively through his hair as he fought to regain the control that she knew he so cherished. She didn't move away. She didn't speak. She just let herself be held, knowing that Matthew needed it as much as she did.

It dawned on her as they sat there, wrapped up in one another, that this man was her husband. *Hers.* For the rest of her life she would have this—this comfort and joy. And, yes, this fear. For loving someone was no guarantee that there would be no hardship—in fact, if anything, it was a guarantee that there *would* be. Because you had so much more to lose when you truly loved someone. If misfortune struck, the consequences were so much greater.

The feeling of Isabelle's hand in his hair was like a dream—one he never wanted to wake up from. Her body, nestled as closely as possible against him, was so small and frail, so light, that he was immediately worried about the weeks ahead.

He raised his head to look at her, his beautiful wife. 'Please, don't ever do that to me again.'

She smiled tiredly. 'I intend to live a long time yet, my lord.'

She placed her hand on his cheek, drawing his mouth

down to hers, and Matthew sighed into the kiss. For one long moment he allowed himself to taste her, sliding his tongue between her lips to gently stroke hers. But when she wrapped her arms around his neck and pulled him closer, her breath wheezing, he pulled back.

'Matthew…?'

'No exerting yourself, love.'

'I hardly think that's what he meant,' she replied, but the words lost any force because of the way she rasped them.

He lifted her easily, repositioning her in the centre of the bed. 'We have a lifetime. There's no rush.'

Matthew started to move away, all too conscious of his body's response to Isabelle, but she caught his hand in hers, stopping him. 'Please…' she patted the space beside her '…stay with me.'

'I don't think—'

'I want to sleep with my husband,' she countered. She yawned once and curled into the covers. 'I think I am allowed that much, considering I was deprived of my wedding night.'

Matthew, wanting nothing more than to hold her, took off his shoes and climbed onto the bed fully clothed. Isabelle moved over, making room for him, and the moment he lay down beside her shimmied closer again, snuggling against him as if she needed his body heat. She closed her eyes.

Matthew repositioned himself, shifting onto his side so that he could hold her as close as possible and touch her, his fingers trailing down her arm and the soft fabric of her nightdress.

'I don't want separate rooms,' she said suddenly.

'Hmm?'

'Wherever we end up living, I want to sleep in your bed every night,' Isabelle clarified. 'I don't want separate rooms.'

'All right.'

It was the easiest demand she'd ever make of him. He'd give anything to have her like this, soft and cuddly and pressed up against him every night.

'And I want more babies. Not until Sera is a little older, but maybe in a year or two…'

Matthew froze, even as he began to harden at the thought of her pregnant with another one of his children. 'As many as you want,' he promised.

She nodded sleepily. Matthew was watching her face, so he saw the frown pucker her brow right before she opened her eyes.

'What did Gareth want?'

'To fulfil his "familial obligation" and ensure that you had not been taken advantage of,' he said drily. 'Duchess…?'

She opened her eyes and turned to face him. Her hand found his face, immediately soothing.

'What is it?' she asked.

'The scandal is coming,' he said honestly, hating to alarm her, but wanting her to be prepared. 'The gossip columns were already speculating. And now, with your cousin…'

She nodded seriously, but she did not seem as alarmed as he'd expected. 'We are prepared for the possibility, Matthew. All that's left to do is protect the children as much as possible.'

'I agree. I don't want Luke and Sera subjected to speculation,' he admitted. 'I think we should close up Everett Place and remove the household to my family's country estate. My father and Briggs can handle your business from here until the season ends.'

'We should let the rumours die down?'

Matthew nodded. 'In a few years, nobody will care. We can return to London once some time has passed—when Luke goes to school, perhaps? I would like to be nearby for his first year. But until then we can remain separate from the *ton*. I can manage my family's land and estate. We can choose those friends we would like to come and visit us…spend time with family…' He ran his hand down to her stomach. 'Add to our own family…'

'Yes.'

'You must think about it.'

'I don't need to. I trust your judgement. And Sera… We will protect her for as long as we can. At least until she's old enough to understand.'

'She will carry our sins,' Matthew murmured regretfully.

'But she will carry them knowing that she is loved unconditionally. And one day she will meet a man who sees her for who she is and not for how she was born, and he will love her fiercely and love her regardless.'

'But not for many years,' Matthew said, sounding less enamoured of the idea than Isabelle was.

Isabelle laughed. 'I think I would rather enjoy living solely in the country for a few years.'

'You are known to be quite reclusive,' he teased. 'But I should warn you that living with my family coming and going all the time is hardly going to be what you're used to.'

Isabelle sighed happily. 'No, I don't suppose it will be. But I am glad nonetheless.' She kissed him. 'I rather adore your family.'

'Me too,' he admitted.

Isabelle repositioned her head on his arm. 'I suppose I should pay a visit to my parents soon and inform them of our marriage.'

'I wrote to them.' Matthew didn't want to hurt her, but he couldn't hide the truth from her. 'Yesterday, when I thought…'

'And?'

'Your father replied, asking me to keep them apprised of your condition.'

Matthew had not penned a reply to that, knowing that her parents did not deserve one.

'Thank you for doing that.'

'You do not seem surprised.'

In fact, he thought, she did not seem affected by their negligence at all.

'My parents are not like yours,' she said simply. 'How could I be surprised or upset when I have never known or expected anything different from them? I was a disappointing alternative to the son my father wanted, but never sired. In their minds they are excellent parents, for no other reason than that they raised me to be a fit wife for a duke.'

'My parents are yours now too,' he pointed out, feeling angry and sad for her. 'You have an entire family you never bargained for. And you will probably be sick of their attention within a fortnight.'

'I know—and I couldn't be happier.' She burrowed against him. 'I can't wait to get started on the rest of my life with you,' she murmured sleepily. 'It still feels like a wonderful dream I might wake up from at any moment.'

Matthew kissed the side of her face.

'I'm so tired…' Isabelle mumbled, yawning again. 'I know I've slept for three days, but I rather feel I could sleep for three more.'

Matthew brushed her hair back from her face, revelling in the silky strands between his fingers, memorising the gentle weight of his wife's head on his arm and her body curled against his.

'Sleep, my love.'

'Don't leave.'

'Never.'

Matthew waited for Isabelle to fall into a deep sleep before finally closing his own eyes after almost a week of wakefulness. And as his body gave way to exhaustion and his mind began to shut down, he had one last singular thought: *I don't deserve to be this happy*.

Epilogue

London, 1844—two years later

Isabelle gripped her hands together to stop herself from reaching out and smoothing Luke's hair, aware that he would be humiliated by any maternal gesture in front of his school friends.

'You will write if you need anything?'

Luke smiled nervously. 'I will.'

'We will see you at half term,' she reminded him.

Matthew, perhaps sensing her struggle, took over. 'You are going to be fine,' he said quietly. 'But any time you need us you will write and we will come. And, Luke, if you hate it here, we will bring you home.'

Luke expelled a tight breath. 'I know. I'll be fine,' he insisted bravely.

'Ashworth!'

Isabelle turned to greet the approaching stranger as Matthew came to stand beside her. The man was tall and thin, with an elaborate moustache that Isabelle instinctively knew his wife must hate. A young boy trailed behind him.

'Talbot.' Matthew returned the greeting, shaking the man's hand. 'Allow me to introduce my wife—'

'Ah, yes! The Duchess of Everett,' Talbot replied, pointedly ignoring her pregnant belly, which had already attracted a few scandalised glances. 'I heard your marriage caused quite a stir, Your Grace.'

Isabelle smiled indulgently. 'I prefer to be known as Lady Ashworth, Lord Talbot.' She curtsied. 'It is a pleasure to make your acquaintance.'

'Yes. Quite.' Lord Talbot smiled kindly before dismissing her to talk to Matthew.

Isabelle, sensing the two young boys' awkwardness, stepped in to make introductions. 'May I introduce you to our son, Luke, the Duke of Everett?'

Luke stepped forward, his hand outstretched towards the Talbot boy. 'It's a pleasure to make your acquaintance.'

'Graham,' the boy replied informally, and returned the handshake.

The boys assessed each other for a long moment, as if deciding whether or not to strike up an alliance. Isabelle held her breath as the silence stretched, only expelling it when Graham nodded his head in the direction of a small group of students standing nearby.

'Come on. I'll introduce you to my friends.'

Luke nodded, smiling brightly at the possibility of meeting more people. 'Let me just say goodbye to my parents.'

Isabelle's throat burned with unexpected tears. It wasn't the first time he had referred to them as such, but hearing it still affected her as much it had the very first time.

Matthew had started it—introducing them to his acquaintances as his wife and children as naturally as if it were complete fact. But it had taken Luke over a year to overcome his self-consciousness enough to reciprocate.

The first time he'd actually said, 'Perhaps we should ask my father,' had been in response to a question that Mr Briggs had asked regarding the estate, during one of their monthly meetings. Matthew had cleared his throat and attempted to answer the question casually, despite his emotion. Isabelle had excused herself to go and cry in the corridor.

Since that first awkward acceptance they'd fallen easily into their roles, and now it was strange to think that there had been a time when they had not been such a close-knit family.

Isabelle pulled Luke into a brief hug. 'Be good,' she whispered, and released him almost immediately.

Matthew shook Luke's hand. Neither of her boys said anything, but Isabelle saw and read the silent messages conveyed between them before Luke took one last big breath and turned away too.

She watched him for only a moment, not wanting to embarrass him. But turning and walking away was one of the more difficult things she'd ever had to do, made easier only by Matthew's supportive arm around her.

* * *

Matthew handed his emotional wife into their carriage and pulled himself into the conveyance after her. He sat down and, reaching over, lifted her onto his lap and into his arms immediately.

'He'll be fine,' he promised when she sniffled.

'I know,' she replied as the carriage began to move towards their London home, where Seraphina was waiting with Tess. Isabelle rested her head against his chest, her hand coming to fidget with the buttons on his waistcoat. 'It's just… He's still so young.'

Matthew's own heart clenched in his chest. 'He is. But he's clever, Duchess. He'll be fine. And if he's not he'll come home, and we'll find an alternative.'

He kissed her face, pulling a shiver over her skin.

'Luke is a duke,' he went on. 'His path will be a lot easier than that of most of the other boys there by default.'

When a single tear trailed down her cheek, Matthew placed a hand over the swell of her stomach—which, although partially hidden by her dress, was still clearly visible in contrast to her tiny figure.

'Don't fret, my love.'

'I'm not usually this nonsensical,' she insisted, wiping her face. 'It's the baby. I'm hot and bothered *all the time*. Which makes me waspish. I can't sleep.' She slouched against him. 'I feel so *lumpy*.'

Matthew sounded his disapproval deep in the back of his throat. 'You're not "lumpy"; you're beautiful,' he whispered. 'Maybe you just need a distraction.'

His hand reached beneath her skirts to trail up her stockinged calf and—to his absolute delight—straight beneath her chemise to her soft centre.

'You're not wearing drawers, love,' he observed huskily.

'I can't stand them against my skin,' she replied breathlessly. 'So many layers…'

Matthew took her mouth in a gentle kiss as his fingers parted her damp flesh, running over her repeatedly until she arched her back, pressing herself wantonly against his hand.

He groaned his approval. 'Do you like that, Duchess?'

She panted her reply. 'You know I do.'

He laughed and dipped his head to lick the top of her breasts, which seemed to grow heavier each day in her pregnancy. 'I want these in my hands,' he murmured, breathless in his excitement.

'Yes…' Isabelle ground her bottom over the hard length of him in reply. *'Yes.'*

He quickly unlaced the ribbons at her bodice, thanking God that her condition made corsets ill-advised and unnecessary. He spread her dress open to reveal her chemise and, too impatient to remove the last garment, sucked her hard nipple gently into his mouth through the fabric, making sure to be careful with her sensitive breasts.

Isabelle moaned her pleasure. Her hands sank into his hair and tugged, trying to pull him closer, and when Matthew reached beneath her dress again, sliding a single finger into her wet core, she moaned and ground herself against his hand.

'Please, Matthew…'

Matthew complied, shifting his mouth to her other breast as his fingers thrust in and out of her and his thumb found that little bud of nerves.

Isabelle's body clung to him, pulsing and drawing him in as she moved closer and closer to orgasm.

Mad with lust, crazed with the smell of his wife filling the carriage, Matthew released her breast with a small pop. He brought his lips to her ear. 'I love your body, Duchess,' he crooned, his fingers never stopping. 'When we get home, I'm going to strip you naked and let you ride me, so that I can watch you on top of me.'

'Yes…' she hissed, enjoying the fantasy she knew they'd play out as soon as they got home. It was no secret that he loved to watch her, full of life, pregnant with his child.

'I'm going to squeeze your full breasts and suckle your nipples until you are screaming my name.' Her body tensed for one perfect second. 'I'm going to worship you,' he whispered, just before she shattered.

Isabelle's back arched. Her hands tightened in his hair. Her body took his fingers greedily, as if she might prolong the sensation if she could only hold on to them for longer.

He kissed the side of her head as she collapsed against him, her breaths heavy and ragged.

Isabelle was quiet for a long moment as she regained her composure, but as soon as she became aware of his hard length pressing into her she shifted on his lap, making space for her hand to find him beneath his trousers.

Matthew hissed out a sharp breath. 'Not here, my love. I want you in bed. Naked.'

Isabelle raised her eyebrows. 'Anyone would think you quite debauched, my lord. Lusting after a pregnant lady.'

'Perhaps,' he conceded. 'Although lusting after one's pregnant *wife* seems the gentlemanly thing to do.'

She laughed and shifted again, moving to the seat to begin fastening her dress. 'I still don't understand why you find my condition so appealing,' she said off-handedly.

Matthew gently swatted her hands away and began helping her, deftly re-lacing the front of her gown as he had hundreds of times before.

'It's not only your condition, Duchess, though I *do* find the idea of my child growing in you sinfully delightful.' He watched the blush spread over her face, enamoured of the fact that he could still embarrass her. 'It's you,' he said simply. 'It's only ever been you.'

Isabelle sighed and rested her head against his shoulder. 'Who would have thought that a simple favour could lead to this?'

Matthew leaned down to kiss her. 'Not me,' he replied. 'Though I am exceptionally glad I was first on your list.'

* * * * *

Author Note

Thank you so much for reading *One Night with the Duchess*! Researching and writing this book was so much fun, and I can't wait to continue this journey with you.

If you have ten seconds to spare, I would be eternally grateful if you left a review of *One Night with the Duchess* on Goodreads. It could be only a few words, but every review helps spread the word!

If you enjoyed *One Night with the Duchess* and would like to stay in touch with the Widows of West End, Willa and Leo's book is coming soon! Follow along on Instagram (@author.maggie) for updates, promotions, and sneak peeks.

Warm regards,
Maggie Weston

COMING SOON!

We really hope you enjoyed reading this book.
If you're looking for more romance
be sure to head to the shops when
new books are available on

Thursday 21st
November

To see which titles are coming soon, please visit

millsandboon.co.uk/nextmonth

MILLS & BOON

MILLS & BOON ®

Coming next month

THE LADY'S SNOWBOUND SCANDAL
Paulia Belgado

She hesitated, then straightened her shoulders. 'I've come to ask you not to evict the residents at number fifty-five Boyle Street.'

'Boyle Street?' He rubbed at his chin. 'Ah, yes. I purchased that building from a Mr Andrews...no, Atkinson.'

And it had been a fine deal as well, as Atkinson had been eager to sell to stave off his creditors. Desperate sellers always offered the best bargains.

'But why would I need to evict the residents? Isn't it some shop or factory?'

Lady Georgina's mouth pursed. 'I'm afraid it is not, Mr Smith. Number fifty-five Boyle Street happens to be St Agnes's Orphanage for Girls.'

'An orphanage? In the middle of a busy commercial district?'

She let out an exasperated sigh. 'You bought it, didn't you? You didn't know it was an orphanage?'

'I did not.' He frowned. While he had instructed Morgan to clear the building, Atkinson definitely hadn't mentioned there were any occupants, nor that they were orphans.

Damn.

'Oh, now I see!' She clapped her hands together. 'There was a mix-up then? And you really aren't evicting the girls?'

'I didn't say that.'

She blinked. 'You mean to throw over two dozen orphaned girls onto the street?'

Elliot ignored the knot forming in his gut and erased the vision of shivering waifs out in the cold her words had conjured in his mind. He'd made many cutthroat decisions in business before, and this one would be no different.

But his next move would no doubt be the most ruthless one he would ever make.

'I could change my mind. I mean, *you* could change my mind.'

'Me?' Her delicate brows slashed downwards. 'And what is it I can do to change your mind?'

'Marry me.'

Her bright coppery eyes grew to the size of saucers. 'I—I b-beg your pardon?'

'You heard me. Marry me and I will rescind the eviction notice.'

'You can't be serious.'

He was deadly serious.

Continue reading
THE LADY'S SNOWBOUND SCANDAL
Paulia Belgado

Available next month
millsandboon.co.uk

LET'S TALK
Romance

For exclusive extracts, competitions and special offers, find us online:

f MillsandBoon

X @MillsandBoon

⊙ @MillsandBoonUK

♪ @MillsandBoonUK

Get in touch on 01413 063 232